T0354319

SEBASTIANUS:
THE WAR BEGINS

Keegan Holmes Walker

iUniverse, Inc.
Bloomington

SEBASTIANUS: THE WAR BEGINS

iUniverse books may be ordered through booksellers or by contacting:

iUniverse
1663 Liberty Drive
Bloomington, IN 47403
www.iuniverse.com
1-800-Authors (1-800-288-4677)

Because of the dynamic nature of the Internet, any Web addresses or links contained in this book may have changed since publication and may no longer be valid. The views expressed in this work are solely those of the author and do not necessarily reflect the views of the publisher, and the publisher hereby disclaims any responsibility for them.

ISBN: 978-1-4502-5580-6 (sc)
ISBN: 978-1-4502-5581-3 (ebk)

Printed in the United States of America

iUniverse rev. date: 8/26/2010

PART ONE

THE DEATH MARCH

Chapter One:

The Death March

Slowly edging along the sides of an old barn, the young boy held a bag of stolen apples in his strong hands. He was only nine. He had stolen the apples from the farmer, having been homeless with nothing to do for food as no one would hire such a young age. His heart skipped as the barn owner appeared from the darkness, armed with a machete sword, cutting down long, stiff plants, roaring, neck veins bulging.

"You are worthless! You think that you are better than anyone here?" demanded the cruel, rugged middle-aged man. The boy was only eight years old and scared. He had taken one piece of bread and the owner of the food had now a wooden cane as he mercilessly beat the boy. "This", he said, pausing to smack him across the ribs with the cane, "is your lesson."

Crying, the boy attempted to limp away. He had been an orphan for years, living in Hestour's kingdom after his parents had died. "Answer me!" roared the man's voice as he forced the cane upon the child's face. "Answer me!" he repeated.

The man swung the cane once more, and unimaginably, the boy reached his hand and he caught the stick, shattering it into hundreds of small pieces. Dumbstruck, the man demanded, "Are you a witch? Were you sent by anyone?"

No one had ever seen such a thing happen. It was truly unheard of. "He is no witch!" roared a voice only eighteen years of age. This was the voice of the leader of the nation Hestour. "I'll take him. He has something about him. I've heard the villager's complaints. I've eyed the boy and he is only gifted by goodness. I will take him in. He will be just and believe me, a powerful weapon."

The child was never an outcast ever again, but was in the makings of a brilliant hero.

The nursemaid of several young boys was very old, and very unkind. She was not tolerant. Though, she was credited for her amazing ability to tell tall tales. She told hundreds of stories. Some were of happy adventures of warriors who conquered dragons and saved people. Others were of matters much more important. Stories of creatures that loomed in the dark and served all powerful evil were common. Some were of the spirits that controlled death and afterlife. The boys were very young and reacted atrociously to all of the stories, being more scared that they had ever been. That was all but one. The nursemaid never really knew that boy's name. He loved the stories and took everyone in by heart.

The nursemaid loved that boy, too. But eventually, she was fired. But on the third day of each week, she still sneaked into the castle of Hestour, where the boy lived, and told him the tales. He took these as lessons. He believed that this was what every other young child was learning. He became more knowledgeable than them all. Eventually the nursemaid had died. She told every story to that boy and he recorded down everyone and could recite more than half by heart. The boy grew, and he still remembered those tales.

The boy was very talented. He could anything. He could name anything. He could recite word from word of legends. He could take pain. He could inflict pain. He could do anything. Some may say he was perfect. Some thought he was too perfect. Either way, that boy possessed more talent that anyone that had ever lived.

A long time ago, longer than anyone can imagine, was a different world where great things and horrible things would happen. This was a world of unbelievable magic. Trees will touch the clouds, crazy men at sea, giant creatures, and worst of all: crazy kings and false rulers.

This world was separated into many parts, but the ones here are two famous parts. One of them was the land of Lord Titus. His land was a fair land wooded all along the borders, called Hestour. The other land was of the darkest and upmost evilest called the Crusalands, more known as the Dark Lands. Lord Titus was a kind man and a fair man. He was very young for a lord, nearly thirty five. He had long black hair and a short thick beard with one stroke of grey that he, so embarrassed, tried to cover it up so often that people laughed when they saw ridiculous scarves of necklaces and other failed attempts.

But the Crusalands was a horrible place where nothing but trolls, dragons, and any horrible thing you could imagine lived. Rotted trees curled and shriveled upon the rainless desert like lands. Damp caves lay across the land, lined up in the forest forming some sort of ring around the Black Forges of the trolls. The Crusalands was once ruled, though it is free now, by a horrible man known by everybody as the King Crusak. He was a dark Warlock, one of the very last since the dark leader called Latorin. Crusak brought in trolls from the caves and monsters from the swamp to forge him weapons and armor. Crusak was strong, too big for a mortal to kill and, too big for any regular sword to slay. So to settle it, a man called Hestour Vinco forged a sword of the most mysterious magic, and he brought Crusak down and imprisoned him in an inhumanly chest of the strangest powers. No one knows where Vinco hid the chest, but that is why no one has opened it. Years after, Vinco, after accomplishing so many more things, died of old age. His body is buried in the highest mountains of far beyond, perfectly still and unaffected by time, no trace of dust, there forth giving him the name St. Hestour. Crusak still remains in the chest, waiting eagerly for a fool, a follower or, to be honest, anyone to open the chest that lies deep below in the dark, calling out.

Hestour had been safe for nearly two hundred and fifty years. No one thought that possibly a hero was needed, but there was a hero needed. He had not been called by destiny yet to help the kingdom of Hestour. He was called Sebastianus the No Name. A descendent of God as you could call him. You could easily recognize Sebastianus if you saw him. He green eyes stuck out like a sore thumb, he was also a very fit and talented man, he was quite muscular and he was always careful. He was also very intelligent, though he was never properly educated in a school. No one thought of him as a hero. He had been an orphan since the age of four. His parents were killed in a brutal accident while hunting of which he was not told how ('Too gruesome for one to describe", Lord Titus had once said). There forth Sebastianus had been raised in the Royal Kingdom of Hestour, Titus as a father of some sort and his old nursemaid as a mother. But now he lived as one of the Royal Court members as a servant to the general Juerous, who was currently away to Arka, the last land that contained those who were pagan as almost everyone, thanks now to St. Hestour, were people of God.

The peaceful steady beat was wished to never end. Almost everyone in the kingdom of Hestour was at the once every year festival to celebrate the long years (two hundred and fifty-two now) since the death of Crusak, Latorin, and the dark empire that had almost taken control of the world. There forth, the day was established as 'St. Hestour's Freedom Day. Loud conversations' were heard and they rang out from everywhere. It was always a warm, sunny day in the Hestour, as the nation lied underneath the warm sun always. Everyone was enjoying traditional food and entertainment. The oldest of traditional music cried through Hestour with a soft and steady beat, bringing all joy. The tune, though playing lightly, was so familiar, even when it was the faintest music to those who couldn't hear it as well, that everyone heard it well and in fact, most sang along to it. Everyone was dancing, laughing, eating, and some even puzzled from the questioning performances, riddles, and jokes.

But there was one thing everyone in the kingdom and few throughout different lands, such as the Occupo, Muse, and the Disterra, (which happen to be some of the finest, richest, and most powerful places you can find) all came to the sporting events. The most popular of the events was historically racing (which was racing on whatever beast they owned, not on foot) and then there was of course cheeky, fun tricks done by magicians, who were often fake performers. The magicians could pull of the grandest of entertainment, but it was usually not as enjoyable because of the dirty lies. Though at the time, the one everyone loved the most were the fights. All of the greatest warriors would battle each other for glory. The land of King Titus was a very popular place indeed.

The ten thousand villagers and tourists stood in the coliseum, cheering, chanting, and screaming. Everybody was enjoying the fight between the former winner of Hestour, Aursca the Great and the former champion of Occupo, Minsilcus the Mighty.

Aursca took his opponent down in the first minute and proceeded to beat him. But the promising Minsilicus arose and took Aursca on to the ground and eventually claimed the match and the title of Hestour's fighters'. He jokingly celebrated by dancing around the battleground set up for fighters when he froze pale to hear a threatening and shrill voice cry, "We're taking over this kingdom and the land of St. Hestour is to be ours!" Everybody in the kingdom froze like Minsilicus did when they heard the threat. Many years ago, a man named Rusmol claimed that a possessed man would come to the land of Crusak's defeater and unleash the powers of evil. The possessed man would come to the village and scream random things. The story was a legend, though. The screamer then stepped forth so all could see him.

The villagers' response was to laugh aloud and fall on the ground as a sign of arrogance and that they had no fear. "You are nothing but a weak old man", a man from the crowd remarked. It was true the man was nothing but an old and dusty being. A long grey beard hung from his wrinkly face, and the man's scalp was bare. He wore a long, black cloak that draped upon the clean grounds of the fine Hestour. The old man's eyes looked as if flames burned within them, but as you looked closely, you could see the man's eyes were black. He was indeed possessed by an evil spirit. It could not have been Crusak's doing because of course, the imprisoned warlock had, in the old legend, chosen the toughest man in the entire kingdom to invade and spread the word of his being.

It was just then that Lord Titus stepped forth, a smirk upon his face. He was, as usual, covering the grey streak of hair on his thick beard by stroking it. He chuckled and asked jokingly, after looking at the crowd for his attention, "So, my good man, as much as a small and pathetic thing you are, what do you intend to do to my people? Were you sent to wipe your own shame upon this fine kingdom?"

The old man's reaction was to pull from his cloak, a small chest, wet and damp, with a cross carved upon the top and keyhole. It was covered with many designs, God, the Holy Spirit, and that of which is good because the box needed to stay sacred, protected by the Archangels. This was the chest. An evil smile curled up on the man's lip. Then a cold wind crossed Hestour that gave the warm land frost and all shivered in the cold as the sun grew smaller and smaller and the sky became darker and darker.

Storm clouds formed and lightning shot, rain poured, thunder boomed. The man slowly opened the chest, laughing not in his own voice, but in another's, a deep and dark one that sank into everyone's souls.

A red blinding light shined over the kingdom for a minute that never ended. When the light drifted off as quickly as it had formed, there were feathered, scaled, furry and slimy beasts everywhere: on the streets, on houses, in houses! The sky was darker and much stormier. Parents eagerly raced for their children and children raced for their parents. The creatures of which people had not seen for hundreds of years had returned to destroy the human world for the cause of all evil. "Go my children, to wreak havoc upon man!" the prophet of evil called out. Everybody in the kingdom ran around like maniacs, screaming in terror, and then a very deep voice that everybody knew shook the ground below them. The words were so horrifying that almost everyone forgot about the beasts. "Serve me and I will serve thee justice and mercy, against me and thou shall receive darkness! For I have returned, body and soul", were the words that came from the sky that swirled black clouds. "Today all humanly rights and justice fall from the hand of God into mine. The sun will fall and I will rise, water and earth on my side. For I have returned, body and soul, as the great, the ultimate, Lord Crusak."

Meanwhile Sebastianus, the Royal Court servant of the general, was at his cabin, which had been owned by parents before they died, a thirty minute walk outside of the kingdom in the North Forest enjoying his nap until he was awoken by a loud *Buzz!* "What is that awful noise?" Sebastianus asked himself. As the noise cleared away Sebastianus realized he had just missed the festival. In pure disappointment he then decided that he would hunt for dinner since it was almost time to eat and because he needed to take the depression of missing the most fun event of the year off his mind. Sebastianus flung the door open, armed with a spear.

After nearly an hour of hunting there was no luck yet. "Something must have frightened the animals badly", Sebastianus muttered to himself. Finally, with a silent sigh of relief, Sebastianus spotted a deer. It was odd though, different from the usual. It was larger and the tail was a peculiar color. It had a large black stripe on each side. *All the merrier* thought Sebastianus. *New food to try, I guess.*

At that moment, the creature turned round, obviously hearing some sort of rustle from its hunter. At this, Sebastianus fell back in terror. The creature's face contained one large eye, like an eggshell, completely white with one black speck painted right in the center. Its snout snorted roughly and the mouth, now opened wide, spat orange muck that stained the large, ten fangs on both top and bottom. It looked at startled Sebastianus, roared (another odd thing) and charged teeth ready and obviously it was hungry as its mouth foamed eagerly for dinner. The mediocre hunter did not know what to do at a time like this, so he stuck his knife out in front of him and, unable to stop, the beast ran right into it and surprisingly died quick. So Sebastianus wrapped up the beast and brought it home. It crossed his mind that it was not right to eat a creature like the one that he had just killed. It seemed inhuman to eat a one of a kind beast that he had never seen and would most likely never see again. So he, hoping that some good luck in return would come out of it, set the beast down and continued to hunt for a regular creature that would not attempt to eat *him*.

Sebastianus continued deeper north into the woods until he could see the sparkling crystal clear water that gleamed and glistened as the sun reflected upon it. The warm weather and lack of water had concluded four deer to thirst, so they drank from the cool, brilliant, and clean water of the Northern Hestour Bay. Sebastianus snuck behind them, tip toeing in the dirt that was now mud from splashes of water. One deer turned and faced his hunter. Though Sebastianus was quick to throw his spear and claim the beast. The other animals, in fear, fled the area, scared off by the starving hunter – or as they saw it, a savage murderer. Sebastianus picked up his meal and wrapped it in his blood stained cloth. He lifted the wild and heavy deer back to his house.

As Sebastianus stepped into his cabin, struggling to carry the rather large beast, the faint buzzing returned to taunt him again. It was not bees, wasps, or locusts. Anyone who lived in the woods would know that, as all beasts' sounds were familiar. But, so his meal was not spoiled, Sebastianus tried to ignore the sound. Though the thought seemed to cross his mind that still, he had no clue of where this peculiar noise was sounding from. This of course, reminded him again of the odd beast he killed. That thought crossed his spinning mind as well. Where were the strange symptoms of an off day coming from?

Nearly an hour later, when Sebastianus had gutted his kill and let it bake in the fire and when the food was cooked, Sebastianus enjoyed the meal so very much, and he almost ate it all before remembering to sacrifice some to God, like the law was stated. He did so and then wiped his mouth, having a great time on his week off from serving the arrogant Jeurous. Then again the noise came, louder than before, buzzing upon his property. It was as if it were trying to egg him on. So, as Sebastianus had lost his temper, he swung his front door open furiously and followed the buzzing. He was bare footed and moaned to himself when he noticed his filthy feet. He decided that he would go on, though. He passed the Red Branch Tree, which was the tree that bordered the North Forest and Hestour to the Unknown Lands where many feared to tread. Sebastianus had not noticed when he passed the border, but continued until he reached a spot where he bare foot felt a sharp pain. It was a branch that he had stepped on. But this branch contained small little sacks of some sort. They were spider eggs, he guessed. But they were two big. The unfamiliar eggs then popped like a balloon as small deformed wasps stretched out and took Sebastianus by surprise. The eighteen small little insects went into a thick hedge where the sharp buzz of a noise continued. So, the curious Sebastianus Within two minutes he had reached a wasp nest. Though there was a problem with it. It was twice the ten times the size of his house and the wasps inside were as big as raccoons. He hesitated and then ran as fast as he could, screaming, back to his house. Something was going on. The freak deer and the giant wasps had either scared away or eaten the other animals in the forest. There were probably more, too. But where could they have come from. Crusalands was a three week journey and besides, the creatures never left the land of Crusak.

"What", he said as he took a big breath, "is happening?" he asked himself. His question was answered when the wood fell from his door and a swarm of wasp bigger than himself crashed in. Buzz! In terror Sebastianus panicked not knowing what do. He then flipped over the table and used it as a barrier.

As Sebastianus cowered he then remembered that he had his blade. Sebastianus then ran from behind the table. He held the hilt with both hands, with his pointing his blade toward the monsters. He was horrified and began to shake like crazy. A bit of drool dropped from his mouth. He licked the drool of his chin with his tongue. He took a deep breath and charged at the wasp. Then in the blink of an eye, Sebastianus had jammed his sword through the monster, it then fell dead to the ground, dead.

The wasp swarmed in at him, all coming with their sword like stingers first, directing at his face. Sebastianus dropped his sword and ran behind the table where he was safe. The wasps must have been blind because they did not see even the slightest movement from their target. They stabbed air, and, being satisfied, moved backward. Sebastianus, with all of his might, forced himself to use his muscular arms to lift the small dining table and throw it all the insects, throwing three out of the five knocked dead on the ground, spilling green thick liquid and blood upon the wooden floor of the cabin.

The two wasps were the largest of the bunch, and they each made odd noises that scraped Sebastianus' eardrums. They were coming toward him, surfing on the wooden floor with their thin black and awfully hairy legs. They seemed like arachnids from the view that Sebastianus now saw them, thin hairs pointing from their fat bodies, and six odd legs as well as the four eyes instead of two. As he braced himself for the creatures, Sebastianus now noticed that his sword lay behind his challengers, where he had dropped it before fleeing to the table.

Quickly trying to think, Sebastianus maneuvered himself over the insects. As he leaped nearly two feet up and six feet forward, he felt the jagged teeth nibble at his thumb. He screamed as the wasp had bitten the nail of his thumb and nearly split it in half. It bled worse than any previous wound he had ever had and stung more than anything. He took a small moment's hesitation, observing that the wasps were very slow moving creatures, though wider than ever, to stop the blood from dripping. He reached down and grabbed his rusty sword.

He turned to his challengers and slashed at the first, stabbing it three different times. It made an awful noise and spilled nearly a gallon the disgusting green thick liquid as well as blood. He looked at the other monster that roared beside him and quickly thrashed at its side. It cried loudly in the air before Sebastianus put it out of its misery by stabbing in three more times in the ugly face that it had before the wasp fell dead.

Sebastianus' plan had worked. He was almost glad until he realized the mess that had been made. He thought of the days, possibly weeks that he would have to put into cleaning. And then he thought of the money it would cost to repair his old house. He quickly mumbled to himself, "That is enough! I must find the source of this!" He roared to himself. Sebastianus thought that would be the worst moment of his life, but none did he know much worse were yet to come.

Later on that day as Sebastianus was cleaning up the mess of the wasps as well as his aching cut and the many things that broke and were knocked down, such as the door and the table, he heard a soft knock on his door. When he arrived at the tall and oak wood door nobody stood to greet him. The backside of a familiar man was facing him as he walked south .But there sat the brown, faded, dead grass before him a fine rolled up note that was whiter than the whitest of all snow. In perfect scripture familiar handwriting:

Dear Sebastianus No Name,
You missed the fair today as I knew. Assuming that you have been attacked by one of the fowl creatures that now openly roam my kingdom, we can discuss the ending to it. It will be seven tonight in the Grand Hall. Bring my letter to the guards and they will allow you inside.
- Lord Titus Licesio II

Quickly Sebastianus made his mind up. He would go to the castle, but be careful crossing the woods, which he feared now he had faced the wasps and the warnings of Titus. He wrapped the note in his cloak and prepared to leave, also bringing his sword. Knowing that he would most likely have to face something on his way, Sebastianus left at five, which only a moment after he had received the letter. So he took off, out of the day, one thought coming into his mind. What had happened? The fair had been ruined, but by who or what?

Sebastianus had chosen his cloak carefully. It was dark and thin. This way he could blend in to the dark so he could not be attacked by a passing by creature. It was thin so he could move swiftly through the woods.

While crossing the Hestour River on the bridge, he felt the presence of something. A creature was following him. He ignored it at first, to lure the creature closer. When it was close enough, he would murder it the first chance he had with his sword. As the creature now was only feet away from him, Sebastianus pulled his sword and swung fiercely behind him. A similar sword was thrown in his direction, but he dodged, nearly falling into the Hestour River.

"Stay back, creature!" demanded Sebastianus, the sword steady in his hands as he held it in front of him. The beast he was up against was short as ever and dark from the shadows that the setting sun casted.

"Sebastianus? I thought you were one of the creatures. There have been three that have attacked me lately. I'm sorry", said Raphael. Raphael Venger was a Mealin. They were mainly human, but they had many animal instincts and the majority of them were savage. The only difference between a Mealin and a man is that a Mealin is slightly shorter with large hands and feet. Raphael had been found as an infant by humans and, being mistaken for a man, was raised by them. His true identity was not figured out until seven years later where he ate an animal live and raw in front of his foster parents. He was disowned by the people and from then on, Raphael swore never to use his Mealin instincts ever again. He had a muscular body and a shaved head, with no facial hair, but thick black eyebrows. "How are you doing, Sebastianus?" he asked, putting away his rusty sword.

"I'm doing decent...except for... ", Sebastianus stopped himself. As quickly as he could, he explained his miniature battle with the wasps back at his cabin and how it was completely destroyed. Raphael offered to help him later, but Sebastianus refused the kind offer. The two, having nothing more to say walked for forty minutes in silence.

After the journey, the two crossed the moat bridge of the wonderful, but small castle of the Royal Family of Licesio, who were believed to descend from Hestour Vinco himself. The small drawbridge was dull and faded, so Sebastianus carefully stepped. He realized that he had lost the note from Titus. "Sir, we need identification if you have lost your note."

"I am Sebastianus No Name, raised by the Royal Court. I am the assistant of the general, former apprentice of the messenger. I was invited by Titus."

The guards gave a small look to Sebastianus. It was a questioning look. "He's with me, too", said Raphael, showing his message.

"Please forgive me. Go on, the both of you", he said, signaling the way in with his large and burly hands.

The Grand Hall was magnificent. Hundreds of painting hung upon the brilliant walls. Paintings of hundreds of the Licesio lords and queens all the way back to the largest painting that Sebastianus had ever seen. It was Hestour Vinco, who stood proud in his portrait, holding a sword that looked even more brilliant than his own painting. There were twenty-one tables in all, three rows of seven. Appearing from his throne in front of the room was Lord Titus. He looked worried and sad, but yet furious. His golden crown was tilted. He removed it from his head and seated it upon his thrown. He maneuvered around the dining tables and gestured toward Raphael and Sebastianus.

"How are you?" asked Titus, his voice deep but proper, proving the royalty that spread across his blood.

"Not so well", answered Sebastianus, deciding not to tell him about the incident of the wasps until he heard what Titus had to say. He leaned carefully close to Titus.

"So, why is your life so bad at present?" Titus asked.

Deciding that there was no point in not telling Titus about his incident with the giant wasps, he told his kingdom's ruler. After explaining his crisis, Titus sighed. "I am afraid this is why I have gathered so many of you here today. Please take a seat. I'm assuming many people came early, as well for numerous reasons, so this will start at six."

"I am sorry, Lord Titus, but this needs to start now. I need explanations!" roared Sebastianus.

Titus was surprised that Sebastianus had the audacity to speak to him, a king that way. Then Titus sighed "That's why I invited you here to my secret meeting with the rest of the Royal Court. Just listen to my addressing", said Titus.

Now that more were gathering to the tables, Titus decided to break their conversing by loudly banginbg his silverware against his golden goblet filled with wine.

"It was many years ago, that Hestour Vinco took the stand. He fought Latorin and the pack of darkness. One of the most notorious of these dark men was Lyock Crusak, who was promised much land by Latorin. The land he was rewarded for his brilliance in battles was the finest of western lands.. These were countries, Arka, Rebucia, Gonjeaux, and the Sezelands. He renamed the Sezelands to the Crusalands, after himself. He found the darkest in the eastern land and gathered them to the Crusalands to work for him. After years of work, they had built him the Fortress of Crusak, in which was the finest temple anyone had ever seen. Beside it were forges were the trolls worked. Outside, an empire of creatures roamed freely.

"Seven of these creatures would guard Sezeland Path, so no civilization found to the hidden empire of Crusak. In order to do so, he had to sell the last of his mortal soul to Servius Death, the Red Nexuela. Once the mortal part of Crusak was murdered, his soul would belong to the Red Nexuela forever. So the Red Nexuela gave him the most dangerous beasts in the world. That is why Hestour Vinco trapped him inside the Chest of the Archangels along with the majority of his empire and hundreds more. But the seven beasts remained untouched, hidden forever in unknown spots.

"Crusak was imprisoned by Vinco two days before the Final Battle where he killed Latorin. But Crusak was not dead. And four people know where the box had been hidden. The people that know were Lord Reabius Azell, King Okkor Osmani, Liberius Volde, and I. We never told a soul, but somehow, the cousin of Liberius Volde, Bartholomew Van Sevets, found out where the chest was hidden. He thought that power would come his way if he freed Crusak. But instead, he was possessed and came to our kingdom like a prophecy of the wise Sobalus Muse stated. Bartholomew came to the fair and he unleashed forty-one beasts into the kingdom. By now, I can guarantee that more shall come. This will be the time that we must face our fears.

"Many nations may march to the Crusalands, but many will not. Those who do will not make it in time. As you know, we the third closest nation to the Crusalands. The first is Arka, who have feared to travel the Death March. Rebucia have turned round their sides and the majority of them followers of Latorin. So I wish to gather at least four hundred men from Hestour to travel to the Crusalands. You see, I have found the map of the path to the Crusalands. It has been painted larger for all to see."

As the crowd peered to the large painting, Titus announced one final thing. "Please tell every man you know. All men here I hope will be able to go. Women and children's lives shall be spared and they will be left to defend Hestour. We would be gone for a month at the most."

After the meeting, Sebastianus met with Titus, Raphael at his side. "We shall come", Sebastianus said proudly.

Titus thanked Sebastianus and looked at Raphael. "Of course I will come!" he said. Raphael now seemed to be offended. "I would go even if I was guaranteed a one hundred percent death", he snapped.

When Sebastianus arrived back at his home, he sent out messages to several blacksmiths, asking for armor. The first one to reply gladly made him a brilliant body of silver armor. It was not too thick, but not too thin, light and perfectly fitting. He put it around himself after receiving it four days later. Sebastianus found himself reading a letter from Titus a day later.

Dear Sebastianus No Name,
The Death March proceeds at dawn.
- Lord Titus

At this moment in his life, Sebastianus was more ready than he had ever been in his whole life. As he watched the window that night, hoping to see a large group of travelling archers, knights, and villagers walk the Death March. The darkness in the sky was beginning to fade slightly. As Sebastianus saw the men at the march, he left his house with his blade and joined beside Raphael and Sir Samir. He looked ahead of him, seeing the dangers before they had come. He peered over at the four hundred-fifty men and sighed, seeing the many deaths that were going to come. The darkness was rising again, like the times of Vinco.

Chapter Two:

The Journey Begins

Titus's men marched on. After a day and night of walking the group came to the Caesar Mountain range. The mountains stood high, higher than the small mountains that Hestour had on the very southern tip of their nation. These were in Arka, which was a fairly small nation. The mountains had small paths that rose to the tips and back down again on a path of seventeen of the largest mountains.

"We'll set up camp here for the night", Titus told those of the Death March. Nearly everyone in the group dropped down, exhausted. Most of the men were praying to God, asking to keep their lives. Night passed and as the day came in, brightness swirling in the air, Sebastianus awoke and stepped to Titus, who looked more tired than ever.

Sebastianus looked at the worried face of his lord, Titus, who was sitting on a rock, obviously not sleeping at all the night before. "Titus, you look awful", exclaimed Sebastianus.

"Thanks", said Titus sarcastically.

"I'm sorry. You look like you have not slept yet. Why?" asked Sebastianus, worried it could be involved with the March of one of the beasts that were to fight.

"This is believed to be the area that one of the creatures located. People have reported deaths at this spot and many have seen the creature and it's on the map. I am worried because it might spring from the least expected time."

Sebastianus felt the heavy hale poor against his shoulders. He realized something, though. This was one of the warmest parts in the world. Why was there hale? "Titus!" Sebastianus roared. "The hale, they're pebbles! The beast is coming!" Sebastianus was knocked off his feet and landed on a rock, cutting his forearm. He rushed to his sword that sat upon a flat surface. As he tried to pick it up, he felt the even surface split and form uneasy cracks and lumps. Managing to grab it, he roared to the camp, "Hide!"

"*Those of the Death March fear and plead for your lives, because this creature that you face is a god of stone and mountains. Roman of the Rocks shall kill each and every one of you!*" roared a voice in the air. This was the voice of Crusak as he sent the beast, Roman of the Rocks, to murder the camp.

Running for their lives, Titus, Raphael, and Sebastianus saw many crushed beneath boulders falling from the sky. Blood spattered upon Caesar Peak and eventually, boulders were being thrown from an invisible force on the very tip of the mountain. One hurled toward Sebastianus, but he darted faster than Raphael, the quickest man that Sebastianus had ever met. The man behind Sebastianus was the unfortunate and was smothered by the boulder.

As Sebastianus ducked, confused, he saw another massive boulder above him. The boulder barely brushed Sebastianus' hair on the back of his neck. Roman of the Rocks was fifteen feet tall and twenty feet wide with arms like a gorilla's, his knuckles brushing the ground. He was made of pebbles and boulders. He slid down the mountain on both feet, controlling the rocks to fly upward and land on the camp as he rushed down. Green eyes and a mouth that glowed with red blood were placed on his face.

Sebastianus and Lord Titus immediately took cover in a small cave where the Roman of the Rocks could not see them. It was located down the path of Caesar Peak. Many people followed him, while others split up. Those who were too slow were slaughtered. As they hid in the small, dark damp cave, they could hear the horrible screams of many warriors. Soon, the majority of the group had found their way to the cave and was in hiding far back. Three warriors remained outside the cave fighting off Roman of the Rocks. One was running for his life, toward the cave.

"Come on! Come on!" Sebastianus whispered to himself hoping that all three soldiers would make it back unharmed.

His prediction did not come true as two were slaughtered mercilessly. Finally Mathias, one of the three warriors was inches away from the cave, sprinting, and his sword miles behind him where he dropped it. "Help!" yelled Mathias, but as soon as one foot entered the cave he was swept off his feet and was pulled up the mountain by the Roman of the Rocks. He was dragged and his face was sweeping the jagged rocks. When he lifted it to cry out in pain, it was slathered in blood, an eye ball missing and his ear cut off. The sight of him was gone, though his sobbing continued. Luckily Mathias did not give them away so the Roman of the Rocks still had no clue where the soldiers were hiding.

Then the warriors thought of a clever plan. The soldiers marched out the cave as Roman of the Rocks remained on the other side of the mountain, devouring his prey. The soldiers split up. One half gathered hundreds of large rocks and tossed them at Roman of the Rocks. The other half gathered all sorts of metal that had been left behind and tried their best to force them to together of rub them against rocks. Finally, they had sparks. The sparks turned into small flames. They had fire.

With burning swords they chucked them at Roman of the Rocks and slowly he was melting. With more fire he would began to turn into lava. But only small specks of him were beginning to soften. As Sebastianus turned round, he saw Titus pulling from a small case that was under his cloak he had left in the camp.

Titus opened the case and slid it out. Sebastianus' eyes lit up when he saw the finest craftsmanship he had, and ever would see, laying there in Titus'ss hands. Titus then tossed him the sword. The sword then began to glow a blue color as soon as it touched Sebastianus' hands'. Titus then commanded "Use the sword." He powerfully tossed him the sword and Sebastianus caught it by the hilt. He felt more powerful, like he could do anything.

Running up to the Roman of the Rocks, Sebastianus then thrashed the blade through its arm. The fowl beast then screamed louder than anything heard to the human ears. The giant creature's arm had turned to dust, crumbling pebble by pebble.

The Roman of the Rocks seemed more furious than it had ever been. Several pebbles from the wreckage of his arm formed back together, but not enough before Sebastianus sliced it again and now it was shattered completely. It roared and then ran toward Sebastianus, rumbling through the aftermath of the mess that it had caused. It came toward Sebastianus, but it was only coming toward the blade that now sliced his other arm in long, slow slashes. It had no arms, but still was one of the most dangerous beasts in the world. It cocked its large head toward Titus and now began to beat the king with raining boulders. Titus was feeling piercing pain that stung his wounds that were filling with dust and rocks. He looked at Sebastianus, signaling that he needed desperate help.

The sight of his injured king made Sebastianus very angry. He leaped toward Titus, dodging the Roman of the Rocks. Sebastianus jumped up surprisingly high, higher than usual. He aimed his sword toward the creature, but it was easily dodged. Roman's reflexes were good, but for some reason, when he held the magnificent blade, Sebastianus' reflexes were even better, along with strength, courage, ways of battle and brains.

In rage, Sebastianus jumped up at least ten feet high. With his right hand, he jammed the sword in between two of the rocks in the back of Roman of the Rocks' head. He pushed to the right and the boulder fell from his face, his mouth falling as well. The small hole that was his throat spurted blood. Roman of the Rocks fell upon his knees, the rocks slowly coming apart, boulder by boulder. The beast was demolished and behind one of the stones that tumbled was a smaller black stone shaped as square. It was carved in fine handwriting '*Lyock Crusak presents the First Guardian, Roman of the Rocks of Caesar Peak.*' It was the beast of

Sebastianus got on his knees and began looking through the dust. He found the tablet, and on it was a red and black triangle. Then as Titus walked over to Sebastianus, he whispered "The symbol of Darkness." The small stone turned to dust and the aftermath of Roman of the Rocks glowed green and disappeared in the sudden dull and cold wind that blew strongly, swords and shields of dead men being swept across the ledge of the mountain. All cheered when they realized that Roman of the Rocks had been massacred. The cheers burned the ears of Sebastianus, who, for some reason, was not cheering. He knew that this was only the start to the madness. As Sebastianus looked at the ground, knowing Roman of the Rocks was nothing compared to what he was going to meet, Raphael walked up to him. "I'll always be at your side", he said.

Sebastianus now glanced at Titus. "What is this?" he asked, gesturing towards his brilliant sword.

"The sword you hold is one that has been kept and cleaned every day for over three hundred years. That is the very sword that Hestour Vinco used. The sword you have used is the Sword of Vinco", Titus replied with a smile and nod.

But little did the citizens and brave warriors on their quest know, they were being watched. "Fools!" Crusak said out loud in complete fury. "No!" Then Crusak thought of a deadly plan. "The Arachnid shall take care of them!" he said to himself.

The wind had died down and the Death March had moved to a small valley at the edge of Arka, the Crusalands woods. They slept with their cloaks over their bodies. The armor did help, but it was still unbearably cold as they were traveling south now and it poured rain. It was dark, but in the visible dim light were the only two men that were not sleeping. Sebastianus sat with his arms crossed, looking at Titus, wanting answers.

"Titus, what is all of this about? There is so much you have not told any of us, I can sense that. And I know that you want to keep something to yourself", Sebastianus firmly whispered.

"Sebastianus..." began Titus, biting his lower lip.

"There is no excuse of you leaving out life changing information!" said Sebastianus, now slightly waking few of the soldiers before they drifted off to sleep once more.

"Sebastianus, you have no last name as you know. You were brought up in the castle as an orphan with skills of all sorts. You did have parents that I knew. Your mother was from Arka. Her name was Rosih. Your father was from Hestour and his name was Collos. Rosih and Collos were notoriously rich and wealthy with seven sons. The six first sons were Gerard, Crinco, Leonardo, Vincente, Laarioz, and Harizo. When Rosih and Collos were almost at the end of their lives, Rosih gave birth again to a boy named Dramilius, which meant Night.

"Rosih and Collos, before they had to the children, had come from a long line of the Lator Family. The Lator family was the richest in the world and clearly the most powerful at a time. Their powers had crumbled, but were slowly rising again. Lator means Dark, so the family is now known as the Family of Darkness. You might have guessed by now that Latorin comes from the word Lator. Latorin was the first person of the family. Latorin the King of Darkness was the founder. Rosih and Collos had settled the North Forest and had declared it Lator Property and tried to open a church for Latorin. So my father, Sedove, who was the lord of Hestour, was forced to send the soldiers to kill your parents. All of the family was brought to be executed. All of your brothers escaped and fled the nation back to their homeland, in the Crusalands, where many in the Lator were born. Laarioz and Vincente returned to the aftermath of their parent's death to turn themselves in. They were murdered by angered villagers before even doing so.

25

"Dramilius was only an infant and had not been baptized into the religion of darkness. He was brought to me when I was a young lord, only nineteen. With my queen I was forced to raise him, to use him as a weapon against the dark if they ever rose to power again. I raised him and he was very amazing and I realized that he was perfect at everything, but gave him low rankings so he could learn to respect those who were higher."

Sebastianus understood now. The boy named Dramilius was him. He was Dramilius, the son of Lators. He was related, somewhere back, to the greatest evil that had ever been or ever imagined.

"Where are my brothers? Where is the rest of my family?" questioned Sebastianus, raising his voice.

"The weaker ones were murdered, but before they were executed, the majority sold their souls to the Red Nexuela so they are partially alive, but in a way you could only dream of. The stronger ones have rampaged across the world after the seven years of over two thousand deaths to the Lator Family and followers. This was called the Red Aftermath as so much blood was spilled. One thousand innocent people were viciously murdered before the dark settled down, but that is more frightening. If the dark has settled down, they obviously are doing something awful, something that will threaten all of humanity", Titus said, his voice a whisper.

"But why?" asked Sebastianus. "Why do they want to destroy the very world that they live on?"

"The way Latorin works is complicated. I have theories, but I think a more likely one is that the world is blocking his way to something. He needs something unearthly. If he's destroys this, he can do whatever he wants."

A thought was now occurring to Sebastianus. This man was related to him.

After walking through all the mountains, which took three whole days, they came to a large petrified and ancient Oak tree. It was massive. It rose three hundred feet tall, the tips of the stone like leaves rubbing at the end of low clouds. All took a slow moment to admire the famous tree that had been said to be up since the times of Vinco. Nobody knew where Vinco's body was, but many had theories that it was underneath the tree. Sebastianus did not admire the tree, but only stare at it with confusion. It was such an odd sight.

Titus spoke loud and clear for all people to hear. "This is the symbol of the swamp. We are now past the mountains and the first of the Seven Guardians. We are now a step closer to the end of our journey!" Everyone then began to cheer.

By the time the Death March had reached the swamp, the men decided they would set up camp in the swamp because the giant had destroyed the other camp in the mountains. It was quite risky because the swamp was a hot, damp, and humid environment, which proved to be extremely dangerous at times. Quicksand had settled near the camp and small spots made a mottled design. Thin water devoured the very bottom of the tents and the long grass poked through. The animal skin tents were soon destroyed in the swamp, there forth, the Death March was forced into the nearby cold and damp cave. Many more caves were all around the area, the majority small. Some were very thin, but seemed to never end and seemed to be flooded with water and moss.

Soon the dark poured in. It was only evening, but the large, soggy trees covered the setting suns. Sebastianus turned to the Death March who were all talking at once. "Hey, can anyone get some firewood?" Sebastianus called. The exhausted Death March did not reply simply pretending they didn't hear so they didn't have to get out of their comfortable positions in the cave with remains of the animal skin tents as warm, thick blankets.

"Sure thing, Sebastianus", the sudden reply of a cheery looking fellow said who seemed to be only a teenager, just two or so years younger than Sebastianus. The boy saw that he was not known to the person he was talking to. "My name is VGabriel", he said, cheerfully. "I saw some sticks about ten minutes back."

"I appreciate that", Sebastianus said with a plastic grin revealing his yellow teeth. This was not an uncommon thing to have at the time. VGabriel was soon immediately off, in a small jog.

Thirty minutes had passed. Sebastianus was worried. "A man is missing!" he called to the Death March. They turned their heads, half of them looking concerned. One half simply started their conversations again.

"Does no one care?" demanded Sebastianus.

"Sebastianus, we respect that you caring for one of your fellow men, but you have to understand", said Titus, coming from his circle of people that he was conversing with.

"What do I have to understand? A man is missing!"

Titus tried to be calm at the moment. "Sebastianus, I hate to say it, but many of us, if not, all of us, are going to die. In fact, our mission is to distracters for other nations. Few of us have a chance of living. We have been given a name that suits. We are the Death March. We will march to the death. We are going to have to face that death is approaching our way. If he dies now, then it will only be a day, perhaps two days, less."

Sebastianus tried to take this in, but yet he still feared that someone was dying slowly in the swamp. He could imagine it. But it was more than imagining. He was seeing it. Someone was in the middle of a puddle. This was VGabriel. He was being tormented, tortured. He was screaming and was unable to move. But nothing that Sebastianus could see was causing him pain. "Help!" he was yelling, "Help!"

Hushed voices were whispering into his ears and he was screaming more, and more. He was dying. Only then did Sebastianus scream himself. VGabriel lifted his hand and it was beginning to blacken at the tips. It was crisp. Somehow, a force was burning him alive. "Mercy!" cried VGabriel. Now the burning was spreading down his arm. He was almost dead before it stopped. VGabriel tried to squirm away, crying now. But as soon as he did, he was dragged backward in direction by an object that Sebastianus could not recognize. VGabriel reduced his screaming with only sobs and weak cries. He knew it was useless. Then the vision blurred to red. It was now blurring, though. Blood was spattering, covering Sebastianus' image. It now faded and Sebastianus saw Titus rubbing a cloth over his forehead.

"You were out for a while", he said. "Are you sick? Did you drink the swamp water?"

"VGabriel...he's dying...I saw it. I saw it in my mind. It was a real image. Something is tormenting VGabriel", Sebastianus moaned. He leaned to his side and vomited for what seemed like forever. Blood was now spattering.

Sebastianus now began looking around. Many people were like stones. They were cold, pale, and motionless. Titus saw the expression on Sebastianus' face. "A sickness has come. Two have died, three paralyzed and eight infected. The rest are by the fire. They're okay. You, though, do seem to suffer the same illness as the others. You are having something different."

"I am not ill, just shaken. For I have seen in different eyes, the eyes of the trees that are blocking VGabriel and his cries. Something dark was burning him to death with fire that could not be seen. The tormenter was not there, too."

Titus sighed. Raphael was now coming from the left of him. He said one word that stunned everyone. "Latorin."

"What do you mean?" Sebastianus asked nervously.

"Latorin is a very strong force. This could not be the work of Crusak, because killing a man through his own mind and burning him is something only the darkest could conjure. Latorin may only be a spirit that is trapped, but on occasions, when the dark seems strongest, he can leave his prison for moments, just enough to kill a weak little lad like VGabriel. Latorin then was forced back. But this was a sign. He does not put images in one's mind for no reason, Sebastianus. He wants you dead. He wants to kill *you*!" Raphael exclaimed.

"Lord Titus, we think you need to see this!" cried one of soldiers. "It appears that several caves are at the very back of this one. One seems very peculiar."

Sebastianus wearily jumped from his position, stomping his boot accidently in his vomit. Once he had heard the word *peculiar,* he reached for his special sword and followed the scurrying bunch as they traveled into darker parts of the cave. The dark cave now appeared to become lighter and lighter. A torch had been lit down the way. It had been lit for almost three days. A man had been here for some sort of ritual.

Anyone could tell that this was a place where rituals or worship was preformed. There were statues of things that Sebastianus only had nightmares about.

"Here are the caves, Lord Titus", said one of the men. He stepped aside. The first was normal. The second was normal. The third was normal, but the fourth cave was indeed, very peculiar. It was possibly cotton or silk, but something was stretching upon the walls and ceiling of the cave. "What is that?" demanded Titus, his voice quivering.

"It seems as though it's webs. I think they're spider webs", Raphael mumbled. He looked down and picked up a small stone and threw it at the mysterious silk. The stone stuck as though it were connected. It blended in to the white silk. It was a web, and immediately, it began to vibrate, shaking slowly. A small sound was in the distance. One would have guessed rats or any other creature that would lurk in a swamp cave. But Sebastianus thought. He had not seen even a small ant in the cave. Perhaps they decided not to roam in these parts, but even so; at least rats, cockroaches, or flies would be in there. There was a predator in the cave. As Sebastianus looked closely, he could see that bones were placed on the white silk. He had not noticed them, before. They were small bones of rats. Shriveled up insects that had once been large were stuffed inside.

"There's an opening, big enough for a man to walk in", Titus pointed out. "I think it would be best to see what lurks in the cave, to know what we will face."

Sebastianus didn't feel right the very second he stepped into the cave, he felt like he was being watched. The place was covered in dead rats and insects and many other small creatures. It was then that Sebastianus inhaled the smell of not dirt, or slime, but blood. He smelled fresh blood. He looked around, only to find the brand new rat that was almost completely dead. It twitched once more before dozing off to its death. Not a drop of blood was inside it. Sebastianus had smelled a dead animal *and blood*. How could he smell blood if there was no fresh blood about?

The very man that had brought the soldiers to the cave now was lying on the silk, dead. It was his blood that was filling the air. He had been murdered by an unknown source, the source of which inhabited these caves.

A shrill cry was made out from behind the soldiers. It was VGabriel, stuck and wrapped in silk to block the entrance of the cave which they had come from. He was barely alive. One of his eyes was bulging out of its sockets, almost melted from the invisible fires. His arms were loose from his shoulders, both crisp black. His hair had been burnt and his neck had been bitten, blood pouring from the throat. He moaned in agony before the entrance was completely blocked and it was all dark.

Hissing silenced VGabriel before his death. The hissing was shrill and high, scaring all of the men. Raphael roared, "Help! We're stuck in the cave!" It seemed to be no use as no sounds were coming from behind the slaughtered body of VGabriel. The layers of silk in the way were worth pounds. The shrill hissing continued along with sounds of clicks, taps, and scurrying. If there was a living source in the cave, there was more than one.

"Get us out of here!" screamed the other man that had guided Sebastianus, Titus, and Raphael to the caves. He was now roaring; spit flying from his unwashed mouth. "Get us out of here!" he was no almost crying.

Sebastianus removed the Sword of Vinco from his side and thrashed the silk. He stopped for a moment to halt the other men. He listened closely and heard the rustle of clicks, scurrying, and hissing from behind a large clump of silk. Sebastianus swung his blade at the layers of silk and took it out, finding smears of blood and oozing green liquid just like the wasps from before. He tore away the silk with his sword to find the dead mangled body of a spider. But this was a spider like no other. It had a body the same size as Sebastianus' torso and hairy legs the size of his own limbs. Its large fangs were filled with enough poison to kill a quarter of the Death March. The spider's murdered body twitched until death finally came to it.

"That second challenge. This was the simplest guardian that Crusak could ever conjure!" the man that had overreacted before chuckled to himself.

A small sound of scurrying scraped the eardrums of Sebastianus. No one else seemed to hear it. Sebastianus eyes the smallest movements that were appearing from under the silk. "There are more!" Sebastianus warned the others. Thirty spiders the same size as the first emerged from the silk, hissing and throwing their disgusting legs forward at the men. Sebastianus thrashed, slicing it into two. Others came in pairs, merciless.

The only man that did not bring a weapon was the very man that Sebastianus had been following. The man was immediately screaming, running in circles. He was bitten by a spider large spider that had come behind. His leg was oozing blood. The spiders licked the fallen blood and then wrapped him in silk they squirted from their own bodies. The spiders bit their fangs in and began slurping in for minutes before their victim was a shriveled piece of what appeared to be a thick paper

Sebastianus sliced the majority of the spiders that had been slurping upon the man. All of the humungous spiders were all dead, forever to rot in the silk. But Titus, who was a little clumsy, tripped. Raphael helped him up, but now he was falling. Normally Raphael was one to keep his ground. All were on the ground because a force was rattling, coming down the way. Fifty more spiders and behind them, a creature bigger than Sebastianus, its eight hairy legs rubbing against the silk. The spiders were coming in all directions, including from the ceiling and floor of the cave. As Sebastianus could see, this was the mother of the spiders. The eyes were red like blood and the fangs were thin because they had not feasted on a human in such a long time. And now that three large and well built men stood before them, with warm blood, it could not resist but to back the baby creatures away to take the prisoner there and feast upon them. Titus took his sword and swatted the children spiders away, making his way towards the dead body of VGabriel that blocked the entrance. The mother spider tried to make her way toward Titus, but Raphael and Sebastianus found themselves fending her off. They slashed at her, but it only lightly scraped her skin.

Titus was now using his sword to scrape the body of VGabriel off the spider webs. He was successful, but behind the body were many of the spiders on thick layers of silk. Titus stabbed them, slicing them in half. One of them was inches from biting him, but Titus was quick to defeat the creature with a swift slash through the body. He was now scarping through thick webs.

Sebastianus and Raphael were having a hard time. Raphael had almost been bitten on several occasions, and Sebastianus was not having an easier time. The smaller spiders were squirming all over and coming as common as mosquitoes swarming over a hot pond. The largest spider seemed to lose interest in the two that her children were battling. She stood behind and nibbled on the remains of the man that they had killed just minutes before. She now seemed to be seeing that Titus was straight in view and in easy reach. The mother spider raced on her webs, crawling sideways and straight past Sebastianus and Raphael.

Titus was already through, jumping at the last second. But now the spider was chasing him through the cave and she was twice as fast. Titus turned and round and faced his sword forward and thrashed hard. It was harder than he had ever imagined and blood spilled from the mighty beast. The arachnid was suffering, but nowhere near dead. It was now angrier than it ever was and stared at Titus, its eight eyes ready to see its legs tear apart her victim.

The large spiders were coming from all over, ready to bite their victims. Sebastianus was now going full blast, running at the creatures instead of them running to him. He was using the webs to his advantage. He wrapped the silk on his sword and stabbed the spiders inside their mouths so the sword stuck in and could move from the blade. Raphael was beginning to catch on the ruthless tactics of Sebastianus and soon, had the spiders dead, severely injured (waiting to die), or run off. It was a massacre in the end. As Sebastianus clarified the deaths of the arachnids, he turned round to see the entrance clear and Titus struggling with one of the fiercest creatures ever.

Raphael sprinted and Sebastianus followed behind. The two were some of the most athletic that there was to offer. They each were most likely the fastest runners in all of Hestour and were soon at Titus'ss aid in moments. They thrashed at the spider, threatening it back into its lair. When the creature had refused, Sebastianus jabbed the Sword of Vinco towards one of its legs. The swift and flexible villain dodged the attempt and soon was trying to bite Raphael. It was then that Titus thought of his idea. If they lured the creature backward, then it would be facing four hundred-fifty soldiers that were all trained, armed, and devoted to defeating the creatures of the world.

Titus ran backward. He kept jabbing his sword at the arachnid, though. Soon that his companions were beginning to understand what their lord was trying to do, they were soon following him, doing the same.

The three were almost helpless this way, though they were not completely vulnerable. They managed, several times almost being killed. But eventually, they were in reach of the camp at the tip of the cavern. The camp soon saw them and heard them. Within moments, the creature was dead. No one knows who had the winning stab, or if the creature simply died at the numerous stabs at the same time, or if it collapsed dead before anyone could touch it as it did seem rather old. But many say that they saw Sebastianus stab the arachnid last before it died. So twice was the most unexpected man the hero.

As the mother of the spiders fell dead, its blood seemed to, like the dark magic, form dripping letters on the cavern wall: 'Lyock Crusak Presents the Second Guardian: The Arachnid and Her Children of the Arka Swamp Caverns.'

Sebastianus sighed, though all seemed to cheer and hug each other in joy. Raphael seemed to not be able to join the happiness either. He looked across to Sebastianus and they could read each other's minds. They both knew that what was yet to come was going to be much worse than this.

"Titus, there is so much you never tell me. I need to know, because this journey seems to involve me more than it should. And you know all of this, but you never tell me", Sebastianus whispered as the group reached the borders of Arka. Large fields stood before them with small streams from the swamp that led to the Larkon Sea.

Looking more seriously than Sebastianus had ever seen, Titus turned. As his body turned, so did his demeanor and he had a grim face, dull and pale. He turned again; making sure no one could hear him and whispered, "What do you want to know?"

"I want to know everything. Start from the beginning. You cannot leave out a single detail", snapped Sebastianus, trying his best to keep quiet.

Titus cleared his throat and began from the very beginning. "Herattan Lator was of the most ancient from a hidden land called Arishba. He was a prince in the country, son of the most powerful man in the world. His mother was dead and he had three brothers that had died in war. So all there was to his family was his beloved father.

"You see, Sebastianus, Herattan was born with several things that differs his mind and abilities from the average man's. He was born completely insane and with physical powers like no others. And another thing that was plugged into his mind was curiosity and brains one hundred times bigger than mine. So, he wanted to be king of Arishba so some of his fantasies could come true. But his father was in amazing condition and there was not even bad words thrown at each other it was so peaceful. To conclude, Herattan murdered his own father. He was declared king for almost one month before the arrival of Sobalus Muse, who was possibly even wiser than Herattan. This was how it all began.

"Muse was such a wise, positive, kind, brilliant, and outgoing man, that Herattan was declared Duke of Arishba. His replacement was Sobalus Muse, who ruled magnificently. But one day, Sobalus found himself half dead in the woods. His attempted killer was obvious. When Muse returned, a ship had been sent out with hundreds of men, including Herattan. It was Herattan's idea to explore the rest of the world.

"Heratten found many things. He was the first to see all ninety nine nations, which were completely empty. He explored all seas and many more places. He saw mysterious places such as the City of Souls, which I believe in completely", said Titus when he saw the look of doubt on Sebastianus' face. He began again, "He also saw Torninoa, the city of the dead. But all of his men died when they journeyed to 'The Land of the Forgotten.'

"Many believe that the Land of the Forgotten is a myth that Heratten came up with. Others believe it is real. Remember when I told you that I think our world blocks a force that Latorin needs, well I think that this is that force. He said it was indescribable. His execution for the attempted murder of Muse was postponed when they heard of this story. Sobalus wanted to know more. So then Sobalus set out to journey to this land with the guidance of Herattan. But he was double-crossed as Herattan killed all of the men on board while they slept. He sailed the voyage back to Arishba and was crowned king. This was when the worst came.

"Herattan claimed he saw a spirit that had come from the Land of the Forgotten to tell him everything. The spirit was called Krausin. He said that 'in' at the end of a name meant 'dark and brilliant.' Krausin said that if Herattan changed his name from Lator to Latorin, then he would have successively become absolutely perfect and all powerful. When he changed his name, the good in him had been drained away completely, turned into evil, and spat back at Herattan. He was now Latorin.

"Latorin ruled Arishba darkly. If he thought of sick pleasures, he would use the citizens to fulfill them. He thought of combining man and beast to one creature. He did so and started finding that monsters were formed. He loved his creations and soon inspired the first dark wizards that would help him. His followers were those who did not want to suffer. But Latorin managed to actually form darkness in the minds of his false companions and soon this led to Crusak and people of the sort. He used his own blood to make things only in the darkest nightmares. When Latorin found out that people were leaving Arishba to be free of his reign, he called war on the free leader whose name was Liberius Volde.

"Liberius' wife was once a widow because her old husband was Sobalus Muse. He had a son who his wife named Sobalus Muse II. Liberius himself had relations to the Lator family and hid them. His brother had closer connections and slightly darker than he was. His nephew was the famous prodigy, Hestour Samaras Vinco. Another was among them and his name was Reabius Azell."

Sebastianus recognized the name Reabius Azell. He realized that he was a current nation leader of a place named after his family. The nation was Azell.

"You are probably wondering about the current leader of the nation, Azell. I will get to that later", Titus began again. "There was a pond of eternal youth that these four found out when Liberius was getting older and the four children were in their twenties. They drank from the fountain and stayed young forever. They were rebels and when they returned from their journey to the fountain, their village had been slaughtered by Latorin. From here they began their famous run as the four rebels that defeated Latorin.

"The four all possessed powers, but Sobalus and Reabius were only real legitimate wizards. Together, with a long, long process, they were able to defeat Latorin with special weapons given by a notorious blacksmith. Liberius lives by the Larkon Sea on his boat, the *Prince Alexander*, which is named after his son that was killed, Alexander, the prince of freedom. Reabius Azell now runs his own nation, who are considered the wisest and most powerful. Sobalus' death is not confirmed, but no one in the world knows what happened to him. As for Vinco, he was killed as he killed. Latorin stabbed him in the heart while he stabbed Latorin in the heart. They died at the same time.

"Ever since then, the dark has been stirring. Many say that it is the disappearance of Sobalus and the death of Vinco that will raise Latorin to power. The most notorious of the dark's servants were Solomon Bruno, who has changed in a way and now leads his own nation, Servius 'Death' Tirmilen, the undead king who now is known as the Red Nexuela, and Lyock Crusak, who you know.

"There have been heroes in the past. Obviously our four greatest are Vinco, Volde, Azell, and Muse. There were also the Protectors for a short while, the Hunters, and I believe that you will succeed further than any. More villains seemed to appear. Many are mortals selling their souls to Latorin's spirit. I've heard of werewolves and vampires as well. Then times were silent was many years. Then came a possessed man who I received information that his name is Gregory. This man must have been very adroit in finding things because the chest was one hundred feet under the ground in the City of Souls. There, a ghost guards it inside the Fountain of Youth. Several other chests are bound there and many are in Torninoa and some lie in the darkest depths of the world. Vinco was one of two to know where the Land of the Forgotten was.

"Gregory seemed to travel and remove the box, spirits of Latorin growing inside him until he was completely possessed, no longer even man. He received the chest and came to the right spot at the right time. It was the middle of the fair that celebrated the very reason that Gregory was shattering. He opened the box and one thousand creatures swarmed upon Hestour to wreak havoc and vengeance against mankind, those who imprisoned them. The leader of them was Crusak. I don't know what happened to Gregory then, but I feel sorry for him. If he is not suffering to a beast in the dungeons at this very moment, he is dead. But yet, he deserves it. It was not Latorin that came to him, it was he was moved toward Latorin. And now we are in the middle of the biggest crisis since the days of Vinco."

Sebastianus nodded and then a thought appeared to him. "Will we meet Liberius?" he asked in a curious, childish tone.

"Yes, we will. We shall travel with him across the Larkon Sea as he is only one who knows the waters so well. And just for the knowledge, Sebastianus, Liberius will beat you or threaten to throw you overboard unless you call him Master Volde or Lord Volde. He does control a nation, you know." Titus smiled and then mumbled to himself, "But he doesn't do much to show that he's the lord."

"What do you mean?" Sebastianus questioned.

"Well, Liberius has lost much sanity in the wars he has been through. Also the things that he has seen…" Titus stopped himself there. "He's just forgotten he's the ruler of Volde. He just seems to live out on his boat for ten months out of twelve. Never does he make new laws or put people in prison. He just forgets his job. But trust me, watch him. He'll be gentle and kind one minute and the next he'll be threatening to kill you. But the anger is nothing compared to the nights. At night he goes on dock and talks to himself and says things that are so real and so horrifying that he screams. He'll try to kill himself, but stop with a moment in time. He chants rituals of ancient beasts that live all over. You can never look at Liberius in the eyes, either. They are lifeless, motionless. Honestly, I think they're stone. If you look at them for too long, you see things in them. You see things he has seen. He's an odd fellow, Liberius. But you cannot help to feel sorry for him. It's just he's older and his history is enough to make you cry. He's seen his wife murdered and all of his children murdered. He's seen his nephews, brothers, sisters, cousins, nieces, and best friends slaughtered. Be careful. But this obstacle, Sebastianus, shall not cross our way for the next five days or so. So be patient and never forget that."

"The fields of are rough, so be on your guard, Sebastianus. This is a great place for creatures to roam. It's warm and has many animals. There is even a great place to hide. This grass is at least ten feet tall. Also, watch out for the holes. Holes are covered by grass. You fall in and in there for weeks before anyone notices and you'll be dead by then. They're twenty feet deep. I've fallen in one before. It took nine days before someone came back to look for me", Raphael said with an energetic burst.

The Death March had reached the Villkin Fields. The long fields of tall grass were mossy with faint dampness from the swamp. It began as a bog but soon transformed. The Villkin started in Hestour, only swiping the tips and formed a thin steak down Arka but spread in the Crusalands, swallowing half of the northern tip. Titus believed that a guardian was in here.

The group of warriors soon came to an area where the tallest of the grass roamed freely. Many of the men pulled out their knives or swords to cut the tall grasses. "Start a fire", commanded Raphael immediately. "We must burn the grass. If we do so, then nothing can come up, nothing can hide, and all will show."

A soldier came towards Raphael's way and snickered and sneered. He was twice the height and weight of Raphael, with bulging muscles. He bent down so his face was close to Raphael's and spat, "You want us to put the whole risk at camp with a burning fire because you think something in there. A flower will come and maybe spray a couple of bees at us!"

Raphael himself now conjured a smile. The soldier looked disgusted. "Why are you laughing? You're nothing but a dirty cross over breed of an animal and man! So I ask you again, Mealin, why do you laugh at my authority?"

"I laugh", Raphael said, his demeanor changing quickly into a serious face, "because you are definitely going to get eaten, slaughtered, or fall in a hole and never come out!"

"And I presume you're going to be the cause of this?" demanded the soldier. He looked at his audience of over four hundred soldiers. They reluctantly laughed when he gave them a sharp look. The soldier went on again, "And if I were you and you were me, dirty animal, I would keep my mouth shut, walk away and burry yourself six feet under." He turned to the other soldiers and they unwillingly laughed once more.

Raphael laughed again and folded his arms. "If you act like such a leader, I would like to see you beat me. Take me on hand to hand, no weapons."

The soldier hesitated and then laughed. "This seems like quite the act for a creature with no soul. I'm sure that all will remember you were brave before death."

The miniature fight began. Sebastianus turned to Titus, but the lord of Hestour just continued to drink water and kick the dirt around under his feet. When Sebastianus checked back to the fight, Raphael's face was drenched in his own red blood. The soldier was grinning. But then his grin faded when Raphael shot a ferocious punch to the face. Raphael hit again and again in the same spot. When the soldier was realizing the technique, he put his hand out to block, but Raphael ended up curving his punch in the middle of the air so it landed in the side of his opponent's head. The soldier was on the ground, begging for mercy. But Sebastianus saw through this. Underneath him was his sword. He was going to kill Raphael.

The solider had already swung his sword through the air, cutting through time itself it was so swift. Sebastianus had now chucked his sword through the air to Raphael. Raphael caught the Sword of Vinco and blocked the soldier's blade. He hit it out of the soldier's hands and jabbed his blade through the heart.

No one gasped or cried from the death, all knew it was fair and that Raphael was doing the right thing to kill him. Sebastianus just sat there. He was motionless. He was not angry, surprised, shocked, happy, or any other expression. He just shrugged and took the Sword of Vinco from the dead man's heart and wiped the blood off with grass. Sebastianus nodded to Raphael, signaling that it was fine with him. Raphael nodded back with a shrug and a yawn before he drifted off to sleep.

The Death March awoke to sparks. Titus had been starting a fire in order to burn down the grass. The others of the group helped Titus as he struggled to spread the fire to several large branches he found. The men lifted the huge branches and threw them into the grass. A large circle burned, but only enough for a rock. The branches died out and crumbled into ashes.

The ground shook ferociously and the grass was flattened a mile wide and all could see what was underneath the grass. Numerous holes fifty feet deep all around formed a circle. From the holes came green slime that filled high. And rising in the center of the scene was a plant of some sort. It was a thick, burly root covered in thorns big enough to stab through a man's neck and out the other side. The top was a large circle covered in spikes that opened and closed, ready to eat something.

The large plant now released oozing green liquid from its disgusting body. The thick goop quickly spread itself all over the place, becoming a large juggernaut. It devoured the land and absorbed two men under itself and there was no way out. They were stuck in the goop until there was now air to breathe in. Sebastianus raised his sword, ready to strike at any time.

From the holes that were clearing of the green liquid, a terrible smelling aftermath appeared. Soon openings for large roots to sprout from came into the hole, digging as though they were an acid burning the way. The roots were thicker than the plant, almost twenty feet tall and five feet thick, and they were twice the weight of any man in the Death March. The roots seemed to be able dig underground and appear in completely different places, threatening the Death March incredibly as they brought men under, swallowing them to whatever force was feasting below. Even with Sebastianus' Sword of Vinco, he struggled to defeat the twenty five roots that shot up from the ground, ready to kill.

Sebastianus found himself jabbing at a giant root with his sword. It was cut severely, but no dead. Sebastianus waited to see where the beast was going to come from. He peered all around him, glancing and checking for slight movement in the ground. "Sebastianus look out!" roared a voice that was not recognized. Before he could move, Sebastianus found himself being thrown up in the air by the familiar white root. It got him, gripped him, and squeezed him. The root squeezed him so hard, his ribcage was almost flattened and crushed and lungs about popped like balloons. Before the worst could be done, the root released its rough grip. Sebastianus tried to breathe, but struggled. When his lungs were releasing air properly, he turned to his side and saw Raphael grinning. He smirked and mumbled to himself, "That would be one for me, and absolutely nothing for Sebastianus."

Grinning, Sebastianus thanked Raphael and once again, was taken by surprise as a large plant-like root sprouted from the ground and lunged itself at the two. Within moments, the Sword of Vinco was slashing and slicing the root into bits. Raphael smiled and managed to say, "One to one."

Titus had joined the two in the next minute, bringing a man named Oloak, who was very large and fit, and a knight for the Hestour army. He proved his swordsmanship with a brilliant strike at a nearby root. When the roots were dying down, Titus was quick to think of a brilliant plan. "There is obviously a large force underneath that plant", he pointed to the large plant that the roots surrounded. "If one can manage to go in one of the holes and go through an empty root opening, he can defeat what is underneath. But it will be safer if two go. We need two distracters for the roots, as well."

"I'll go", Sebastianus said at the same time as Raphael.

"Then Oloak and I will be the distracters. Come on, let's go, while the roots are calmer", Titus said, holding his sword. He dove into the first root he saw and same with his companion. Sebastianus and Raphael were sprinting and swinging their swords in air to make sure that if a root came near them, it would be sliced.

Raphael jumped into the hole and found himself tunneling inside a very tight space. Sebastianus did the same thing and the two eventually squirmed inside.

Once through the tunnel, small spots of light from the holes showed images of what lurked. A green circular monster sat on top of grass that grew underneath the surface of the ground. It was lumpy and had a very large hole full of red organs. There were other holes as well, but none as big as this one. The hole led to the inside of the creature. The roots were coming from all over its body. As Sebastianus could see, a root was dragging back a dead body. The root swung the body into the hole, which was clarified as the mouth now.

Sebastianus looked at Raphael, who was also disturbed greatly. "We have to jump down onto the creature", Raphael suggested. His companion nodded slowly but soon felt something grip around his waist. A white, squirming, but thin root had grabbed hold of him. Sebastianus' arms were free, so he grabbed his blade and stabbed it dead. He then took his blade and cut the rope like root and landed on a soft green lump that almost felt as if it was wet and slippery, but Sebastianus still had a good grip on the lump. Raphael fell behind him, stumbling on the mossy like creature. He managed, though and then the two began to whisper again.

"We should slice all of the roots", Sebastianus said confidently. Raphael agreed and soon the two were at the job. Sebastianus stabbed a root several times before it dozed to the ground with no life. Other roots came at Sebastianus, but the Sword of Vinco was powerful enough to slice them all in half. He thrashed his famous weapon at them and they were pale and icy, dead. Raphael had soon eliminated the rest of them. The monster itself had almost no reactions with the exception of a three small twitches (these twitches were small to the beast, but short earthquakes for Sebastianus and Raphael).

Now stab marks covered the large green and leathery creature as the two soldiers were gashing their opponent with their swords. The long and perfectly crafted Sword of Vinco cut right through the thin skin of the creature.

Raphael was lifted reluctantly off the creature quicker than Sebastianus could think, by a thick, white root that had sprouted straight from the mouth of the creature. Raphael had not known what had hit him. Sebastianus was now fending himself as another root came at him. This one was thicker and taller. Sebastianus gashed at it, but he was tied up within a matter of a minute, the root controlling him and tossing him carelessly inside the mouth of the juggernaut of the fields. He still had his sword, and he knew that Raphael had his, but still, Sebastianus could only think of his death.

The two soldiers were in a black hole, where roots were sprouting everywhere. The humungous roots lifted them up and tossed them in a large, red, and plastic like tube that went for what seemed like forever. It was lighter inside the tube, and Sebastianus could clearly see through the tube. He saw plant parts, sacks containing murdered bodies of the Death March and water. He saw what looked like brown chunks of meat that he guessed were the organs. Raphael had closed his eyes tight, hoping to block the images from his mind.

Sebastianus felt a large loop form and within a split second, he was upside down, spinning in circles. Raphael was cursing the beast, but it did not stop as the two were eventually hurled downward into a large red pit. Water was pouring from every side. The water, that Sebastianus thought he was going to drown in, soon drained. It was flowing into small holes that led somewhere in the monster. "Raphael, where do those holes lead?" demanded Sebastianus.

"I've not a clue", said Raphael, his sword still high in the air, prepared for the monster to strike at tbhem any time.

"They could lead out", suggested Sebastianus.

Raphael hesitated and then looked around. There was no way of seeing this or knowing. He looked at Sebastianus and sighed. "We will have to guess."

Sebastianus nodded in agreement and stuck his foot inside one of the holes. He felt the dampness on his boot and it filling with cold water. It was deep. He dipped the rest of his leg. Eventually he was completely in. Raphael was following and soon the two were in a small tunnel, completely under water. There was only darkness, but they could feel the soft and cushiony sides of the creature as they tried to find their path through. Soon enough, they were out of the water and gasping for breath. Their heads poked out of an opening where they found themselves in a large circular cave. They jumped out, hoping to find a way out. But there was none that they could see. Raphael checked everywhere and even attempted to find his way up the sides (walls) for an entrance. There was not a single place to even begin an escape.

"Sebastianus, we need to get back in the hole!" demanded Raphael. Sebastianus looked at him, puzzled. Raphael pointed upward to what appeared to be a mouth. The mouth-like body part of the creature revealed teeth. The teeth were like hundreds of swords and they were slowly coming downward to chomp the victims. "Come on, Sebastianus, find the opening!"

The two soldiers looked around for the opening only to find a small slit. It had closed. Sebastianus and Raphael were trapped in a cave of the juggernaut of the fields. The teeth above then began to close in on him. "Help me!" Sebastianus roared over and over again. Raphael kept calm. When the teeth were only inches away, he kneeled down and folded his hands. In the darkest time, Raphael always relied on prayer. He mumbled and his mouth was barely moving.

Sebastianus nodded at Raphael and knelt down on the soft, damp, green surface of the cave. He folded his hands and said to himself, "God, I usually don't pray, but if you're listening, let me live." He sighed as there was no given reply. Sebastianus put his head in his hands and cursed.

"Look over there!" demanded Raphael, pointing his index finger to the left of Sebastianus.

A large hole was forming in the side, blinding light coming from it. It led to the outside. The light coming in was the sun. Sebastianus rejuvenated with Raphael. He gripped the Sword of Vinco tightly and began stabbing every area of the creature. He made sure that every spot was gashed. Then he widened the opening in the side of the monster with his sword and began to clear the goop. Sebastianus stabbed the creature even more, Raphael copying him, before he saw that the teeth were coming down quicker. The two were soon squirming though the hole and trying to get out. After what seemed like forever, Raphael and Sebastianus were breaking the surface. They were in a small ditch were a lifeless and pale root had been detached. They were facing fresh air once more, the sun shining upon the fields. But in the distance, havoc was spreading.

"Raphael", Sebastianus finally decided, "We need to get some sticks. I have an idea." Raphael and Sebastianus found two sticks with ease as they poked through the grass. Sebastianus began rubbing them together with all of his might. As he did so, Raphael was catching on and found dry grass. Raphael shoved the grass down the hole as Sebastianus started sparks. And then there was a fire. He put the fire on the grass in the hole and within moments, the fire was spreading down into the creature. Though it was not dead, it was weakened. Every root was down and they were going to be for a while.

"Let's get out of here!" demanded several of the soldiers.

"We have to finish the job", many yelled.

Sebastianus and Raphael shared the idea with everybody they could and told them to tell others. Within moments, every soldier was starting fires in the root holes. The creature was going to be dead any time.

They knew that the creature had been finished when a large hole in the center of the fields softened in, as though melted. There was an acute roar and the roots popped from the ground, only to melt suddenly to white paste.

The ashes and paste and grass had mixed into a repulsive mixture that smelled worse than the corpses that Sebastianus had seen. For just five seconds, all could see clearly that it has spelled out for all to see: 'Lyock Crusak presents the Third Guardian: The Juggernaut of the Fields'.

"We should set up camp here", suggested one of the soldiers to Titus, who was smiling at the aftermath of their victory. Titus shook his head.

"This place smells worse than dung, there are dead bodies everywhere, it's unsafe, and this root paste could melt skin if you touched it", Titus replied. "We will walk to Liberius. He has a beauty of a boat that we can all sleep in."

Chapter Three:

Traveling With Liberius

After the short walk, Titus and his group came to the Larkon Sea. From behind a large pine tree, a crazy looking old man jumped out of his fine golden brown painted ship. On the side of it written in gold and amazing hand writing was: *Prince Alexander.* He had a trimmed grey beard and an almost bald head. He had bright green eyes that made his pupils almost seem invisible. He was very muscular for his age and he wore a dark cloak with the hood down. Liberius eyed every man in the Death March before nodding.

"Hello, Liberius", said Titus with a plastic grin. "How are you? How is the nation?"

"Hello, Titus. I am very good. The ship is doing fine, as well", was the reply of Liberius. His voice was raspy and young sounding. Sebastianus took in mind what Titus had said about Liberius and the state of his nation and how he did not control it, though he was leader, and how he did not answer Titus's second question.

Sebastianus thought it would be a good thing to introduce himself to Liberius, so they could get on the right foot. "Good evening, Lord Volde. My name is Sebastianus", he said, putting his hand out for handshake.

"What is your surname?" demanded Liberius.

"I am an orphan. I do not know it", said Sebastianus calmly with a fake grin. He did not show a sign of emotion besides happiness and calmness. Liberius did not like that.

"You will be served dinner", Liberius changed the subject and turned to the Death March. "As for lunch…" He cruelly grinned.

His wicked smile gave Sebastianus a shutter as he stepped to the side from the dock to the fields. He came back to his spot a minute later with a bloody rabbit he had killed in a matter of seconds with his bare hands. "You have ten minutes to get whatever you can find."

No one moved.

"That is your choice", Liberius said without emotion. He seemed as though a stone. "Dinner shall not be served for another two hours."

To impress Liberius, Sebastianus tried to look like a helpful person by making sure everyone was on the *Prince Alexander* before him. He was the last one to step in, but was grabbed with cold hands and pushed out. It was Liberius. Sebastianus saw his face. It was blank and his eyes, Sebastianus could have sworn, were black for a second. He was sure that for a moment, his eyes were pure black. He put his purple lips (from the amount of red wine he drank) to Sebastianus' ear and whispered. "Beware the waters, lad. Never trust the water. I've been out here so long and I know things that lurk here. And others, I'm not so sure about. But all I can say, boy, is that it will never be safe. The only reason Volde isn't overflowed with awful water creatures and witches, is because they have someone protecting them. That someone is me. So watch your step."

Sebastianus still could not understand what he was being told. He was too distracted from the stone like face of Liberius. It was enough to make him scared enough to run back to Hestour right at that moment. "What do you mean by that?" asked Sebastianus nervously.

"Listen boy. You're young. You can still enjoy life for a lot longer. I would recommend you do your best trying to live! Go back now…or risk your life." Sebastianus looked at the man with mixed demeanor, like his feelings were at the moment. It was silent for a second. Sebastianus then walked slowly up the rest of the board into the roomy *Prince Alexander*.

The *Prince Alexander* was a massive ship. There were twenty five rooms, two restrooms, with a deck bigger than homes. The captain's quarter was like a small house. There was a treasure room full of things Sebastianus had never dreamed of. And the bottom had many barrels. One was full of money, one filled with wine, and several contained weapons. The ship was a small village. And in every room was a painting of Hestour Vinco, Reabius Azell, Sobalus Muse, and Liberius.

Liberius had prepared a delicious stew in a pot bigger than a full grown man. Beside him was another pot. He had two of them! Sebastianus wondered how the boat carried all of the weight. "Let us say Grace", announced Liberius. The Death March sighed, but prayed just the same. After that, they received a small bowl of stew. Sebastianus could tell it was rabbit stew and was disgusted, knowing it come from the creature that Liberius had killed before. Liberius saw the look of disgust on Sebastianus' face and wickedly smiled. His mouthed the word, '*Enjoy*' to Sebastianus.

The rooms that the Death March were given were fair size. There was only one bed in each room. The two highest ranking people in the room were given the bed. A real knight named Heinze proudly gave his position to Sebastianus, who he felt earned it. Another actual knight by the name of Montar gave up the bed to Raphael. Raphael slept on one side of the bed as Sebastianus took the other. The rest of the ten soldiers managed on the hard floor, but were given layers of comfortable sheets from Liberius to keep them warm. Overwhelmed by his tiredness, Sebastianus only had to blink before his eyes were fully shut.

It was all dark. Not a movement could be heard or felt. Even the breathing of nearly three hundred-fifty men was light. Sebastianus awoke. He slowly peered around him and guessed the time. It was somewhere between twelve o'clock and one o'clock in the morning. Sebastianus had always had a gift for telling the time even if there were no clues. Within seconds he was back asleep.

He woke up later to the sounds of the waves, and the water slowly and roughly rocking the ship. There was also a slow howling wind, although it could have been something else. Sebastianus tiredly sauntered up to the deck of the ship, from the warm cozy room he slept in below. It was the middle of the night and was raining gently and slowly. He looked down at the water. The moon reflected on the dark foggy sea. He thought about it and guessed the time was three o'clock in the morning.

As he wandered upon the mile long deck, he nearly stumbled with surprise when he heard noise and saw a figure dangling on top of Liberius' room. The figure was humming softly. "Mm-mm-mm." Tired, Sebastianus quickly identified the figure as Liberius. His bulging calves were in plain view and Sebastianus was impressed. As he turned his eyes to Liberius' face, which he could see in the moonlight that directed straight at it, he saw the black eyes once more just for one second. But it changed and his eyes were gleaming. The bright moonlight sky made his twinkling green eyes stick out much more than in the day. *"And she comes to me. I see what she sees. I feed her them, my black heart will not mend. I am so regretful, and even more as the regret grow."* Liberius hummed. To Sebastianus, it sounded like a chant, and a very dark one. The chanting began again, only to frighten Sebastianus more than he had ever been. What he was hearing was in tongue. Liberius was now chanting in a language Sebastianus had never heard. And to add to this, his small eyes had turned color once more. They were pitch black, blacker than Sebastianus had ever seen. He stopped in his chanting, and, without turning his body or (seemingly) his neck, turned his head completely to the left to face Sebastianus.

"Why are you up here so late?" he whispered, calmly. His eyes were now pale green.

"I-I, well, uh, just uh, I was just -" Sebastianus was then cut off by Liberius as his craziness returned.

"You heard her, didn't you?"

"What?" Sebastianus was discombobulated completely.

"Ancient evils roam Larkon Sea and it got its name from the very reason. Larkon means 'dark'. She's been roaming for a very long time. She never stops. She was down for a little while and then some idiot had to bring her back. She feeds and feeds. Out here, you get eaten or you shove people in place so they can get eaten. It is the only way, you see. I've been providing her since her resurrection. Volde must pay her, but I cannot pay. I've paid for my life already. I should be dead, but I'm never going to die. Never will the Angel of Death come my way."

Sebastianus understood. Liberius had been feeding one of the guardians so he could live. "You're a flipping psycho!" roared Sebastianus, sickened by the work of the man.

Liberius' eyes were dark again and he lost the last bit of sanity that his eyes could hold. "Know who you speaking to, son? I am Lord Liberius Volde. I single-handedly brought down the empire of Latorin. I killed Crusak. Vinco is a lie. I was a king among mortals, but he wrote things down and his writing went down in history. He was announced a hero. I, Liberius Volde, withered and was deprived of my mind. I rotted slowly until I was casted here!"

"You lie! You're lying! Vinco killed Latorin and you merely *helped* bring down the empire. Vinco killed Crusak. Vinco wrote all of the names in history, but he was a hero because of killing Latorin. You lost your own mind. It is your choice to give the sacrifices. You chose to come here! This is your entire fault!"

It was silent for a minute, or so, Sebastianus was no longer tired, but angry. He wanted to say awful and dirty things to

Liberius. He was angry enough to grab the Sword of Vinco and slice him in half. Though his mind nearly overflowed with nasty thoughts, his mouth did not speak a word out of place. He kept his temper. They both stared at one another, for a while the staring never stopped. Not a word was said. The silent moment was broken up when Sebastianus shook his head no. He was disappointed in the man and simply said, "You say you dread withering here, well only you can stop that. It was your choice, and when the time comes, you will be exposed to death."

Sebastianus walked back, hoping to get some sleep. He felt a nudge on his back, realizing who it was. Liberius planted a large punch to his forehead. Sebastianus slumped down, feeling blood matting down the tips of his hair. His vision darkened and before he could do a thing, he felt his body being dragged across the ship deck and down a hard wooden staircase. Sebastianus was unconscious before he could feel the soft bed mattress beneath him.

Awakening on a soft bed, Sebastianus looked around. When Sebastianus decided he was alone, he came up from the bed, yawning and stretching. He was in Liberius' room. "Hello, boy", said a familiar voice from outside of the room. The large wooden doors opened and Liberius walked in, armed with a sword. Titus was beside him.

"You had quite a bad knock, there, Sebastianus", began Titus. "What happened to you? Did you fall on one of Liberius' wine barrels? The same thing –" Sebastianus cut him off and began the story as it happened.

"Liberius punched me in the face. He confessed to murder, too!" Sebastianus roared. He picked up the Sword of Vinco, which had been laid next to him, and pointed at Liberius.

"I did no such thing!" offended Liberius cried out. "In fact, I tended your wound when I found you on the deck. Then I brought you to my room and you blame me!"

Sebastianus figured it out. Liberius was two men. There was something living inside him. It was something dark, nibbling at his soul. When his eyes were black, Liberius belonged to the creature, when they were green; he was a regular man, untouched by the evil.

"I must have tripped, knocked my head, and had a bad dream", Sebastianus said with a fake laugh. Liberius laughed and Titus laughed.

Sebastianus left the room. It was early in the morning. Before he did so, though, Liberius caught up to him and explained he saw him injured, so he bought him to his room. Sebastianus just nodded and smiled. He thanked Liberius and walked down the large staircase to the fifth room on the left in the humungous hall.

There, Raphael was just awakening. He was naked except for a sheet wrapped around his waist. He said hello while yawning to Sebastianus and put on his clothes. Sebastianus said hello back and clarified that there was no one else in the room. "Where is everyone?" he asked.

Raphael yawned again and replied, "Everyone went to breakfast. Liberius is serving bacon and eggs. I wasn't hungry, so I slept more. The rumor is you had a knock." Raphael pointed out the bruise on Sebastianus' forehead. "How did you get it? It looks pretty nasty."

"It's a long story, but falls into what I want to tell you", replied Sebastianus, who glanced at the open door before shutting it. "I was up on the deck last night. It was very late and I heard odd humming by the captain's quarter. It was Liberius, humming a chant to a creature."

Raphael's face twisted in confusion, though Sebastianus kept on talking.

"His eyes are strange. Have you noticed?"

"Yeah", quickly replied Raphael.

"They turn black. His eyes were black and he told me that he feeds people to the creature so that it does not eat him. I told him I thought he was insane. So I turned around and before I could do anything, Liberius had punched me right in the face. And then he brought me over to his room and tended my wound. Isn't that strange?"

"He's flipping insane. We need to tell Titus. If he does one more thing that I think is even remotely peculiar, I'm killing him. I think he might just be lying about his times as a hero."

"I believe that at one point in time, he was a hero. But now, he is completely dark. I think that the cause for this is a spirit. And as far as I am concerned, very few spirits lurk around the earth. Latorin is still weak, so I doubt he could do so, and on such a strong person as well. And there are many others who could be held responsible, but there is only one that is truly the most powerful spirit of them all."

"Who is that?" demanded Raphael.

"I am speaking of the spirit that created Latorin. The spirit is Krausin", Sebastianus said. Just at the name came out of his mouth, a chill spread down his spine. The air seemed frigid, though the sun was poking into the room.

The morning went by quick, it was soon a bright and warm afterAndreyn. Sebastianus asked Liberius about his past, with the guess that it was obviously a very enjoyable tale. Liberius shuddered with the question and decided that Titus would be a better person.

"Why?" Sebastianus questioned.

"Listen, boy, my past is long and it has some very bad memories. I don't want to talk about it. I lost so much of my family, it's hard to count."

Sebastianus nodded in respect of Liberius' opinion. He walked away and descended down the long staircase to the room of Titus, where he asked him about Liberius. His response was long, too long. It was nearly an hour when Titus was done. He told about the defeat of Latorin and the conquering of Volde and the peace treaty between the werewolves, which was signed with his name and the blood of a werewolf.

"How come you asked me to tell you the story? Liberius is the one who did all the amazing things", said Titus. It was silent for a moment. Sebastianus was getting sick of these silent moments. It just seemed to be a part of his life now. It was always quietness when there wasn't blood being poured. His life seemed to be hesitation and war.

"He didn't want to talk about it", Sebastianus mumbled.

"He's a tough man, he could handle something like that", Titus replied. "I wouldn't know why he would turn down now."

Sebastianus wanted to tell Titus about his theories about Krausin, but he felt it was never the right moment.

Liberius was humming again, his voice seeming more shrill and high. It was as though a rugged sound coming from his throat, scratching away. He was now singing to himself, "*I look at her black eyes, so cruel to never cry, the eyes that will never tell a lie, they tell the truth but why? They will kill you cold-blooded, the soul is blackly flooded. The Beast of the Waves, within the darkest caves, in man's blood it bathes, as if it gave. But it takes; it takes from the Larkon lakes.*"

Sebastianus was up there that night, spying on Liberius, who sang a demented song. But what intrigued his ears was 'The Beast of the Waves.' Sebastianus could not help it and sneezed, his nose twitching more than it had ever. The noise shook the deck's silence, shattering it as though glass. Liberius turned his head, his eyes like black stones.

As lithe as he could be, Sebastianus stretched himself behind two barrels, making him invisible from Liberius' angle. The possessed man raised his head to the air and sniffed powerfully. His nose twitched and eventually, his lips moved. They were purple from the red wine that he had gorged. The lips slowly moved apart and sound came out once more. It was not Liberius' voice. "A man is struggling on this board. His name is Liberius Volde. Another man joins the struggle. Dramilius, I can see. He is behind the barrels, waiting as I sniff him out. He smells as though one of us, though his trace shows man and the godliness of his soul. This is a good god."

"What is your name?" demanded Sebastianus, appearing from his hiding spot. He was face to Liberius, who was now just one step away from him.

"Krausin is my name. I am born from sorrow, pain, fear, and the darkness in the day. The night is meaningless because it must be black, dark. In the day, it is special. It is important that I feed when I must. I save Liberius' soul only to beat it. It is mine and I can make him suffer. One of the greatest living souls is in my control. Shall I use it for my own desires? Shall I use it to kill? There are many I must slaughter, and he shall be last. Reabius Azell must die. Titus Licesio must die. There are many more. Liberius shall die last, but you will be slaughtered only a moment before him. But it shall not be to my hands. The hands that will take your life shall be His. The Dark Lord, Latorin, who I gave life to, shall squeeze the life from your body. I am Krausin, from the blackest place in the world. This is the place where no one dares. It is the Land of No Return. It is the Land of the Forgotten. I am the spirit of evil. I am the ambassador of death."

"Then you will spare my life?" Sebastianus asked. He was nervous, but could not reveal this to Krausin. The spirit would use anything against him. Krausin would steal the very life from everyone on the *Prince Alexander*.

"Your life shall remain. Liberius will live. Titus Licesio will live, Raphael will live, and all will live. This is the regard of tonight. You must not die, but suffer. I have been assigned several more tasks, and as far as I am concerned, you are weak and undeserving of me taking your soul. You are protected by the Sword of Vinco, but if the sword were to separate from you for a time, and it was far from you, I could squeeze your throat until your head fell off the shoulders and not a drop of blood seen. Remember Dramilius that I am always here. I am always somewhere. When Liberius seems different from when I am in control, it is because

I vacation and feast upon those who do not serve me. Remember this, Dramilius. Now go. I mustn't speak to you."

"I have more questions, though!" Sebastianus pouted like a little child. Liberius (Krausin) turned round, his back facing Sebastianus. And to the soldier's surprise, Liberius' back seemed to fall. It was as though the skin was a costume for what was underneath. And what Sebastianus saw underneath scarred him for life. It was a figure with large hands and long, bony fingers. The feet were the same as the hands. The whole thing was so thin that Sebastianus could see the bones poking. The ribs stuck out further than the shoulders, which slumped to his chest uncontrollably. How his legs took the weight, no one knew. His face was large and gaunt. The eyes were black holes with a flicker of fire for his pupils. The mouth stretched far across so that it nearly touched his disgusting and deformed eyes. The teeth were black and sharp. This was Krausin, the real Krausin. And Sebastianus was never more scared as the creature stretched his body, arms flying in the air. His full height was nearly seven feet tall. It was the definition of spindly, but in a more atrocious or horrifying manor.

"What is the Land of the Forgotten?" demanded Sebastianus, his head raised to face Krausin's. Krausin smiled his black eyes dangerously close to Sebastianus' as he bent over.

"Imagine, young Dramilius, a place where there was a brilliant sun, but yet there was only darkness. Imagine a place where there were hundreds of crops, but only one a year would sprout. Imagine livestock by the dozens, but as soon as they were born, they died. Imagine this. Now, Dramilius, imagine that not a soul with even a hint of goodness lurked on every corner. Imagine a place where there were hundreds of people like me and Latorin. This is worse than hell, this is the ultimate evil. It is the dark made land. And we worship the blackness in day. We pray to the pope of sin. The Land of the Forgotten is the definition of evil. Do you hear, Dramilius? Do you understand me?" Krausin smiled, and then his smile faded.

"You say that everyone in the land is the dark made flesh, but yet you spare every life on the *Prince Alexander*. You that you are evil, but is blood being spilt? You are not good, but you are not evil?" Sebastianus asked, showing no emotion upon his grim face. Krausin started at him, a smile widening on his face.

"We shall see about blood upon this ship. I may not be the killer, but I did not say I would not be responsible." He took his bony hands and stroked Sebastianus' face, and where his bony gaunt fingers had been, there were bruises, blood, and Sebastianus felt the spraining of his nose bone. Krausin wiped the blood from Sebastianus' face and shook it on the ship floor, and smiled. "Blood has been spilt on the deck."

The smile on Krausin's face faded and he looked toward the skin of Liberius on the ground. He reached downward and pulled himself into the skin. Liberius stood there again and his black, beady eyes turning into green stones. And Sebastianus sprinted back to his room, leaving Liberius standing like a painting, blank and clueless.

Sebastianus was careful around Liberius. On occasions, he would see a faint smile from him, like he was showing that Krausin was still there, always. *No* thought Sebastianus. He knew it was not Liberius all of those times, it was Krausin taunting.

The ship was very slow, and Sebbastianus knew that Krausin was stalling something. Perhaps it was a night where he could kill. They were half way up the Larkon Sea and it was dawn when Sebastianus asked Titus about the Beast of the Waves. Titus answered with a shudder down his back. And Sebastianus prepared for another tale.

Long ago", Titus began, "in the times of Crusak and Latorin, many claimed to have seen the Beast of the Waves. The Red Nexuela was asked by Crusak to create beasts. He thought that the land's elements could depend on the beasts. To create the beasts, he used drops of his own living-dead blood. This blood was enough to disturb the balance of the elements, able to make a figure crawl out. When the figure crawled out, he gave it life and shape and meaning. When he spilled blood into the Larkon Sea, the water bubbled for three days, and all of the fish died. The sailors' ships caught on fire and the grass around it fell back into the earth. The creature that came out was very horrifying. It was half a mile long, with fins and scales like a snake. It was said that the Red Nexuela spat into the water, and then the creature attempted to attack him. But the Red Nexuela knew what to do, and he cursed the monster so that it could only move from the bottom of the Larkon if a ship passed over and near. And so, it is the only creature that we know off. Hopefully, though, we are not passing it. Liberius should know where it is. So I trust that we are safe."

Sebastianus thanked Titus with a nod and slumped out of the room, searching for his own. He stumbled across the room, where Raphael was reading a book. It was in gbreat condition, and that was rare in Hestour. The only books in Hestour were *Laws of Hestour, History of Hestour,* and *The Vinco Sagas.* Sebastianus peered closer and saw that the book was not of Hestour, and titled *Theories of the Dark and Powers of the Dark by Liberius Volde.*

"Where did you get that?" demanded Sebastianus.

"I found it in the treasure room. There is a lot of interesting things in here. It is in three parts. The first is about spirits and ancient hidden lands. The second is about the Land of the Forgotten, and the third is about certain evils, such as Krausin and Latorin. You should read it."

Sebastianus skimmed through the spirits, and the Land of the Forgotten. Once he had arrived to ten thick, worn-out, handwritten pages about Krausin, right after flipping parts about Latorin, Krausin, and even a small part about Crusak. He began to read rapidly.

KRAUSIN

Chapter Four

The Source of Power

M any people are under the influence that spirits are souls flying through airs, and that the average man cannot see them unless they possess a person. This would be very true, except in the case of the darkest spirits. The Largona Spirits can take the form of terrible beasts or men that can petrify one in fear of their looks. They are the highest rankings of dark spirits.

Krausin has a body similar to a zombie or a soldier of the Army of the Undead. He is believed to appear as a very spindly figure with a long mouth that stretches to his lifeless eyeballs. This is of the description of Sobalus Muse I, the old king of Arishba (See the Latorin Sagas or A History of the World). King Muse saw Krausin fly across the kingdom on corpse horses of some sort and to the palace of Latorin, who was then Heratten Arishba. Muse recorded this in his journal before writing several chapters of A History of the World, which is by numerous authors, including myself.

Muse was frightened by the creature he saw, as he passed the roads. He, who was going at an incredible pace, halted himself to glare at Muse. With the glare of Krausin, Muse began to bleed from his face, ears, chest, and palms. Krausin smiled before Muse fell unconscious and ill for many days. Krausin later became the creator *of Latorin, converting him and giving him powers. And ever since, the land has darkened, with the power of Latorin, which could very well be called the power of Krausin.*

But where has that power come from? Many experts would agree that the darkness of the day strengthens him, and that the evil in good can also have the same effect. But this is truly not an explanation how Krausin could start what has become the world's largest fault. Wars, murders, betrayal, creatures of the dark, pain, and corruption was invented by Krausin, but simply passed on to Heratten (Latorin). Where does the power come from, then? My theory is that the power is a source of complete and whole evil, a force that lies hidden in the Land of the Forgotten.

This source is wholesome. As one like Heratten has a heart, mind, a history of goodness in his childhood and earlier years, and other human parts. Krausin is much like that. But this evil is simply the anti-God, or the anti-sun. It is pure. And perhaps, one of the first men ever found his way to the Land of the Forgotten, when traveling. There, he discovered this power and became the first to inhabit the evil land. The power can easily be what the average religious man would call the Devil. Of course, completely in my opinion, I would see that all of the facts can be put together for evidence almost exactly like this. I put together knowledge of a regular man and concluded to what this is. But of course, this cannot be his entire power source. A pure evil could not fuel him fully and still stay evil, as well as filling hundreds a day every day. There must be something else.

Latorin once made his famous speech, in the first dawn of his reign, and said to the people:

"People, I have become a new man. I was once Prince Heratten, the king of Arishba, ruler. I was foolish though, young. But then my eyes opened wide as the spirit named Krausin appeared to me. He was kind, and showed me the ways. For a new mind inhabits my head. For the reign of the Arishba family shall end. The new rule is of me. This is the reign of Latorin, the conqueror, the great, the creator!

"Your greed and sin becomes my joy and my amusement. There are things that you people do not know of. There is murder. Murder is when you are a killer, when you purposely bring death to someone. Murder can be because of many reasons. And then there is what I call fuel. Fuel is very new. Fuel can only be used by me. There is fuel in two ways. The first is a pure thing that gives me strength and my mind. The second is a gadget inside me that makes me what I am. When one murders, sins, or offends, it becomes a good to me. It is a fresh breath of air that I may inhale."

That was the beginning of Latorin's speech that scared many. It was horrifying, as many knew that life was coming to an end. In the speech, he talked of the pure evil, and the sin of people that helped him. Read the rest and you will hear the darkness that hints a possible hidden power that shows what the source of Krausin may be.

"And with the people's work, worship, blood and bone, I will rule powerfully and know all. You will help me, and I will help you. I have chosen my government carefully and all shall follow. Praise is to Krausin and darkened blood, which makes me whom I stand before you."

He mentioned the words blood several times. Latorin has many times been seen holding a golden wine glass dripping blood. In the famous painting Ill *by Zetr Millicicioz, he is shown drinking blood and crushing his scepter. This is because Krausin, Latorin, the Red Nexuela, Crusak, and all evil have a vampire like characteristic. They all have a yen for blood. It gives them strength. How it works, I do not know. But I simply am only aware that blood is a source of power. I do not know if has to be human blood, beast blood, dark blood, animal blood, good blood, or sinful blood. But I do know that these creatures have a craving for blood. This is a large strength for them. This also helps prove that their meaning in this world is of darkness (see* The Meaning of the Madness *by Curos Munomus).*

-Liberius Volde Volume II from A History of the World

Sebastianus thought, his head twirling with thoughts as they only made him more confused as he tried to concentrate. Krausin, Latorin, and everyone and everything else made his brain ache and yearn for sleep and ice.

"So, should we keep it?" asked Raphael, eagerly. "There are some helpful things in there. The chapter about the Red Nexuela is over one hundred pages long, and Latorin is even longer. And I would assume that there are some things in there that could help us defeat Crusak."

Though he felt bad about taking an original copy book, he knew he should. "Yes", replied Sebastianus.

"Can we take more?" Raphael said with a smile. "The shelf has at least one thousand books, and some of them look very useful in our work. One was entitled *The Seven Guardians of Crusak.* There are nine that I saw we should take, and several others I didn't get a chance to take a look at."

Sebastianus hesitated before agreeing. "Let's go later tonight, just before we leave. Do you have a bag?" Raphael nodded and turned his eyes to the direction of a leather bag smeared in thick oil so the water did not affect it. Nodding, Sebastianus made his way out of the room and through the humongous hall. Liberius was lighting the candles along the room, and nodded with bright green eyes. It was getting darker, and Sebastianus knew that soon Liberius would become Krausin, and would torment him. Then he saw him turn slowly. Liberius' eyes were green, but darkening and frightening. "It's here", he said slowly. "The time has come. Sebastianus, tell every man to gather weapons."

Sebastianus spread the word as told, knocking on every door and rattling the words barely out of mouth before he was already gone, due to the speed he was going at. Quickly, Sebastianus was on the dock, and there, he saw the clouds swarming like bumblebees above him. The waters seemed blacker, and it was still half an hour of a journey to the coast.

The Larkon was pitch-black now, enough to scare someone out of their wits. And small ripples could only be barely seen, far in the distance to the east. There was no surprise that it was the beast of the waves. All soldiers were pushing and shoving up the staircase to the deck. The bustling crowd of fighters were prepared and kept their swords tight. Titus squeezed his way through and roared into Sebastianus' ear. His words were, "Get Liberius now!"

Sprinting, all of his muscles pounding, Sebastianus was in the large room in a moment. As he tried to catch his breath, he knocked on the door. When no response came, he pushed it open. There, lying on the floor, his arms and legs out like a star, was Liberius. He was wearing no clothes, and his body was covered in markings. They were peculiar markings, those of the devil. His face was bare and cold. He was dead, and Sebastianus knew so. Liberius was dead, but Krausin was alive.

His conclusion was shattered like glass as Liberius began breathing. His eyes were black, and he was holding large candles. They were black, made from the fat of animals. With a black flame, the candles began to grow to the size of an animal. *"Atra Erus, come to thee. Atra Erus, make me holy like your brilliant self in the blackest Sabbath. I honor you so. I honor you as the king, and you refuse to speak to me. Please, my lord, speak! Please speak! Speak!"*

Atra Erus, Sebastianus knew, was the language of the Black Sabbath, the anti-divine. He had heard it spoken only once before, in the Hestour Theatre where one spoke in the language, acting as a demon. Atra Erus meant Dark Lord. Liberius was referring to Latorin.

But it was not Krausin speaking. Krausin was the only one in the world who Latorin would show respect to. There were more demons in Liberius. They were demons after Sebastianus. *"Speak to me, Lord! Please, speak to me!"* The voice was not of Liberius, or of one demon. It was the voice of hundreds. It was so threatening that Sebastianus leapt from the room, sprinting to the deck.

As soon as he was united with the soldiers, Sebastianus gripped the Sword of Vinco harder than he had ever. And he prayed. It was not a prayer to defeat the creature, but for the soul of Liberius, which was contaminated in filth and waste of the evils that lurked within.

The *Prince Alexander* shook ferociously and the water rippled slowly. And then it was quick. And then it was slow. Sebastianus and the soldiers could not bear the wait. Within moments, though, the wait was over. The water exploded on the surface, and from it, emerged a long neck, towering over the ship. All quivered in fear as the large black eyes stared them down. The creature was blue and green, with crabs and seaweed slathering his body. It had a large snout with a mouth of hundreds of sharpened teeth. The teeth were in layers, nearly seven all together, that went down, almost in the throat. Fins were all over its body, and small spikes. The black, lifeless eyes were much like those of Liberius'. And Sebastianus was frightened. The beast showed dominance and roared, almost as though taunting.

Then the beast stuck its head further out of the water and hesitated to bite. None could reach the beast, but with one snap of its head, it could make a hole in the ship and devour five soldiers. The beast of the waves blinked her large eyes and then, in a very breath, had snapped its jaws and taken a man in her mouth. His limp, blood covered leg poked from in between the teeth, but was slurped up like a pasta. And the wood was broken on the ship, holes revealing the rooms below the dock. The beast roared at the rest of the men, and took another snap of its jaws.

Everyone wondered how a beast that size could be defeated. And not a soldier who was fighting knew. But on the floor, panting for breath, and his voice of animals and unearthly creatures, was Liberius. And somewhere in the back of his brain, behind the thoughts of the demons that were controlling him, was how to kill the beast of the waves. Liberius twitched and his body was now bleeding. His throat was closing, and he felt death coming his way. But a better word for his experience would be repossession. The demons were inside him. The servants of Latorin would bring good news to him, because they were now completely in control of the one of the strongest fighters of the light in the world. But the demons had come after the departure of Krausin, meaning that somewhere out there was the spirit capable of destroying mankind with the right strategy, and the only other possibility to defeating him was going to dead, a victim of the beast of the waves.

Sebastianus was throwing abandoned swords and any other weapon lying on the deck. He was even so desperate as to throw his own armor, which left him was only a thin mail coat over cloth covering his torso. He jabbed the Sword of Vinco into the air, missing several times. His eyes were closed and he was simply just stabbing into the air. With luck, he had hit something, which he now knew was a spot just above the lips of the beast of the waves.

The beast was beginning to bleed black blood and growled lightly before snapping its jaws at Sebastianus. But at the right moment, Sebastianus jumped out of the way, and was surprised to be rolling on the slanting wood into the hole that the beast of the waves had created. Sebastianus was now in the murky water, and saw a spot in the water where the sun was shining. Through the water he was able to spot where the beast of the waves' body was visible. For a mile, the blue serpent stretched out into the east where it had come from. And as Sebastianus looked to his west, he could see land that was very near. The beast must have pushed the *Prince Alexander* further.

And as Sebastianus looked to through the ship's sides that had been crushed, he could see at least fifteen miniature boats, and all supplied with oars and several had compartments that the men could use to store some of their excess arsenal.

"Titus, get the men to the hull!" commanded Sebastianus.

The lord of Hestour nodded as he rounded up everybody to the hull of the boat. The water was rising higher though. And by the last man who jumped to the bottom, he only had to dive a head's length before he was covered. And, diving further and further into the water, the men were soon almost drowning. But they were nearer to the safety escape boats.

But little did they know, they were nearer to death. Now that they were in the waters, they were in the origin and element of their opponent. They kicked their legs like horses, bruising their own companions' faces and bodies. The soldiers were weakening slowly and only one sensed this. Sebastianus felt his lungs beginning to crumble in the water. The boats were as though permanently stuck to the wood of the *Prince Alexander.*

Sebastianus swung the Sword of Vinco. The safety boat came apart from the ship and soon everyone was bustling and battling to jump on and float up with it. Fifteen men managed. Sebastianus cut two boats with one thrash of his sword and more floated to safety.

Breath was running out. Sebastianus jabbed and jabbed, and more soldiers behind him gathered their strength to do the same. All of the boats were loose now, and jiggled themselves free. Sebastianus entered the last boat, Titus with him.

The soldiers floated up quickly and Sebastianus gasped. He had almost died and for the first time, it was not from an unearthly creature. He breathed harder than he could ever remember before his stomach turned round and he vomited, almost all of it water. Titus did the same. "Well, thank God you did what you did, Sebastianus."

Sebastianus smiled. His grin was only placed upon his face for no longer than the snap of the creature's jaws. The beast emerged from the Larkon as though a cannonball and massacred one of the small boats, all the men dead. Their blood stained the blue sea.

"Get away, beast!" roared a voice in the distance. The man appeared from the ruins of the *Prince Alexander.* He stabbed the beast in the neck several times with what Sebastianus thought a sword like no other. The sword the man held was identical to the Sword of Vinco. It was the same craftsmanship, and of the small man's hands. The man slaughtered the beast and then confronted the soldiers as the creature fell into the waters behind him. The splash rose like fires and he stood before his kill. The man was Liberius, bulging muscles and clean skin. His eyes were bright green. Behind him, all could see, for a time so short it almost did not happen, the water had formed words. *Lycok Crusak present the Fourth Guardian: the Beast of the Waves.* "Hello, my people. The soul has been renewed, and I truly tell you hello for the first time."

Liberius nodded toward Sebastianus. He knew everything and he knew that Sebastianus knew everything. But as for the rest of the world, those whose futures would never be as twisting and unexpected as those two, they were clueless of the events.

Chapter Five:

Land of Crusak

The white horizon was apparently snow. It was whiter than anything ever seen. It shined as the snowflakes fell onto the blackened surface of the Crusalands. The sky was grey and there was no distance. There was no east and no west. It had become colder and colder, and eventually frigid. They had been traveling for nearly two hours, and not a single living creature had passed them.

Liberius, Sebastianus could not understand. His ways were mysterious. His body was strong, his mind sharp, though his soul was weak and lost. It was lost in the ways of the darkest, in a place where demons could travel inside of him as though he were a door.

"Titus, what direction are we to travel? I have not been in these parts since the days of my youth." Liberius smirked. "I apologize. That was when I was *truly* young." Sebastianus knew he was referring to the fountain of youth that he, Azell, Vinco, and Sobalus."

Looking through his bag, Titus managed to find his compass. He pointed to the left and the soldiers took a sharp turn under the command of their leader. Titus looked at Liberius, as though trying to tell him something through his face expression.

Liberius seemed to understand. "In the frigid weather of the Crusalands, there is bound to be the Latorinous. They are all sorts of awful creatures. The Latorinous are originally a pagan cult or church-like group. They have been since the olden days, the oldest days. They were the hooligans of Arishba, and some were deformed or crippled. Many believed they became the first beasts. When Heratten was first in power, and the majority disagreed with his choices, the Latorinous, who were then the Kings of Shadows, were loyal to him. Many of them became his followers and first soldiers.

"And then Heratten became Latorin and his followers took on a new name and new customs. And then the Latorinous powered with the witches, vampires, and werewolves of Arishba. Together, they made Margius Aloksius. Margius Aloksius means *Day of Bloodshed* in the language of the Black Sabbath. That was the first worshipping day. They sacrificed one of each of the races. Then they killed one human and offered them to flames. Together, they would make potions, cast curses, and invent spells. Soon, the Latorinous had instituted a church (though it was more of a cult). It was called Church of the Five Royals. They five royals were the children of evil: Latorin, Florence the Witch, Malum Estone the Vampire, Arig Herjolfsson of the Latorinous, and Helgareth de Rellias the werewolf. Together, they would wreak havoc upon the world. They succeeded. But one Margius Aloksius, Latorin thought of an idea that would change life forever.

"With one drop of blood each, the five were able to stir up a potion. Legs from a Latorinous member had been thrown in. Arms of a witch, torso of a werewolf, brains of a man, and head of a vampire had been stirred into the potion. They were reinventing man in their own way. The man they created was Servius Death, who would become the greatest general of all time. He would lead every battle of Latorin. And one day, he was mortally injured. Since evil loved Servius so much, they granted him afterlife to live up to his name. He became the leader of the dead armies. He was given a red cloak to hide the blood that would of stained everywhere on his body. He became the Red Nexuela. And he, like the story of Crusak, was able to grant the members of the Latorinous their sick wishes. He rotted the human inside of them. The hearts turned black and the blood evaporated. The skin was grey and the stomach became a stone. The Latorinous were beasts. They vowed to live the life of the Red Nexuela, and became immortal. They lived in the cold, where Latorin ordered them to stay until his return."

"What day is Margius Aloksius?" asked Sebastianus, who was the first person to speak after a moment of a long silence.

"The date is between the Latorinous, and some of the ancient witches, vampires, and werewolves. But it doesn't matter anyhow, because they will sacrifice you any time if you cross their territory. Legend says they have a new creature they feed humans to."

The thought of all of this sent a chill through Sebastianus' body. It added to the frigid weather of the snow..

"The beast that some of the locals once claimed was one of the seven guardians. Gelu is a beast of the frigid weather. His powers go beyond those of Roman of the Rocks, the Arachnid, the Juggernaut, or the Beast of the Waves. It is a creature of pure coldness. At its fullest and strongest, it can turn your blood into ice and turn your muscles to snow. Gelu is what I guess you could call an ice-vampire."

"What about the Latorinous?" Sebastianus questioned. Liberius raised his eyebrow. "What do they look like? What can they do to someone?" added Sebastianus.

"As a second passes, even if it is in the smallest way, the Latorinous change. After ten years though, they will have completely transformed. Their behavior switches and their bodies can switch. It is though there is a demeanor that contains parts of Latorin in it. They may look like anything or anyone to be honest with you", Liberius replied.

Wind knocked several men down, including Sebastianus. It was stronger than anyone had ever seen it (perhaps not Liberius, who had seen a lot of things). The snow was coming harder, the skies were greying, and the clouds piling. Thunder and lightning just made the scene look more threatening.

The time passed, and the weather became worse. Two men had died, and three had gone missing. And this was just the beginning. Gelu and the Latorinous were yet to come, and, no one could say that that was it.

Looking at his middle finger, Sebastianus sighed and shivered. The tip of the finger was blackening. Raphael would, always keeping his humor even though how ridiculous it was, would make fun of him immediately. Sebastianus wondered, where had his friend gone. On cue, he saw Raphael to his left, carrying his oil-drenched bag. It was full. He smiled at Sebastianus and managed to make his way side to side.

"I got the books, mate", Raphael smirked.

"Cheeky", Sebastianus replied, chuckling.

"It's flipping freezing!" he exclaimed. "What about you?"

"I know. Look at my finger", Sebastianus said, holding his finger to Raphael, where he could see.

A rumble broke the two apart. Sebastianus dropped his sword, and Raphael dropped his bag. They picked up their belongings, and stumbled back to the ground as another rumble had hit them, this time, harder. The two found the possessions and carried on, only for two paces before the snow acted as glue and they were forced to be on the spot.

"It seems that we have visitors", said a voice. It grumbled and mumbled until another identical voice took its place to grumble. No one knew where the voice was coming from.

"Or trespassers", said another similar sound.

"Why do you come to our land and haunt us?" questioned the first voice. "All we do is wait patiently until he comes back, and then the people act we're animals and come to hunt us down and kill us!"

"Who are you?" demanded several soldiers, including Titus and Sebastianus. There was no reply, but only fiercer weather. Liberius mumbled to himself, and Sebastianus guessed that he knew the answer.

"We?" laughed one of the voices. "We are the hail, the snow, the grey skies, the thunder and lightning, the rain. We are gods high above you. Your kind killed us off, and we are the last of ours. Forever, we will always seek vengeance!"

There was a pause in the air before lightning emerged from the air and struck a hole, missing the soldiers. Still, the ground rumbled fiercely.

"Then they are the Sky Demons!" concluded Liberius. "They are the Giants of the Sky. Whatever you soldiers call them, these beasts here to annihilate us."

Sebastianus had been told stories more than once from elders in Hestour about the Sky Demons. They had been followers and creations of Latorin. The Sky Demons acted as though gods of the sky and caused all kinds of havoc. When the race was weakened after the war, man had decided they needed to eliminate the giants. They did so.

The false gods made the weather even worse and eventually, Sebastianus was at the point where he knew if the giants were not defeated, he would freeze to death. One of the giants moved clouds with his head sized fingers. His face was hideous, covered in snow and gashes, as well as bruises and scars. He had two green and wild eyes. "Brothers!" he called. His greasy hair stretched down the sides of his face and into a beard as long as Sebastianus.

He leapt from the sky and onto the land. He was easily the size of the *Prince Alexander*. Cloth hung from his waits and, attached to it were many bags. On one was the dark language, where the name Gelidus. Behind him several other giants jumped, almost all identical. They each had bags marked with their names. The Sky Demons were Gelidus, Tempestas, Caelum, Frigus, and Procella. "Newcomers?" bellowed Caelum with a savage smile. "I thought no one dared to come over here?" he said. All the other giants nodded in agreement.

"I would think that they deserve to be eaten!" Gelidus roared. "For seventeen years, we haven't a meal!"

Suggestions of what to do to the Death March spat out. Torturing them, eating them, stepping on them, and using their live bodies as tools to do work in the land were some of the Sky Demons' cruel suggestions.

"We will kill them slowly!" the monster called Tempestas grinned and then reached in his bag. Sebastianus could not believe it but Tempestas carried hail. It was hail the size of fists. He gripped it in his burly hands before tossing them as hard and fast as he could at the Death March.

Sebastianus ran for his dear life. Raphael was nowhere to be seen. But Liberius was quick at the side of Sebastianus, running equally as quick and elegant, dodging the hail and jumping over slaughtered bodies as though they seemed to do it often.

"Lightning!" roared Procella. The Sky Demon reached in his bag, pulling out what appeared to be two spears and a large drum like object. He played quickly. After every strike on his instrument, thunders pounded in the sky, making the earth rattle madly, only proceeding to the running away harder.

Caelum screamed loudly, wind coming from it, knocking back members of the Death March into large rocks and stones. Sebastianus turned round only to find a faintly visible Raphael. He signaled him to come with Liberius and him. Raphael obeyed only to be left behind again, far off in the snow. Sebastianus soon turned to the center of attention where a clump unbelievable and unearthly weather gather, growing stronger. There were the Sky Demons as they dominated the small battle.

Sebastianus ran and ran and ran. The run was ferocious, unbelievable. He sprinted all the way, dodging lighting and jumping over bodies. He avoided where the earth shook. It was the Death Run. Then Liberius grinned. Then Titus did too. The army had all followed, overwhelming and stuttering the havoc.

The beasts soon found themselves running out of their magic, and as soon as the Death March had charged. Sebastianus slashed and jabbed at their knees and shins, as high as he could to. The giants were overpowered and eventually their wounded legs could not hold any longer and their limp bodies fell. The soldiers clumped on top of their chests and stabbed. Sebastianus jabbed in the neck of Gelidus. The beasts were finished. Liberius smiled and wiped the blood from his face. Another battle had been one by the Death March, but their numbers were beginning to give out.

The men smiled in enjoyment, soon traveling to the center of the snowy lands. The Death March was complebtely alone for a time. But the darkest creatures that inhabited the lands were soon to come. These were the creatures that were once men.

The coldness slowly evaporated, though it was scarcely noticed by any of the soldiers.

The thump-thump-thump of the soldiers was no longer heard after they stepped in the two feet high snow that nearly buried their legs, even more than their battle of with the Sky Demons.

"Liberius, you never explained Gelu. He is a creature of the snow and lives on the cold and ice, but what is he. What advantages does he have on the other creatures that we have faced?" Sebastianus questioned.

"Gelu has...an unusual power. He lives with the cold. His abilities are as limited as the temperature of his surroundings. That's why he lives here. That's why Crusak named him Gelu. As you should know Sebastianus, that means cold. I'm sure someone as young as you remembers the old stories as a young in the castle of Hestour", Liberius added.

"He's more powerful than any of the creatures you have faced yet, Sebastianus. And armies more wait if he does not die. The cold and the dark: that is where the evil feed and grow. There are other elements, but in the depths of the catacombs of Gelu, you will find things.

Then a cold shiver streamed down Sebastianus' spine. A creepy scratchy voice began to speak. It was the Dark Language. It was the same language that the demons used. But just as though it were of Hestour, Sebastianus could understand it same. *"We hold the prophecies, Dramilius. We are the servants of the king and you mock us."*

Silence overcame Sebastianus for nearly an hour in the snow. And finally Titus punched his shoulder, breaking the moment of shocked silence. "What's wrong, Sebastianus?" he asked, a nervous look of panic upon his face.

"Nothing", Sebastianus replied. His voice trailed off as he spoke and Titus still worried secretly. So did every soldier, each of their minds twisted in and knotted from wondering. When where they going to die? When was their time?

The remote peacefulness from the cold ended shortly when a blizzard began to spark as though a fire. It got colder and colder. Liberius stuttered on every step, looking to the side of him, making sure that death was on his way.

The cold and darkness of the snow was bad enough. But Sebastianus had another thing to worry about. The Latorinous would be after him.

"We should camp here! If we go any farther we'll run into trouble. We'll be too tired to fend ourselves", Titus seemed to decide for everyone. But he spoke through the mouths of all. No one could bear to walk any further. So they collapsed and crawled into the cave where Titus guided them.

Sebastianus couldn't sleep at all. With no more than a few pounds of body fat, he was defenseless from the frigid weather.

"Latorin will see to it that you are warm", said a voice from the distance. It was high-pitched and cold. It was just then that Sebastianus noticed how late it was and that he was the only one still not into a deep and vast trance, sleeping on the cold snow.

"Krausin?" Sebastianus asked.

"I am not Krausin. I am similar. I stand for the same cause, I descend from the same place", the voice said. "And now, time will stop, and I can meet you."

The wind stopped blowing and snowflakes paused in midair. All of snoring from the soldiers stopped. Only Sebastianus and the creature in front of him could move or do anything of the sort.

"You're part of the Latorinous", said Sebastianus, who was not even looking. "I fear you. You want to kill me. You are a dangerous creature."

The Latorinous member stepped in front of him from a small hole in the cave wall he had been hiding in. "Latorin will help you become warm. You're cold and can become warm. He'll crown you a king. You are a king, but wrongly. Dramilius: son of the dark, fending for the creatures of the light. You claim to be a descendent of Vinco, but you are a descendent of Latorin."

The man was short with ridiculous amounts of hair all over his body, a mask made from small amounts of wood and other materials that Sebastianus could scarcely make out as human flesh and bones. "We are you", he said in his deep voice. Rags covered some of his body.

"Get away from me!" Sebastianus demanded.

"There is a crown to be placed upon your head. It could be a magnificent crown of golden jewels or a crown of thorns. The gems are the envy of your former loved ones. But the thorns stab your head and only bring hardships. The choice is yours: Dramilius the Dark, or Dramilius the Dead. Choose", said the creature.

"Why did you choose Latorin?" demanded Sebastianus. "What sick thoughts converted you?"

"I was born with the mark of the king", he said, pointing to a birthmark on his shoulder. The mark was a triangle with a triangle on the inside. "My parents tried to kill me by drowning me. But a man named Cassius saved me. I knew my life belonged to the ways of Latorin. And Cassius converted me and taught me. I had choices of how I could serve Latorin, and this was one. So

I decided I would become wild and sacrifice everything for the true king. Forever I belong."

"What is your name?" asked Sebastianus.

"My name is Huscol", he said, his voice changing tone slightly. "No one has asked me that in years."

"Now!" a voice came from behind Sebastianus.

Time resumed and there was a rush of excitement as Sebastianus felt a sharp pain. A dagger was going through his stomach. He fell, the dagger was removed, and the white snow became red. Then it darkened. It was black.

Sebastianus awoke by Raphael, who was struggling to get up. Attempting to move himself, Sebastianus failed, realizing he was tied in thick white rope, similar to the color of snow.

He saw around him a cold, dark disgrace of a village. The houses were igloos or forts made of ice and logs with twigs and small stones. There was a sign of Latorin about every meter. Some areas in the snow were cleared as roads. Besides one stairway, the village would have been impossible to leave because it was in a ravine with four ninety-degree angles as walls.

Counting to himself, Sebastianus spotted sixty-four men, built like something inhuman, almost portraying a large wolf or hound, due to the awful amount of hair that made a sheet upon their bodies. They did not feel the cold. Because of the sick transformations, they could stand it without the slightest feeling.

One of the members put his hand in front of everybody to stop them. "These men worship the wrong leader. They believe false gods. As we know, Latorin is dominant. He created the first world and the next. A path that we have not dared to go near was covered in snow one hour ago. We have cleared it now and it leads to the underground caves, the House of Gelu!"

The tied soldiers were carried

"Help me!" yelled the man as Gnomei slowly unlocked the bars. Gnomei grinned as he shoved the soldier in. "Please, don't!" he yelled.

Sebastianus saw that almost half the men were gone. Now Raphael was next. He screamed in fear as Gnomei untied him. Sebastianus roared in pain as he saw that Raphael was about to be killed by Gelu.

"I say we let this troubled man go in with the Mealin!" Cuspis roared out to the crowd. "They'll watch one another die!" Cuspis roared again to the herd of masked midgets. Everyone cheered as Gnomei untied Sebastianus. He threw them in the cave, after he unlocked the bars. "Good luck!" he yelled in. Then he shut the door and laughed.

The cave stretched on forever. It reeked like dead corpses and hairy, sweaty men. The two friends did not dare speak. Nothing seemed to be anywhere. As they looked up, they saw that the cave went up about one-hundred more yards. Caves were all over – almost as if someone had built them that way. The ice sickles were sticking out from everywhere. Each one was about ten feet long. A couple started from the very top to the cold, snowy bottom. Not a sound came from anywhere.

"Raphael, where's the monster, there's nothing in sight?"

"I don't know. Wait, what's –" Raphael said, cut off. Before he could finish, a flash of blue and white crowded over him and then disappeared along with Raphael. The flash traveled up toward the top of the mountain.

"Raphael!" yelled Sebastianus, nervous, scared and sad all at the same time. "Raphael!" Sebastianus screamed, clenching his fists. He took a dramatic gulp as he put one foot on a slippery, icy rock that stuck out of the side. He climbed for five minutes – which seemed like hours – then Sebastianus crawled into an ice covered cave with his one hand. "Raphael!" he yelled as he stood on the slippery surface of the cave. Sebastianus traveled through the caves. Every time he reached a certain point of the cave, there would be a latter like formation on the sides. He simply crawled. up every time to a new cave – which all looked the same.

After about twenty minutes, Sebastianus saw the blood drip from a latter. The one-handed solider climb up the latter half way and then peaked his head up. There was a pile of men. They were all knocked out. Raphael was near the bottom of the pile. His feathers looked black instead of the brown color they were supposed to be. In front of the pile was another mountain of bodies. But this time, they were skeletons. Sitting on top of the dried rotten bones was a giant. He was about twenty feet tall. He had a leathery ice-blue chest, fists, face and feet. Besides that, he was covered in white fur. His eyes were the same color of his leathery skin and his lips were a darker shade. He had ram's horns that matched the color of his skin. His claws were book-sized and grey. "What…what a horrible creature", whispered Sebastianus, as he watched Gelu devour about three men in a single gulp.

Sebastianus looked at his most valuable weapon – the Sword of Vinco – the sword that defeated evil itself. He unwrapped his sword carefully. As he lifted his blade, he smiled. The Latorinous didn't even take his blade. He held the sword in front of him. He slowly climb the rest of the way up the ladder. The fiendish Gelu didn't see him. His ram horns seemed to sparkle like glitter as Sebastianus saw him from a closer distance. He hid behind the living pile. He put his sword out straight. It was silent for a couple of seconds. Then Gelu turned his head. He looked around, ate a couple more bodies and then he spread out white scaly wings then flew down the biggest cave. After a minute or two, Sebastianus became uncomfortable. Gelu took about five seconds to get down to the bottom and come back up.

When cold and heavy breathing fell over Sebastianus' neck, he knew there was something wrong. As he whirled around slowly, he saw a large mouth that had teeth that were the size of fists. They were completely white, except for the fact that the monster had blood stains all over. "Crusak!" he struggled. Then with his claws he tore up air and then was after Sebastianus. He jumped around the caves, chasing Sebastianus. Sebastianus turned around and then he ran towards Gelu. Gelu still ran after, faster than . Sebastianus then pulled out the Sword of Vinco. He pointed it in front of him. "For Raphael, Titus, Vinco...and Liberius", said Sebastianus. He was certain he would kill Gelu in one strike.

Then Sebastianus swung. It was meters away from hitting Gelu! Then everything seemed slow. Gelu them swatted the blade away. He let out a victory cry. The sword went flying all the way to the bottom of the mountain. "NO!" yelled Sebastianus. He had only one choice. He had to look after the weapon at all times. He would also die if Gelu got any closer to him. So Sebastianus put his arms out and backed up. He ran til he was off the edge of the cliff like cave. He fell as the sword did. He fell for about ten seconds then he stopped. He landed in something. As he opened his closed eyes, he saw before him: God.

"Sebastianus, it is time", he said. Sebastianus looked up but could not see as he was blinded from the white glow. Sebastianus was frozen. He couldn't believe it! He was dead!

"But", he said. A little bit of a smile appeared on Sebastianus' face. "You have been brave, wise and strong. You have saved many lives. You have also defeated many. You have a chance. You can die as a hero or you can live to defeat Gelu and go on with your quest."

Sebastianus wanted to have fame as the dead and living. But that wasn't the real reason. If Sebastianus didn't live to kill Crusak, the prophecy said the world will live in eternal darkness as a hell on earth. "I would like to live", he said.

Letum was almost ready to carry Sebastianus off to the Heavens. "What?" she asked confused.

"I would like to live. I must defeat Crusak. To do that, I have to defeat Gelu. I would like to live", he said.

Letum let him go. She didn't speak. She was absolutely shocked. Then she turned into a pitch-black shadow and melted into the snow.

Then Sebastianus saw the sacred sword. It was cracked down the middle. A couple of pieces were shattered. Then the sword slowly came together. The cracks filled in by itself. Sebastianus lifted the sword and then he climb up the caves to Gelu's cave.

He seemed to cLosurb faster. After a couple of seconds, where his hand should've been it was numb. A s he looked at his arm, he was amazed. His hand was back! It was clean and the same as it was before. "Thank the gods", said Sebastianus, smiling. Then he climb again. After numerous times of almost slipping, Sebastianus finally made it to the top where Gelu slept silently. By the time Sebastianus got back, Raphael was only about five men away from being eaten.

Sebastianus then saw that Titus and Liberius lay somewhere after Raphael.

Then Sebastianus thought to himself. He needed a plan. "It's brilliant", whispered Sebastianus to himself. His plan was brilliant. Then Sebastianus ran up the latter. He moved swiftly and secretly. Finally, when he snuck past Gelu, he grabbed Raphael by his vest. He dragged him over to the latter. He then threw him down, ran over to Liberius, threw him down and then did the same with Titus. He grabbed the last fifty and then he went up to Gelu, he pulled out the Sword of Vinco. And then as he was about to stab the terrifying beast, Gelu awoke with a crazy look in his eyes! "Crusak!" he roared like he did right before Sebastianus almost died.

Then he slashed Sebastianus with his claws across Sebastianus arm. He yelled again. But this time, he said "Latorin!" He clawed again. This time he missed. Then Sebastianus slashed Gelu with the sword. It cut his chest and from it spilled snow instead of blood. Then Sebastianus slashed again in the stomach. The beast kept screaming and more and more snow fell out. Then Sebastianus took one more dreadful swing at the face. He ran on top of the pile of bones and he aimed his sword carefully. Gelu, who could do nothing because of his pain, sat, waiting for his death. Then Sebastianus swung and the helpless Gelu fell dead. Then after a second, everybody got back up complaining about headaches and sore necks. They were all cheerful when they hear that Gelu was dead though.

After about ten to fifteen minutes of searching, Liberius finally found a little cave that had a crack in the back that fit about two people at once. The best part was, the Latorinous thought they were dead!

The mountain of Gelu was simply a very poor memory. Everything was quiet. Nobody spoke, nobody but Sebastianus. He needed to know more. Sebastianus could never stop learning. There had to be more. There had to be more clues of what was going to happen, what had happened, what he had not noticed, what he wouldn't notice. He had almost died! He had to know what was next. Each word of the wise Liberius and Titus meant so much more. Though he did understand, Sebastianus didn't. It was too much to bear.

Ever so slowly, the temperature rose and eventually, Sebastianus found that his boots were soaked in what he discovered what was muddy slush of what was once thick snow. For nearly a day and a half, the army marched, finding the journey slowly becoming easier as they merely walked on their way. Soon that of which remained of the slush dripped off a slope into a thin and deep river. On the other side lay red sand, the color of blood.

The sand increased in size and rose up in hills the size of mountains. "The Exuro Deserts", said Liberius "also known as the Deserts of Inculta." He took a very large breath, inhaling the slightest bit of sand, though the air was fresh and warm. Sebastianus still did not trust him. Ever since that incident on the ship, he still believed that a demon roamed inside his soul. Liberius looked at Sebastianus, knowing what he was thinking and tried to form a smile that told that he was now different, changed.

"The Moving Mountain, I can only presume?" Titus said calmly. Then he pointed out a mountain in the distance. It was difficult to tell that it was a mountain due to the hills of glorious red sand. Simultaneously, the soldiers stared at the *mountain*. But large boulders the color of the sand could be seen, if closely looked at.

"The *Moving* Mountain?" Sebastianus asked.

"Just myths", Liberius said.

"Though…", began Raphael.

Sebastianus focused on Raphael. His friend began the tale. "The Moving Mountain was formed the day Latorin fell dead in the Scross Valley. It grew right over his murdered body. The mountain was once believed to be in Rebucia, where Scross Valley was. Then it was spotted in Hestour, Azell, Formighte, and other places. And if you go back to Scross, the mountain will no longer be there. It moves when no one watches. Some people believe that the spirit of Latorin is inside it, somehow controlling the dark from within."

"Do you believe that?" Sebastianus said, unsure what to think. Just some weeks ago, he would have laughed at that idea, but now he had seen the eyes of death and evil and darkness.

"Quite honestly, no one knows what to believe these days", said Raphael still gazing upon the sight of the mountain. "Legends can never be doubted now. Just think, the story of the Angel of Death and his disappearance. The people mourned until he came back to reap the soul of Vinco before leaving once more. He isn't very well liked I guess."

Raphael and Sebastianus were able to laugh at that. They stopped immediately, though. Legends were legends, but how many were actually true? Only living through them would anyone ever knew. "…and he retreated to deserts of blood…" Sebastianus mumbled, remembering the rest of the stories from his old nurse when he was just a little one.

"You know", pointed out a soldier called Holunus, "on the hill next to the mountain, there's a cave. We could rest there."

"No!" said Sebastianus. "Every time we stop to rest, we're almost murdered! We cannot stop, for that is when we are weakest. If we do stop, then a giant monstrous creature will come and kill us!"

"Shall we ratify this case?" asked Titus, his hands being held out, showing the uncertainty that he had in his own suggestion. The men nodded. "But if we do stop", Titus added before the vote could begin, his eyes glancing at Sebastianus "we will most certainly *not* use that time to sleep."

"That's agreed then", said one of the soldiers. Sebastianus turned and gave the crowd a look of disgust, though it was directed to no person in particular.

"Step to the right", Titus began, "if you wish to keep on walking. Stay where you are if you want to stop." Nearly one hundred men poured to the right, where Liberius, Titus, Raphael and Sebastianus stood, disappointed at the decision of the soldiers. But as lord of Hestour, Titus was forced to do what was whatever the majority needed, as long as it was reasonable. He sighed and the men walked several paces before coming upon the hill of blood colored sand. *...And he retreated to deserts of blood...* Sebastianus thought again.

The thought was cleared no sooner that it had come. And now Sebastianus focused on how ridiculous the idea of stopping once more was. He lost his temper easily. He had been through enough and had seen enough.

"Maybe", said Raphael, trying to be optimistic though he saw the risk of resting as well as his friend, "this will be better. I mean we're tired, hot, our clothes are bedraggled from sweat and grime, and well... a stop would be nice...I guess."

The cave in the sand was supported by a massive rock on top of a pile of sand. The sand had covered it up and eventually, somebody dug into the rock. It looked ancient. The soldiers, uneasy, stepped into the dry cave where a single tree sat. It was dead, with a snake curling on it. It was very large, almost filling the cave. Beside the tree was an old man, grey hair dripping over his face and a beard the same. His face was pale and a hint of green. He was sweating and looked ill. His nap, as the soldiers guessed it was, could have actually been his body, dead.

"Arsenio…dead", said an ancient sounding voice. "The illness is killing the few citizens of the desert."

Instead of beginning of the conversation with his condolences, or even introducing himself, Sebastianus spat out, "People live here? It's in the middle of godforsaken nowhere!"

The man glared at Sebastianus, but soon his deep, almost evil looking frown became a mischievous smile. "The migration of the Tyhle village was unexpected, yes. There were roughly", he paused to think, "…maybe seventy people. They came in hope of a better land. There own, as they claim, was destroyed. In fact, ridiculously enough, claimed the Atra Erus returned and Veniauni began to build his forges. How ridiculous is that?"

"You…you spoke Latorin and Crusak's names in the tongue… the tongue of the dark. How do you know how to speak in that language?"

"This is the Crusalands, boy. We were raised to speak in that language, though I am ashamed of knowing so. In fact, I barely knew you could address them otherwise. And I don't like the way you are talking to me. I am more elderly than you and clearly you should respect me! How dare you."

He continued to glare at Sebastianus, but eventually he smiled. "You're the Death March. That little party of yours is quite famous now. You've been brave. It is a dissatisfactory to many of the citizens who still are loyal to Atra Erus."

Sebastianus cringed at hearing the name. It scraped his eardrums, producing sounds as though the screaming of children, dying. The man's voice, now that Sebastianus had time to think about it, was very much like that all of the time when he spoke.

"What is your name?" Titus finally asked.

"Why", said the man, "my name is Presidium."

Presidium glanced at Sebastianus, knowing that he would notice that that name was of the dark tongue.

"Do you...have you a profession?" Liberius stuttered to Presidium.

"I do...or did, in a manner, I guess you could say. I was once very important. Godly stature, I guess one may say. That was a time ago, when I lived in luxuries of Hestour and Rebucia, but those days die." When he said the word *die* it echoed through the deserts. Many of his words did the same: *godly stature.* "Well I'm just a poor soul who was reaped of his magnitude."

Soul, reaped.

Things were getting stranger now as his particular words echoed and scratched. Sebastianus now could only do one thing to prove a theory he had. The theory was one that would have been unexpected if you had not dealt with what Sebastianus had dealt with. His theory was that Presidium was involved with Subvenio Mortuus. That was the act of helping the dead, though it was mainly reaping their souls. It was given that name by those who favored the act of the Angel of Death. It was the tongue for Help Dead. Oddly enough, the name adapted to become a word in the regular language of Hestour.

And what Sebastianus intended to do was to test. The tree beside Presidium held many new leaves, green and full of life while others were dull and grey. Maybe, as Sebastianus thought, the tree was of some sort of significance to the Subvenio Mortuus. To prove this, he stepped to the side, and, to the surprise and anger of Presidium, plucked one leaf.

"We are all doomed. You ignorant fool!" he yelled at Sebastianus before the life evaporated from his eyes. He was dead. From beyond in the cave came hoarse voice, similar to Krausin's.

"A soul for a soul is what I need. And yours, Dramilius, is a wonderful, sweet spirit for me", the voice scratched upon the ears of the soldiers.

"What is happening?" demanded Liberius, raising his sword in the air, removing his cloak and revealing gold colored chain mail that sparkled in the sun.

"*Death*", replied the voice as the creature loomed forward, while simultaneously the dead body of the man Presidium. And once his full form was seen, the stature scared Sebastianus enough that he would

"A sad death", said Presidium. Then he took yet another swing. He aimed for the throat. Instead, Sebastianus blocked his hit with the Sword of Vinco. The sparks flew from the silver surface of Sebastianus' blade. Then Sebastianus jammed the blade bup Presidium's hood. Sebastianus could barely figure out if there was even a face under the hood he wore. His face was completely black from the shadows of his dark hood. Sebastianus let go of the sword. He leaned his head to see if anything was there. Not even a trickle of blood fell. Then after a moment, the cloak fell. Nothing was in it. It was just an empty cloak. Then the cloak shrank and shrank and shrank band…well you get the point. It was soon nothing but a pathetic pile of dust. Then the dust was slowly carried off by the wind. Then the words of the Angel of Death went through Sebastianus' head. *He has sent me, the lord of evil, Crusak. He has hired me to kill you, alone in the dark where nobody can help you. It is my fame with to kill a hero and Crusak' win. Beware of what ever comes to you.*

The desert was scolding. The blazing sun in the morning was enough to blind a city. But there wasn't a city, only about five hundred men left with Sebastianus. Sebastianus could only name a couple, Linos, Alexander, Lionios, Mininem, Gralue, and of course Raphael, Liberius and Titus. The worst part was, they were probably all going to die.

Titus and Liberius had whispering among themselves for a time, Sebastianus had noticed. Eventually, Titus declared that water was nearby, but all had to be on their guard, for it was dangerous.

Everybody looked exited and scared. They had had nothing since they entered the desert. Though the chances seamed slim of living in one of those deadly situations that the men predicted, they all replied yes, hoping that more than just water would be there.

Shortly after, a glimpse of a sparkled river was spotted by Raphael, who had the best eye. "About twenty more minutes", said Raphael. Then he led everyone towards the river.

"Where's your so-called beast, Liberius?" asked one of the men.

"Hiding, that's what he did last time."

Then, one of the men, who were greedy enough, jumped into the water. He drank and washed himself. He caught the fish that came out. "This is great!"

"Stop it, young greedy one!" yelled Liberius.

"No!" yelled the greedy man. Then it happened. He swam and drank and then a flashing horned figure ran out of the water and pulled down the man. Sebastianus, who didn't have much time to look at him, saw that he had two bull horns, a brown head, four legs, two arms, hooves and a horse tail.

"This is horrible!" shouted Sebastianus. Then as everyone began running away, hiding in bushes, or trying to jump the river, the beast ate more and more people. He pulled them under and then they were never seen again. "Titus, Raphael, Liberius, I have a plan!" shouted Sebastianus, after thinking of an amazing plan. The four got together in a bush. Sebastianus told them his whole plan. "It will work", said Titus. "Will probably fail", said Liberius. "It's brilliant!" said Raphael. Then they began.

Sebastianus then ran out of sight, behind a bush that touched the bottom of an orange sandy cliff. Titus ran around the beast over and over again. Raphael did the same, along with Liberius. The beast squealed. It ran after Raphael, but Liberius stabbed the beast in the side. Then it went after Liberius, and then Titus stabbed. Then it did the same and so did the three warriors. It continued til the beast swatted away the weapon of Raphael. He ran for his life, but did not lose control. He ran around in circles, just like the others. Then Titus and Liberius held out there swords. The beast did something of a laugh and then devoured the two weapons. Blood dripped down his mouth, but he didn't seem to mind. Liberius and Titus joined Raphael, running around like fools.

Then Sebastianus jumped from behind the bush with the Sword of Vinco in his hand. He snuck over quietly as the beast tried to kill his victims. Sebastianus then came in fast. He stood behind the beast. It was cornering Raphael, Liberius, and Titus. Sebastianus then aimed for the legs and then when the demon fell, he would go for the chest. So Sebastianus then mumbled under his breath "Thy shall defeat thee, wicked beast." Then he took a swing across the two back legs. "Help!" the best yelled into the air. Then Sebastianus stabbed him in the chest…kind of. He was about any second, but then he heard the stomping of hooves in the distance. Then it grew louder and louder. After about thirty more seconds, a herd of the beasts appeared on the cliff. They were all different sizes. Most of them were bigger, but besides that, they all looked the exact same. So Sebastianus then stabbed the beast and then everyone ran off with the food and bags of water. Sebastianus did not have time to take all the fame. But Raphael did yell "Sebastianus! Sebastianus! He saved us once, he saved us twice! Oh Sebastianus!" And after that they were off.

Chapter Six:

Inculta of the desert

The group ran at top speed for about a half hour until they realized no one was on e there trail. But, just to be careful, they all ran around in circles and in random directions in the sand, so their tracks were not to be seen. Then they all went straight into the hot desert. "Sebastianus", said Liberius "which way is north from here?"

Sebastianus then reached into his bag which carried his compass, good-luck necklace, and right next to it, the Sword of Vinco. Nothing! There was no good-luck charm and no compass. "Curse the Latorinous", mumbled Sebastianus.

Liberius then gave Sebastianus an odd look. "What's wrong?" he asked. "Yes Sebastianus, what's wrong?" asked Titus, who seemed to come from nowhere.

"The Latorinous", said Sebastianus.

"Well, I'm sure at least **somebody** else brought a compass along with them!" yelled Raphael, slowly, eying everybody.

They all seemed to stop, mumble, scratch their heads and besides scratching, they didn't move. They didn't even blink. "Titus, it has been five years since I've seen you. Please tell me the rest of your kingdom isn't like this!"

Titus gave a crooked smile and tried to laugh his way out, but Liberius looked anxious for his answer. So Titus whispered something in his ear.

Liberius started muttering and cussing. Soon enough, he forgot about it. Sebastianus felt ashamed. If they got lost, it would be his fault.

They walked on in the desert. Then Titus held out his hands. "Stop!" he yelled. And then suddenly everyone froze like statues. "Inculta", he muttered. Then one of the men started to shake. The sand below him was cracking and then a flash sucked him in the ground. Then another and another and another. Everyone was running in circles. "Help me God!" yelled about twenty people as they ran farther out in the desert. Then Sebastianus saw that Raphael was well protected. He clung on to the top of a high tree. "Most Mealins live to be one-thousand! I'm only two hundred! This isn't fair!" he shouted. Sebastianus wanted to ask him if he was really two hundred years old. Sebastianus was only twenty seven. Then Sebastianus realized Raphael was way safer than anyone else. So he joined Raphael and climb to the top of the tree. Soon Liberius and Titus were seated safely on another tree. And soon enough everyone was on a tree. "It has to come out", said Liberius. And it did!

He had sparkling green scales. The beast had at least a dozen little horns on his neck and back. But the worst part was that Inculta had three heads. Two heads on top of its body and one at the bottom. Sebastianus estimated that Inculta was about three hundred feet long. The part that seemed to disturb Sebastianus the most was the design on Inculta's back. It was a row of skulls. In front of the skulls was a head with all of its skin, bleeding like crazy from its mouth, ears, nose, and eyes. There was a spear through its head and the man who threw it was Crusak.

"Somebody, help!" yelled one of the men who fell of the tree in front of the deadly Inculta.

Then Sebastianus and Raphael gave each other a look, jumped off the tree and drew their swords. "To Titus, to Liberius and to

Raphael", mumbled Sebastianus. Then he looked at his hand that had grown back when he fought Gelu. "To God, who helped me at my weakest hours." Then Sebastianus heard Raphael mutter something about thanking people and gods. Then Raphael kissed the surface of his green and golden sword and then he went for Inculta. Sebastianus went for the head on the end and Raphael went for the one on the top of the snake. Sebastianus swung his blade. He shut his eyes tight. When he opened, he saw the snake with an only a couple of blood and sweat drops from the forehead. Sebastianus then stabbed the beast even deeper in the forehead. It gave out a painful scream and Sebastianus looked to see how Raphael was doing. Apparently, the Mealin was fending himself well. But no sweat or blood was on the monstrous snake.

Then the snake Sebastianus fought raised its head and tried to bite him. Sebastianus then raised his sword and stabbed Inculta in his cut forehead. The beast's head fell on the sandy surface of the ground. It wailed in pain. Sebastianus took a second to savor the moment. Then he gripped the Sword of Vinco with both hands and thrashed it in the head of the snake. 1/3 was dead.

Sebastianus then ran to Raphael who kept trying to stab the beast. "Liberius! Titus! Help me and Raphael...**NOW!**" Then Liberius jumped off the tree, landing on his feet. Titus slid down the tree trunk like a pole. Then they took out their swords Manius and Delabius. "For the heroes of our land!" yelled Liberius. "And the gods!" added Titus. And then the two took the other head.

Raphael fought great. He didn't get much stabbing in, just blocking. Sebastianus managed to get one stab in. As Raphael blocked the beast, Sebastianus took a swing and stabbed the beast in the neck. It started to bleed badly. The snake head took one more breath and then he passed out for a moment. It was silent for a little bit. The only sound heard were Liberius and Titus trying to defeat the other beast. Then the snake raised its head and took a deadly shot at Raphael. Raphael hesitated and then at the last second, he lifted his sword and blocked the head. Then, as the head struggled to penetrate Raphael's sword, Sebastianus stabbed its Adams apple and then it fell dead. Liberius then took a swing at his own opponent and killed it. Like back at the river, no one had time to cheer. They all jumped off the trees and ran through the desert as the stomping of hooves was heard in the distance.

Chapter Seven:

The Egg of Wisdom

The desert was now even hotter. "Now that the Latorinous has your compass Sebastianus, we will probably end up west, north or east", he said. "The same thing happened to me. I ended up west, where the volcano's of Exuro is."

Sebastianus was silent. After a short moment of silence, they walked on. After about twenty minutes, the sound of hooves disappeared. After a whole hour had past, Liberius stopped. His jaw opened wide. He stared upon the horizon. Everybody stopped with him. Then a lump appeared on the horizon. It got bigger and bigger and bigger until it was the shape of a dragon. It was completely black. Then Sebastianus blinked. Above him, hovering in the orange sky was a black scaled dragon. It's wings and head were blood red with stripes of green. Its teeth were the size of books. It didn't bother to do anything. Then it lifted it tail and an oval-like shape fell out and reached the ground. Then the dragon became the shape of a thumb behind them. Then the oval rolled on the slanted surface of the desert and stopped at the feet of Sebastianus. It was shiny black. It had a blood red skull on one of the sides. Then Sebastianus realized it was an egg. It was only a simple dragon egg. *I wonder why Liberius acted like it was a big deal. It's nothing but a dragon egg* Sebastianus wondered. Then as he bent over to grab the egg, Liberius slid like a baseball player and grabbed the egg on his way. "Fool!" he said as he held the egg tight.

"Liberius, it's only a dragon egg", said Sebastianus with a giggle.

"Do realized what this is? This is the Egg of Wisdom. Every hundred years, the Dragon of Death lays an egg. This egg is a very special egg. The egg of wisdom sees all and knows all. Ever since the armies of Latorin marched through the mountains, the dragon roamed the world. If this egg cracks, we will learn what our destiny is! That's the secret. The Egg of Wisdom is not to be used as a toy! It was the third thing to become…a thing!"

"Well, Liberius you know I have problems with learning and not to good at all with history. There's no need to yell."

Then as Liberius was about to come back with some smart comment, a cracking noise appeared from him. He was wide-eyed. He slowly looked down at the black egg. It wasn't Liberius making the odd noise…it was…it was the egg! Then Liberius set the egg down on the ground. From the cracks, light came out. "Oh, master of the wise ones, tell one of us our future. Tell us the one who will conquer all…and Crusak", demanded Liberius, smiling, knowing it would be him the egg would roll to and talk to. Then the egg cracked once more. Then the shell burst into tiny little pieces. There standing was a regular man. He was wet and naked. He had long, curly brown hair and a short curly brown beard. Before anyone could get a close look at him, Liberius removed his cloak he wore over his armor and then quickly put it on the man. He stretched his back, yawned and then he went over to Sebastianus.

"You are the prophecy", he said in a deep, calm, relaxing voice that made Sebastianus want to fall asleep. Then he spoke a little bit of strange advice. It went like this:

"You have lost much. But yet, much is none. You started with 345, now you have pretty much one. You have almost made it to

the temple of the dark lord. But beware; you must still face the volcano's core. There shall be death to 342. But one will live, another shall live and you survive too", he said pointing to Sebastianus on the last line. Then he just…disappeared. Sebastianus was speechless. The wisest man in the world who only appeared every one hundred years had just spoken to him. Everybody else was silent too. Sebastianus would be a hero. Then everybody cheered but Liberius. He just crossed his arms. Then they walked again to the volcanoes of Exuro.

Chapter Eight:

The Volcano River

The desert seemed freezing compared to the volcanoes. Lava dripped from each volcano onto the ground. Sebastianus, Liberius, Titus, Raphael and the others had to watch their feet. If they stepped in lava…Anyway, Sebastianus then saw a couple of meters ahead of him were a red river. It was all lava. It seemed to go from the biggest volcano to the horizon. "The Volcano Valley River", said Liberius. "We'll have beast luck getting out of here if we cross through the Capital Volcano", he said pointing to the biggest volcano.

"We have to go…in there?" said Sebastianus, gulping. "But wouldn't that be where Exuro lives", he said, still gulping.

"Exuro isn't as bad as everybody says he is", said Liberius.

"Please, Liberius, do not be offended, but yes he is as bad as everyone says", Titus corrected. Then it was silent. Everybody marched on.

"Wait, Liberius, who'd you get past this river…it's all lava?!" asked Sebastianus, panicking.

Then Liberius pulled out five golden coins from his pocket. Each one looked the same with a little poem and skeleton carved on it. "This is what will get us past", said Liberius, shaking and shivering. Then magically, a horn appeared. Liberius picked it up and then blew as soft as he could three times. It made an odd sound, like somebody dieing. "Don't say anything. I'll talk", said Liberius. Then a small sail boat appeared. A man in a cloak was in it. When he turned his head, Sebastianus saw who he really was a skeleton! He looked like the Angel of Death, except he had no tree growing out of his back or snakes crawling from his cloak.

"Purpose for crossing", he hissed in a scratchy voice.

"We are here to fight Exuro in the Capital Volcano", said Liberius with a proud voice. But Sebastianus knew he was trying to cover up the fact he was terrified. Then the skeleton let everyone in. Then as soon as the twentieth person got on, the skeleton started to go away. "Only twenty a ride", he said laughing. Then the rest of the men just stood there. They were shocked.

Liberius pulled out four more coins from his pocket. "Will this do?" he said, nervously.

The skeleton snatched the coins from Liberius and examined them. "Fine", he said "but you owe me a something. What do you have? Any parts of rare objects? Any rare objects?"

Then Sebastianus felt a cold thing under his sleeve. He pulled out – to his surprise – a part of the shell of the Egg of Wisdom. "Will this do…?" asked Sebastianus, when he realized he didn't yet no the name of the skeleton.

"Ducis. My name is Ducis. And what is that?"

"It's a part of the Egg of Wisdom. He just told me my future on this journey. And this is from his egg."

Ducis grinned. It looked weird to see a skeleton grin. "Alright then. Get on, mortals!" Then everyone got on.

It was silent for a while. The only sound heard was the sound of the lava banging the boat. Every time Sebastianus tried to speak, Liberius would stop him by nodding his head no.

The skeleton's eyes were hidden by the cloak that sank down to his nose. He seemed much taller when he stood up. He was somewhere around seven feet.

Sebastianus couldn't but help to ask what Ducis was paddling with. It was white and long. "It's a femur bone of a man who bet I couldn't swim across this river. He bet his life. I simply swam daintily and so the man was mine. I used his bones, muscles, organs and other parts of his body for uses. His femur was perfect for rowing", he said. "Oh", said Sebastianus. *That's probably why Liberius didn't want me to talk* thought Sebastianus. Then it was silent again. No one talked. Finally, the boat stopped. A heap of rock and mud seemed to stop it. It grew large muddy hands and held it. Everyone got out, still silent and shocked. Ducis stroked his egg with one of his skeletal hands and picked up the femur. Before he did that, he took out a couple of jars filled with golden coins. He put the nine Liberius gave him in it and then wrapped up the egg shell in brown cloth. "Thanks", he said with his grin.

Chapter Nine:

Exuro

Everybody couldn't stand the heat. It was so hot, some vomitted and some turned red. A couple got sick. Some fainted. To Sebastianus, everything felt like it wanted to kill him. He was dizzy and tired. Raphael, Titus and a lot of other people took off their armor or shirts. Raphael looked like a giant turkey without his vest and hat. It seemed that everybody with their armor off looked less hot, so Sebastianus took off his shirt. It felt a little better. Puddles of sweat were left behind them. "The…the Capital…volcano…is close. Once…we get past,…we're okay", said Liberius, breathing heavily, taking giant sips of water. Everyone had filled their bags with water. Sebastianus decided he would drink half and pour half on himself.

"Liberius…is there any…way to get past the Capital Volcano without having to go through…Exuro?" asked Sebastianus.

Liberius nodded. "No, there isn't", he said.

Then, they came to the Capital Volcano. It looked like a regular mountain, except for the fact that lava was spilling out. "We must hike", said Titus.

"Can we just go around?" asked Sebastianus.

"The Egg of Wisdom told us we must face the volcano's core. The volcano's core is an old nickname for Exuro", said Raphael. Then everyone began hiking up the volcano.

"What do we do about the lava at the top?" asked Sebastianus.

"I see a clear path up there", Liberius pointed out.

After about two hours, they came to the top of the volcano. The path was easy to get through. It was wide enough. Everyone got through. "How are we going to get down?" asked Sebastianus, looking down at the bottom of the volcano.

"There's an old saying that has worked once or twice. If you hear the rock hit the bottom, you'll make it", said Liberius.

"It's probably the best way", said Raphael.

Then Sebastianus picked up a big stone that was right beside him. "I'm sure this will work", he said nervously.

"I'm sure it will", said Titus as he picked it up. Then he threw it down. After about five minutes, a big CRASH was heard. Then everyone took a big gulp and jumped.

Sebastianus closed his eyes. After one minutes, his feet stopped him. Sebastianus slowly opened his eyes. Then he saw that he was standing on a large ledge. They looked up and saw that the drop was no more than twenty feet. Everyone was only sore from the fall.

"Is everyone –" Raphael was cut off.

"**ROAR!**" yelled a monstrous voice. Then a flash of red appeared behind them. They all looked back. Then the flash appeared in front of them. They all turned again. "Exuro is here", said Liberius. No longer did everyone feel hot but cold.

It was silent for a minute. Then a big *slap* appeared from nowhere. Everyone turned to see a giant bright red hand on the ledge. Its finger nails were long and black. Then it's...head popped up. He had two giant bull horns that sprouted from his ears. He had small horns coming from his forehead and neck. He had two black eyes. Then he hissed and a forked tongue slithered out of his mouth. Then, his whole body came up on the ledge. He had no legs but a snake tail. He had ten arms! Then one of the men went up and tried to stab Exuro. But the monster just swatted him away. Then everyone charged. They all had there swords and shields ahead of the. Exuro swatted somewhere around twenty people off. "You sick fiend! Die!" yelled Liberius as he went in to stab. Exuro hit Liberius with his tail and sent him flying back into Sebastianus. "Are you okay?" asked Sebastianus. Liberius only mumbled something. Then his nose gushed out a waterfall of bright red blood.

Then Raphael, Sebastianus and Titus all ran for the dreadful beast. Exuro put out both fists. As soon as Titus and Raphael got close, he punched them both. They went flying backwards. Then Sebastianus went in. Exuro got wide-eyed when he saw the Sword of Vinco. But, he put his tail out and pushed Sebastianus back.

He landed on top of Titus. When Sebastianus looked down at the bottom of the ledge, he saw the sinking bodies. Then he looked over and saw Liberius and the pile of blood beside him. Then he looked at Raphael and Titus. Titus was concussed and covered in blood. Raphael was bleeding badly.

Then Sebastbianus ran up to Exuro. Exuro only smiled and punched. Sebastianus hesitated. Then, at the last second, Sebastianus dodged the fist. Then another fist came at him. Sebastianus dodged it. Another and another and another came. Sebastianus dodged them all. But he couldn't get a good aim to stab. Then the dreadful giant tail came at him. Sebastianus then jumped over it! With the Sword of Vinco he was able to do those kinds of things. Then, as he came down, he looked at the tail and smiled. He thrashed it through the tail. Exuro screamed in pain. Then he fellb over. Sebastianus had to savor the moment, when he would slit the throat of Exuro, who is by far one of the mightiest creatures. Then Sebastianus took his blade and…well let's just say that was the end of Exuro.

Sebastianus was lucky that was the very moment Titus, Raphael, Liberius and a couple of other people got up. Sebastianus treated their wounds and told them his story. Then they found a cave that lead out of the volcano on the other side. They approached Crusak.

Chapter Ten:

The Army of the Dead

They crossed the wooden bridge over the river of the dead that lead to land of Crusak. It was cold. Everything was black. It was the Southern Forest. Everywhere you went; it seemed that something was watching you. "Should we set camp up here?" asked Sebastianus.

"No!" yelled Liberius. "This is the darkest land ever. If we set up camp here, when we wake up, we'll be dead!"

Then they walked on. It got colder and colder as they went. "Be careful", said Liberius. "Any false move could be the end. Then, out of nowhere, an arrow whistled past Titus's ear and stabbed the man behind him in the chest. "The army of the dead", mumbled Liberius. Then hundreds of arrows went flying from nowhere. They came from all directions. Sebastianus dodged as much as he could. Then Sebastianus, Raphael, Titus and Liberius found a little shelter-like thing. It was a cave inside a giant tree. They all hid inside it. A couple of arrows went past. Then hooves were heard. At first, they were just small gallops in the distance. But minutes later, they were as loud as hooves a meter away. Then they saw the bottom of a black cloak from the cave. "Where are they? Crusak gave us direct orders to hunt them down and kill them", said a whispering voice. Then the horse neighed and they left.

Everyone took a deep breath and then got up. Raphael stuck his wing out of the cave. But then, a dark boot stepped on it. It was almost covered up by a dark cloak! "Filthy Mealin!" he yelled then stuck a bow and arrow at his face. "Where's Sebastianus", he asked.

Raphael's face was red. "Who?" he asked nervously, trying to pretend he knew no one named Sebastianus.

Then the man pulled back his bow and aimed for Raphael's face.

"NO!" yelled Sebastianus. Then he stuck of the blade Vinco to block the arrow from Raphael. The arrow than deflected off the blade and went flying side-ways. Then the man fell back once he got a good look at the sword. "So you are the famous Sebastianus", he said as Sebastianus, Raphael, Titus and Liberius got out of the cave. Then Raphael cut off the head, surprisingly. But the *man* casually picked it up and twisted it back on. Then Sebastianus stabbed it in the chest with the Sword of Vinco. The cloaked man fell dead.

Then they ran off. Soon enough, everyone about twenty people joined Sebastianus and his friends. Then they found a safe place to figure out there plan. "We'll need one brave man to go up there to fight Crusak with Sebastianus", said Liberius. "The rest shall fight the Army of the Dead with me and Titus." No one said anything. But after a minute or so, Raphael said "I shall go with Sebastianus." Everyone looked at him in shock. Then Liberius spoke again. "We will need to protect these two even if it means our lives." Then everyone nodded.

They ran and ran til they saw before them the great tower of Crusak. It was at least three of King Titus's palaces stacked on each other. It stood on a muddy surface. As soon as everyone stopped staring at the tower, they looked at the cloaked men. There were at least fifty of them. Then the soldiers formed a crowd. Sebastianus and Raphael stood in the center. Then they charged. Arrows went everywhere and bodies went flipping over in the sky and showers of blood. Quickly, Raphael and Sebastianus stuck with seven people and snuck out the of the miniature war. The Mealin and mortal approached the great doors of Crusak. Then it opened.

Chapter Eleven:

Rogi the Troll

Instead of light coming out of the doors, darkness and laughs of terror came out. Along with that, a four-foot fiend. He was completely over-weighted with blue skin and rags for clothes. He was completely bald and had pointy ears. "Sebastianus", he said "you have made life difficult for my master! You will pay for your disturbance!" Then he pulled Raphael and Sebastianus in by their shirts and shut the doors behind. Then he began punching the two in the face. "Who...who are you?" Sebastianus struggled.

"I am Rogi. After the Red Nexuela, I'm Crusak' best man", he said in a low voice. Sebastianus and Raphael really didn't really care who the Red Nexuela was. Then he threw another punch at Sebastianus. Then, Sebastianus grabbed his sword. "Don't", he said.

Then Rogi let go of Sebastianus and threw Raphael about ten feet away. Then Sebastianus actually had time to look around and see the inside of the tower. It was covered in fancy pictures, armor, weapons and books. The walls were red and everything smelled really bad. "So it is a duel you want", said Rogi. Then he pulled out two golden swords from a bag that hung on his back.

He then took a swing at Sebastianus. Sebastianus blocked it with the Sword of Vinco. Then Rogi hit with both swords. Sebastianus blocked the one in his right hand. Sparks flew from the surface of the blades. Then Rogi's sword went flying out of his hand onto one of the statues. Then the other sword was also blocked by the Sword of Vinco. Sparks were everywhere. Raphael watched, he amazed and terrified. He knew if he tried to sneak up on Rogi, the troll would kill him. "To Crusak", said Rogi as he swung hi sword again. It hit Sebastianus in the waste.

"Ahhh!" yelled Sebastianus, holding his waste with both hands. Then Rogi kicked his legs and Sebastianus fell to the ground. "Someone help me", said Sebastianus, trying to yell.

Then Rogi laughed as Sebastianus rolled on the ground. "You are nothing but a mortal! You actually think you can beat me", he laughed. Then he took the handle of his blade by both hands and nailed it into the ground. Sebastianus nearly didn't move. But at the last second, he rolled to his right. "Damned sword!" he yelled. Then Sebastianus realized that his sword was stuck. Then Sebastianus went up to kill, but instead Rogi pulled his blade from the floor and swung it wildly. Sebastianus ducked. The sword brushed his black, wavy hair. Then, as Sebastianus was crouched on his knees, Rogi laughed and tried to hit Sebastianus again. Sebastianus jumped a couple of feet backwards and then got up. He took a swing for Rogi, but the blue troll easily dodged it. Then Sebastianus took another swing. "Ahhh!" yelled Rogi. Sebastianus had gotten him in the arm. Then Sebastianus hit again in the arm and Rogi was hurt so badly, that he dropped his sword. Then he tripped Sebastianus with the blade he had just dropped. Rogi punched Sebastianus several times in the face til he bleed. Then the troll grabbed his sword. He was about to kill Sebastianus! Then he fell forward and Sebastianus dodged the body. A sword was in his back. Behind Rogi was a simple Mealin. It was Raphael. "Let us defeat Crusak", he said.

Chapter Twelve:

Crusak, Lord of Darkness

They ran up a black staircase for twenty minutes. The horrid smell got worse as they got higher. The stairs squeaked every time they stepped on it. It winded up a black pillar that had images of wars and Crusak on it. Then, they came to a giant door. It was half open. On it, was the picture of a skull. Then Raphael kicked it open. Before them, they saw that it was the roof of the tower. It was all black and flat. Black railing surrounded the edges. There was nothing, except the giant black and red throne that sat in the exact middle. On it sat an eight foot man. He had golden armor and a golden helmet with two giant horns on it. His whole face was pitch-black for an odd reason except for his blood red eyes. "Sebastianus!" he yelled in the lowest voice ever heard. "You have defeated my demons, my army of zombies and Rogi with the help of a Mealin!" he began to laugh. Then he got out of his throne. His golden armor glowed in the black night.

"You sick, cruel, damned –"

"Please, Sebastianus, pay you respects to the king. Bow and give me the blade. If you do so, I will let you go", he said. Even know his face was completely black and nothing showed, Sebastianus knew he was smiling.

"Never!" yelled Sebastianus.

"Mealin, your life is useless, bow", said Crusak.

"Never would I do such a thing, you fiend!" yelled Raphael. Then he did the thing that Crusak would torture him and tear off his Losurbs for. He spat in the face of the dark man.

"You have made the biggest mistake of your life, Raphael!" he yelled. Then he pulled out his golden sword. It sparkled so brightly, it nearly blinded Sebastianus! "Warrior, set aside! Let me and the Mealin handle this", said Crusak. Then he growled. "Now die Mealin!" he yelled. Right before Raphael could even draw his sword, Crusak shoved his golden blade up his chest. Blood gushed down like waterfalls. Raphael's eyes were closing. "Sebastianus, I'll always be at…your side", he said. Then he died. His feathers were all over.

Then Sebastianus drew the Sword of Vinco. "I will avenge Raphael's death", said Sebastianus, ready to kill the lord of evils.

"Really? You are not *honestly* ready to fight Crusak. I will crush you. Just like I did to Filius and several others who dared to enter my palace." Then he grabbed his sword from Raphael's chest. "Let us battle then, mortal."

Then Sebastianus swung his sword and banged the armor of Crusak. He laughed and the hit Sebastianus. It slit down his arm. Blood stained the black surface of the tower. Then Sebastianus took a hit and once again, it banged the armor and sparks went everywhere. Sebastianus knew from the very beginning that the journey was going to end up like it was. Crusak was going to be killing everyone. Then Sebastianus took another swing and it banged against his bare arm – the only place where there was no armor. "Ahhh!" he screamed. Black blood fell from him and landed on the roof. Then Sebastianus hit again. It scraped up his muscles. "Ahhh! Curse you Sebastianus!" Then he hit Sebastianus in the arm again. It bleeds. Then Crusak swung again. Sebastianus ran to his right and dodged it. Then Crusak' blade banged against Sebastianus' blade. They tried to shove one another down, but nothing seemed to work. The strength of their swords was even.

Sparks burned Sebastianus' face. "I hate you Crusak. With every vein and drop of blood, I hate you. You kill everyone!"

"Of course! That is the only way to entertain myself!" he laughed.

Sebastianus stared at him in shock. He was well aware of the evilness of Crusak, but he had no clue that he would be that gruesome. Then Sebastianus' hands grew sweaty and he lost the grip of his blade. Crusak sent him flying. Sebastianus saw it coming. Then as he fell over the ledge, he saw the railing! He clung on to it. He was alive! Then Crusak forgot about Sebastianus' sword and walked directly toward him. "Help!" yelled Sebastianus, even know he knew it was completely useless. Then Crusak laughed. He lifted his foot and then he stomped on the fingers of Sebastianus. Blood squirted from beneath his boot. "You are pathetic!" he yelled. "You are the great Sebastianus!" Then Sebastianus tried to lift his hand, but Crusak just shoved it back down. Then Sebastianus saw sitting by the ledge was Raphael. The blood from him formed a massive puddle around him. Then Sebastianus could not bare the sight anymore. The man who was killing him was the one who had killed thousands. If he didn't kill Crusak, he would be the cause of a living hell on earth. Then a tear trickled down Sebastianus' cheek as he looked at Raphael again. Sebastianus, with all of his might, raised his hand. Crusak struggled to keep the hand down. But Sebastianus punched his foot aside. Then he did the same with his other hands. Blood leaked from them, but Sebastianus didn't care. He got up and was on the roof once more. He bent over and grabbed the Sword of Vinco. "For Raphael", he muttered. Then he stabbed Crusak through the armor. The spot in the golden armor was now red! Then he stabbed his arms. Sebastianus then slit his lower leg and jammed his sword in the kneecap. Crusak fell. Blood was all over. Then Sebastianus looked at him then Crusak looked back at him. Sebastianus then thrashed his blade in the face of Crusak. Then he lay there dead!

Sebastianus then looked over the ledge. Titus stood there with bodies surrounding him. Instead of the army was dust. Then Sebastianus ran down the staircase of the tower. He ran out the doors. The aftermath of the event was enough to make a full grown man cry. Blood and gore was splattered on the ground, only covered by the dust of what were once Crusak's soldiers, now gone with their commander's existence. Nearly one thousand men had started the journey, only ending with only six hundred. Among the hundreds, Liberius was nowhere to be seen. Making eye contact with Titus, Sebastianus asked immediately, "Where's Liberius?"

"Disappeared."

"It's a week's journey back", Sebastianus stated to Titus, the day ending. It was not at all a celebrated victory. After the death of Crusak, the Hestourians brought down the tower with ropes, axes and fire. A pit was dug with shovels they found from Crusak's men. There, nearly one hundred bodies were laid down, put to peace in the worst way: buried in the lands of the dark, where the fires of hell brewed under Crusak's forges.

"There is one way", Titus said, almost ten minutes after the question was asked. "But that would be too difficult."

"My lord", said one of the knights, wounded and sweating, dirt and blood coming off his torn flesh. "An owl landed half a mile away. It was dead, but it was…one of ours, sir. It was sent from your queen. There seems to be a problem…"

"And that would be…?" Titus began, annoyed with the sentence not being ended properly. He was handed the note with sloppy handwriting.

Dear Titus,

As it seems, numerous men on the shores have spotted war ships of Formighte, Muse, and Apoalan battling on the waters. But they are headed our way. Five Musans declared war upon us and the same for the *Apoalans*. *A fleet of Formightans came toward us and threatened our people, taking almost fifty slaves and burnt down seven houses. Come soon, we need the army. We have but two days until the war begins here.*

Titus hesitated for a moment before he made a statement that was even worse than hearing of the Death March. "Attention, soldiers. I fear that Hestour will be no more in three days time. Nations of Muse, Formighte, and Apoalon have declared war upon us. If we will return in two days, we must travel the darkest path that men have ever seen. I can promise you, this will be the most horrifying moment that you people have ever seen since your birth and may be the worst moment of your lives. We are being forced to travel through hell itself. The city of souls is the quickest path."

PART TWO:

JOURNEY THROUGH THE CITY OF SOULS

Thoughts swarmed through Sebastianus' head. His mind could not conjure such thoughts. Those thoughts were answered almost immediately when unexpected visitors revealed themselves.

Sebastianus was amazed. As ten hooded men moved swiftly through the aftermath of the battle, he recognized them immediately as the most group ever assembled. Some called the group a cult, a society with the knowledge that even the wisest dreamed of, and even others dubbed them evil. The Hunters of Azell were possibly the most clandestine assembly ever. They were the most skilled assassins and soldiers in the world. Why the Hunters had not volunteered to kill Crusak, Sebastianus did not possess that knowledge.

"And we will also be there", were the words spoken by the superior warriors. The words were deep and tingled Sebastianus's spine, as they should have. He had just spoken to the Hunters of Azell. Besides their master, anyone who ever heard them speak was their victims. And their master was one of the most significant persons of all time. Lord Reabius Azell, immortal, magical, genius, former king, leader of his own nation, and one of the men who had fought Latorin hundreds of years before.

"You are familiar with Liberius Volde?" the head hunter stated. Before anyone could reply, he began speaking again. "Well, the dark are strong and he has betrayed us. That's why he is lurking in the depths of the City of Souls. He has plans to resurrect the beast Timos. If you follow us, we can reach the palace of Liberius and defeat him, come back and fight the war just in time."

"What are your names?" asked Titus.

"I am Apollo of the Phoenix, and these are my men: Bartholomew of the Owl, Hector of the Lion, Gabriel of the Tiger, Minos of the Bull, Leonidas of the Ox, Medsus of the Spider, Artemis of the Fox, Mathias of the Tiger, and Icarus of the Wolf.

"Sebastianus", said Bartholomew in a calm voice "we need your help. The prophecy of Monus said it."

"The prophecy of Monus?" asked Sebastianus.

"The prophecy of Monus is a tablet that the leader of the hunters – Apollo – carries. It tells us where to go and what to do", said Hector.

"It knows all and sees all", said Mathias.

"The point is", said Apollo, "we must travel to our destination and then the war of Formighte, Apoalan, Muse and Hestour. We shall guide you to the palace of Timos. But the others", Apollo nodded towards the knights, "will be shown the path directly to the path that will lead to the Castle of Lord Titus. We will be traveling to the City of Bruno and past.

Chapter Thirteen:

The City of Bruno

A cliff stopped the hunters. The horses nearly fell off. Sebastianus looked down. He was amazed! It was only supposed to be a myth! It was the legendary city of Bruno. It stretched far beyond into a foggy distance that smeared the horizon. The houses were temples and towers. They were all golden. In the middle was a gigantic temple bigger than the others. It was Lord Bruno's. Lord Bruno was a myth. He was a king that could never die. He was ruler of the Kingdom of Bruno and the swamps of Hestour. He was once cursed by Azell, ruler of hunting, nature and animals. So Bruno was a freakish beast. "We can't go around it or in it", said Minos.

"Maybe if we remain hidden, we'll be able to go through it", said Icarus.

"We cannot go through the city. If Bruno or one of his minions finds us, we're going to die!" yelled Bartholomew.

"What's wrong with going in the city, it's a paradise?" asked Sebastianus.

"Four hundred twenty seven years ago our immortal king, Azell turned Bruno into a monster because Bruno disrespected him and called him a lazy king. Bruno was turned into a hideous beast. Anyone from the Kingdom of Azell is punished when they enter the kingdom", said Apollo. "But there is no other way. So we must go through. Sebastianus, if anyone recognizes us, you throw this rope around us and say that you are taking us to Bruno."

Then Apollo looked around and saw a large stone. He got out a rope and tied it around as tight as possible. Then he threw the rope down and it almost hit the bottom of the cliff. Then, starting with Gabriel, everyone held on to the rope and slid down. Sebastianus was the third after Gabriel and Artemis. "Keep your eyes peeled for Bruno or his minions", said Apollo, looking every direction and counting every two minutes.

Nothing seemed to happen in the twenty minutes the hunters were down there. It was silent for the next moment. Then Mathias and Hector looked at each other. Mathias whispered to Sebastianus, "Rush hour."

Then a massive clock made a huge sound. It was like a gong. Then everyone sbtarted running out from buildings and riding wagons and horses along the streets. Even animals seemed to be running out of buildings. There were people, trolls, animals, circus actors, gladiators, and all sorts of monsters coming out, such as talking trees. They all ran, walked and rode to temples, houses, caves, secret hatches in the roads, under water, and even swamps. They all went where they wanted to and dbid anything. Some trolls wrestled in the swamp to entertain the other people. "Sebastianus, put on this and you'll blend in", said Bartholomew as he took out ragged shirts and cloaks. Sebastianus took a torn up red shirt and then put on a worn out brown cloak.

"When are we going to be out of city?" asked Sebastianus.

"A couple of hours and we'll be out of Bruno's territory", said Minos.

Then a man seemed to look at Apollo weird. "What is thy name", he asked as he looked at Apollo like he was familiar.

"My name is Laiboran. I work as a salesman at the corner of Bruno's temple. I sell food: chicken, cow meat, fruit and vegetables", said Apollo, sounding unstable.

"That's funny, you look like Apollo, the leader of those filthy bandit hunters", he said. Then he looked at Apollo strange for a moment. Then he walked away.

After a couple of minutes, a big bell rang. Everyone stopped and bowed. Sebastianus and the hunters did too. Then, from the palace of Bruno, a large figure appeared on a massive throne. Giant trolls carried it. On it was around a ten foot man. He had goat horns, lion's mane, forked tongue, a scaly back, gorilla arms that sagged down to his feet, claws, a bird beak, feathery wings, and frog legs. Besides that, he was covered in regular skin like a human's. "Peoples of my kingdom, I have heard that the Hunters of Azell are planning to invade my city! Prepare an army. According to a local man over at the swamps, Apollo, leader of the Northern Hunters of Azell, is already here and plans to kill me." Then Apollo looked at Sebastianus. He smiled and then snapped his fingers. He had a wrinkly, bald, and pale face. Then Bruno looked around at the four corners of his palace. "Last of all", he said "the simpletons, Royal Court, royal family and warriors of Azell have started a war. According to my spies, the hunters plan to start the war here and move it on to the Kingdom of Titus. Formighte, Apoalan, Muse and Noster Multus – the four supreme tribes and the four corners of earth – are the ones in the war." Then the beast of a king jumped off his throne. "Apollo, I hate you from every drop of blood, every vein, every muscle, every bone and intelligence I have. I hate you." Then he ran inside he temple.

Icarus grinned. "Bruno and the Bronese people are not too intelligent. They're also babies as you can see", Icarus said, pointing to Bruno.

Then everyone arose and formed a dozen lines all facing straight and the exact same direction. They faced a giant palace, bigger than Bruno's. It wasn't golden, though. It was black and surrounded by ashes and chunks of metal and scraps of paper. On it was a big sign. It read: THE FORGES OF BRUNO. Beside it were several other smaller buildings. One was simple things like flags and capes and the others were forges. All of the women and about seven men went inside the fabric temple. Everyone else went inside forges. Behind everyone was Bruno. He sat on a white chariot with blue spirals and designs pulled by two vicious beasts. Then he laughed as about 100 strong men came out to him with wood and metal. Tbhen…it began. The men began to build a tower right in front of Bruno's palace. They were going so fast you couldn't see them!

"Bruno has summoned the Speed Demons", said Apollo. "This must be faze two of his war."

Then a Speed Demon put on a flag and the tower was done. It stood about one thousand feet up. It was golden with a giant temple that attached to the bottom. Then the Speed Demons got to work again. They made a golden wall that surrounded the palaces and towers within a minute. Then Bruno looked around with delight. He mumbled something under his breath. He seemed to say something like: "Fools, they actually believe me?" But Sebastianus felt that that was wrong.

"Come on men; we need sleep", said Apollo, bags forming under his brown eyes.

No one argued. Tbhey found an ally that was made of bricks and iron. Medsus, Hector, Gabriel and Minos said, "Allzenso Mionius Rabbocious!" Then eleven tents formed along with several plates of food, fire, clean water, and a bag of gold. They all devoured the food, drank the water and used the fire to talk to one another when it got super dark. They all slept in a tent. They were each different colors and Sebastianus got a black one. And they weren't like the tents you would find a camping trip, they were massive. They were about the size of Sebastianus' house, except a lot nicer. They were covered in jewelry, too! The hunters and Sebastianus slept great. When they woke up that morning, Apollo said that it was time to leave the Gateway of the City. On the way, they bought some horses with their gold for the journey. Sebastianus sat on the back of Apollo's horse and on the way out of the city, the Hunters paid for four dead chickens, and a bag of some vegetables and meat that Sebastianus had never seen. But he still ate it.

"The Gateway of Bruno!" announced Gabriel as he turned his horse around so that everybody could see him. Artemis, Medsus and Minos looked most impressed. "It's so amazing", said Medsus. Minos nodded in agreement. "Apollo, have you ever crossed the gates before?" asked Minos.

"Once, before", said Apollo, sinking his head. "Bruno had just been turned into the fiend he is today. I had just become a hunter. I was forced to find the Three Minions with Minas. Their venom is meant to cure. I was nearly killed by the trolls of the city and made it out with only two of the vipers. I stabbed them to death and then took the bodies to Azell as a gift."

Everybody looked down. "Who's... Minas?" asked Sebastianus.

"Bruno killed him. He was the eleventh hunter", said Mathias.

Sebastianus looked down, too. He felt bad and then he realized that Bruno looked a lot scarier than he once though.

Chapter Fourteen:

The Iron Guards

A round two hours had passed. Sebastianus had napped twice within that time. As Sebastianus slept, a hand poked him in the side. "Sebastianus, awake!" Then Sebastianus was wide awake. Above him, Sebastianus saw Artemis. "It is lunch", he said, eating a dead, skinned, cooked chicken.

Sebastianus got up and yawned. He saw that his horse was beside him and sleeping. "Who cooked the chicken?" asked Sebastianus as he ate the most delicious meat ever.

"I did", said Hector, as he burned the raw chicken under the fire, holding it with a stick that went completely through it.

"It's amazing", said Sebastianus.

"Thank you", replied Hector. Then he ate himself.

"An hour more", said Apollo. "There are...some monsters to face."

"Who?" asked Sebastianus.

"The Iron Guards", said Apollo, devouring his chicken.

"Iron Guards?" asbked Sebastianus.

"They protect the way to the City of Souls. There are seven of them: Metalen, Ijeren, Smeden, Doen, Maken, Bouwen, and Reus. They each stand around four hundred feet. They each carry weapons. They're all different metal clubs. The Formightans made them with the help of the Muses… when they were not at war.

You know, we should be on our way. Everybody store your food in that bag that Minos has."

Then Sebastianus and several others threw their food into a brown beaten-up sack. Hector was given permission to eat on his horse since he cooked the chicken and had very little time to eat.

After another hour or so, Sebastianus and the hunters came to the coast of Hestour. The water was dark blue with mossy green spots and fish jumping around. About a kilometer away was an island. It wasn't the small island you probably think of, it was huge. Nowhere near as big as Hestour. It was their property, thbough. "The Land of the Iron Guards, the path to the City of Souls, and also known as The Island of Fear", said Icarus in a strong tone. But truly, he was terrified, along with everyone. "In the middle of it, you'll see the Dark Abyss. What most call The Entrance to the City of Souls." There stood Leonidas. It was one of the first times he had spoken within the two day journey.

Sebastianus then heard a sound. It was a soft stomp. "Did you hear that?" asked Sebastianus to everyone as he looked around to see anything. But nothing was in sight.

"No, Sebastianus", answered Leonidas.

"The Iron Guards", said Minos, his head sinking low.

"Sebastianus, the Sword of Vinco will be needed to defeat what has never been defeated…by a mortal", said Apollo.

The stomping grew louder. "Men, swim!" yelled Apollo as he dived into the water and swung his arms around like some sort of animal.

"It's useless, Sebastianus", said a ghostly voice in Sebastianus' mind.

Then Sebastianus saw himself in warm water swimming side by side with Artemis. He saw that Apollo was on the Island of Fear. Then he was on the island.

"Apollo, I'm freezing! Don't you have any magic that can dry me?!" asked Sebastianus.

"Mathias and Bartholomew are the hunters of weather. Go ask them", was Apollo's reply.

Mathias was sleeping, so Bartholomew said sure and then "Groshio, Manonionanz, Drimentoebo!" and then Sebastianus was dry and warm.

"Thank you", said Sebastianus.

Then a loud stomp was heard. Everyone was silent. Apollo waved a hand to hide. So Sebastianus and Bartholomew woke Mathias and then the three hid in a small cave inside a hollow tree. They were silent and did not even breathe. Not even the smallest gasp when the giant iron foot landed in front of them! Sebastianus slowly drew the Sword of Vinco. He wanted to take a big breath, but couldn't. A loud screw turned and then a sound of a rusted part falling off was heard. Sebastianus looked out from the little cave, only to show his eyes and hair. It wasn't a part falling off, but an iron arm turning out. It was signaling something. Then Bartholomew got wide-eyed and Sebastian-us heard the sound of trees whistling, rustling and snapping. The other six giants were coming! Bartholomew and Mathias pulled out some arrows that were in a red bag clung to their back. Then they took out their bows. Apollo and Leonidas were hiding in a little cave like thing that went about two feet down into the ground. They then pulled out a small flute. "CAH... CAH!" The red flute sounded of a bird. Then Leonidas chucked a rock near the water. The giant near Bartholomew, Mathias and Sebastianus swung his rusty legs and then ran toward the water.

It stopped right by the sand that connected to the waters of Hestour. He nearly fell into the mossy water. Then Sebastianus realized that iron rusted in water.

"Sebastianus, I have a plan", whispered Mathias as he looked for a stick. Once he found one, he drew out a small map of the island in the thick dirt. "Sebastianus, you and I shall distract the giants as Bartholomew and the others run for the abyss. Once we escape the giants, we go to the abyss where the hunters await us. We will jump into it and then we shall begin our quest in the City of Souls." Then Mathias pulled out a bag of gold coins. "I have a friend down in the City of Souls. But we will need to use these if he's going to give us a ride to the maze."

Tbhen Mathias pulled Sebastianus' hand and led him out of the cave. Bartholomew stayed in.

Sebastianus and Mathias looked around. Soon enough, they found the perfect distraction. It was a giant stick, but Mathias – hunter of weather – could fix that. He rubbed his finger tips together until he caught fire. He burned the stick. Immediately, the giants screamed over the sight. "F...fire!" yelled one of them in a voice so deep, it shook the island. Then it stomped. The other ones did the same.

Then one of them jumped and landed on his knees. Then he swung his hand. The sound of the rusty screw turn hurt Sebastianus' ears. Mathias gasped and then pulled Sebastianus aside. Then he smacked his hand on the ground. His hand made a crater right where Sebastianus had been. "Thank you", said Sebastianus, catching his breath.

"Nothing of the mortal race shall pass us! We will crush you!" said one of the giants. Then he was silent. He examined Sebastianus for a moment. His metal eye balls looked as if they were about to fall out. "F...Family of...Dark...Darkness! Family of Darkness! Nephew of the Dark One! He's a descendent of... Atra Erus!"

The others went crazy as they stomped and kicked and made noise that nearly moved the island. Sebastianus thought of what the iron guards said. Then Sebastianus noticed that that was the biggest distraction he could make.

Mathias stared at Sebastianus in awe. Sebastianus tugged his arm and then they ran for the abyss. Bartholomew and Apollo lead the Hunters of Azell to a massive tree. It stood around fifty feet tall. Sebastianus looked back at the giants who were still going crazy.

"Sebastianus, use the Sword of Vinco to chop this tree", said Apollo.

Sebastianus looked confused and then he pulled out his sword and chopped the tree down. It hit the ground with a large THUMP!

"Sebastianus, look before you what few have seen. Look before you a gateway to the dead. Look before you the Dark Abyss", said Apollo. In the center of the tree was a giant hole with no end.

Chapter Fifteen:

The Truth of the Family of Darkness

Sebastianus jumped after the hunters into the never ending hole. About an hour had past when Sebastianus saw a black surface. The hunters were all sitting there. Their grey cloaks looked black. Not even the slightest bit of light shined. Then Sebastianus fell on his feet. He felt no pain.

"Sebastianus, is it true that you are the ...?" asked Mathias.

"I swear Mathias; I don't know what the Family of Darkness is."

"Sebastianus, has anyone ever used you, your father and the Atra Erus' name in a sentence that only you could here?"

"Once the Latorinous told me half of a sentence that only I could hear. They brought up my name and my father's and the Atra Erus'."

All of the hunters shook their heads. "Sebastianus, the Atra Erus is part of the Family of Darkness. If you go back into history, Latorin wedded. His wife gave birth to several children. One of them was a cruel man. When his wife gave birth, he had a cruel son. His son gave birth to others who became part of the Family of Darkness. The same thing happened again and again til they reached the Atra Erus. He had a sonb, but he died in battle. So

Atra Erus asked his brother, Cato, for his son. Cato refused. Then Atra Erus stole Cato's son, Pravus. But Cato had another son named Sebastianus. Sebastianus was the Atra Erus' nephew", said Apollo.

"That's impossible", said Sebastianus.

"Sebastianus, what makes you saddest or maddest?" asked Leonidas.

Sebastianus thought of Raphael who had died a horrible death. Sebastianus sighed and then a small tear trickled down his cheek.

The hunters looked shocked for some reason. "Sebastianus, look at your hands!", said Apollo.

Sebastianus slowly raised his hands. They were black! They were like Atra Erus' face. They were pitch-black. Sebastianus looked at himself all around. He was completely black!

"Sebastianus do not doubt it. You are part of the Family of Darkness", said Medsus.

"Sebastianus think of the most glorious thing. What you want. What you want most of in the world", said Apollo.

Sebastianus thought of his parents. His mother was dead and so was his father. The Sebastianus looked at him self. He was the pale man he usually was.

"Sebastianus, promise me never to use this power. Tame it", said Icarus. "It may just take over."

Chapter Sixteen:

An Old Friend Visits

They walked for a couple of hours. Everything was cold and dark. Mathias lit a torch.

After a long walk, Sebastianus saw a lake. It was cold and misty. There was some kind of island far behind. Mathias looked kind of scared as he pulled out the sack of golden coins from his cloak. "Sebastianus, my friend's name is Ducis", said Mathias.

Sebastianus was shocked to hear it. Ducis had guided him through the River of Lava before!

"Yes, Ducis is the one who guides the souls from our world to the City of Souls. If I'm correct, you encountered the Angel of Death. Ducis is the father of death, indeed", said Mathias.

Then, Sebastianus saw a little canoe like sailing boat. A cloaked man sat in the back with a long femur bone. "So you made it threw and defeated Atra Erus", hissed Ducis, smiling at Sebastianus. He seemed to have some sort of Scottish accent. "This, Sebastianus, is the River of the Dead. It's also known as Abeo River. It is owned and is the property of Liberius, King of the Dead. An old friend of mine, he is.

Mathias, please give me the money. Or are you just stopping by to say hi!" Then he let out an odd laugh.

Everyone looked at him weird. "You are not a friend to anyone. You are the reason of many things", said Apollo.

Mathias took out the bag of money. Then he pulled out some kind of smooth, shiny, dark blue egg. He whispered something to the skeleton and then walked in the black boat. Apollo, Icarus, Medsus, Artemis, Gabriel, Minos, Hector Bartholomew and Leonidas all jumped in after. Then Sebastianus slowly took a step in. After around a minute, he was finally in.

Ducis was as grey as ever with a dark, dark cloak with a white staff with sapphire skulls on the top. Behind the hunters were three really pale men. They were almost clear. They were completely naked and each shivered when Sebastianus looked at them.

After a couple of hours, Ducis spoke. "I would join your little quest. But because of Liberius, I can't step on land! Unless somebody is willing to give up their life and guide the souls, I can't step on land! I once almost got some man to give their life up. He came from an unknown world. His name was David Jones. He was a horrible man. But he wanted to live and be upon the seas forever. I told him his job. He loved the idea of him sailing a boat all through the land of the dead. He and some other people just like him got on my boat. They asked for a bigger one, but I couldn't do that. They complained, so I threw them into the waters. The souls took the crew to the Swarm of Darkness, where all of the worst of the dead go. Now Plundorios, one of the Ninety-nine Nations, worship this David Jones. They try to act like him. They call themselves "*Pirates.*" They named a place after him. They call the bottom of our seas "*Davy Jones' Locker.*" They say all of the dead pirates go to this horrid place where they are punished and tortured. But, three men from David Jones' crew said they didn't mind the boat's size. So now they're mine...to keep. Right behind you, you'll see Edward Davis, Thomas Henry, and Jonathan Read." Then Ducis pointed to the three white men.

They all shivered again. They stared into space again and then shivered once more. Ducis laughed aloud.

Then the boat stopped. Ducis stopped laughing. He lifted him femur bone from the misty water. It was broken in two. He looked into the water. He bent his head almost touching the water. Then he himself shivered. It was silent. Ducis looked horrified. It was silent for twenty minutes. Then the little boat shook. Ducis rubbed his hand over the femur. It turned into a black sword with a glowing gold tip. Then Sebastianus could have sworn he saw something in the mist. No one dared to move. Then Artemis gulped. That was enough to kill everyone. The sound echoed through out the lake. Then a blue head poked out of the water. It had fins all over and black eyes.

"Sebastianus, this is the land of the dead. Anything that dies comes here. I'm sure that was Crispo, Beast of the Waves", said Gabriel. Then it sunk its head back under the water.

Ducis looked around. Then the beast looked up again and charged for the boat! Ducis laughed. His sword turned to dust as he picked up his white staff. He lifted it and then chanted something. "Bestia reverto ut Torninoa!" The beast then drifted of into the mist.

"Where is it?" asked Sebastianus.

"Torninoa is the world's edge. The beast will fall off the earth. The edge goes to one place", said Ducis.

"Where is that?" asked Sebastianus.

"Exactly, it's nowhere", said Ducis.

"But you said it was a **place**", said Sebastianus.

"No one said nowhere wasn't a place", said Ducis with a smile.

"But it's nowhere", said Sebastianus.

"Nowhere just happens to be a place of eternal darkness with nothing in it. It is filled with anything or one I want it to be filled with. If it is cast to nowhere, then it will never be seen or heard again", said Ducis.

Sebastianus then saw that the boat was moving again. After several hours, the mist and water cleared. Sebastianus found himself on a beach. It was dark and cold. He looked around to see a giant stone wall. He looked to his right. The wall stretched on for miles into the foggy distance. Then Sebastianus looked to his left. He saw the same view. An entrance sat before him. Odd marking were carved into the rock walls. Sebastianus had never seen them before. Even after all of the history he read to keep himself refreshed, he had never heard of it in books or scrolls. "Have fun in the Maze of the Forgotten", said Ducis as he sailed away into the water. Then Sebastianus saw that Apollo was signaling to go in. So Sebastianus did so.

Chapter Seventeen:

The Maze

The stone walls went straight, sideways, diagonal and way Sebastianus had never seen. The walls were coated with an odd language. The walls were grey and only got darker as they went on. The writing was golden and looked like:

▭▭

Everything seemed so weird. Apollo and the other hunters, who were the wisest people Sebastianus had ever met, didn't even have a single clue what the writing met and the way the way through the maze. After around an hour, Apollo stopped. Everyone else stopped behind him. Then the hunter leader announced, "We are lost!" His word echoed into the distance.

Then Sebastianus looked at the writing on the wall. A little bit of mist went by his face. Then it said it into his ears. Something spoke. It sounded like some sort of liar, but Sebastianus knew it was true. It spoke so slowly and daintily, it had to be telling the truth. Sebastianus looked at the wall more carefully. The hunters looked at him. "The writing says left is death and right is chance.

Up is a little bit of hope and down is hell", said Sebastianus. "Something told me. The mist told me", said Sebastianus.

The hunters looked at one another. Then they formed a huddle. Apollo whispered some stuff to his hunters and then they stood straight. "Sebastianus lead the way and you pick which way to go", said Hector. If you can read the writing again, then we may be able to get out of here", said Gabriel.

Sebastianus then did what he was told. He decided that a little bit of hope was better than the other choices. He tried to jog, but everything from the golden writing to the dark skies made Sebastianus tired. Walking felt like the best thing to do.

The writing changed a little bit every time and Sebastianus read each one as clearly as possible and lead himself and the hunters all sorts of directions. The walls got a little greyer and the writing a little more golden.

Sebastianus turned to the right wall and read in his mind. *Only go straight. Do not give up fate. But there is darkness ahead. Beware the dead!* Sebastianus looked a little shocked. "There is one way to go. But that one way is guarded by a demon. Everyone draw their weapons", said Sebastianus, trying to keep calm.

Apollo, Icarus, Artemis, Gabriel, Hector, Medsus, Bartholomew, Mathias, Leonidas and Minos gave each other a look. "The Swarm of Darkness", mumbled Minos.

Then a cold wind swept Sebastianus. He slowly walked straight into the one path the writing told him of. Then he came to a circular room with no roof. Sebastianus examined the writing and then looked up. About five hundred feet up was a giant black ball. Wind spun around it like a tornado in the form of a sphere. As Sebastianus looked more closely, he saw faces spin in, out, and around the ball. "The Swarm of Darkness", said Apollo.

Then everything got darker and windier. All of a sudden, a dark figure appeared. It had jumped from the sky. It was from the Swarm of Darkness! It was furry with two long teeth. It was the size of the room Sebastianus was in. It was a dark brown color and it had a tail like a reptiles. It was scaly and spiked. The beast had giant, long claws. Then it roared and leaped on Medsus and Minos. Sebastianus drew the Sword of Vinco. Then he went for the beast. But the tiger-like creature jumped up from the two scratched up hunters and went for Sebastianus. The creature threw Sebastianus' sword aside and then scratched him in the side. Sebastianus took a spear that he found on the ground (the one Minos had before he was leaped on) and then aimed carefully for the monster. Then Sebastianus threw it. Not a single thing happened! It went right through him! Then the beast roared and went for Sebastianus again. The hunters all distracted the beast with some fire Mathias lit while Sebastianus looked for the Sword of Vinco. After he searched in the dark for about five minutes, he found the sword lying near the stone wall. Sebastianus ran up to the beast and then it clawed at him. Then raised its paw and ripped Sebastianus through the chest. Sebastianus saw that no blood fell. Not even a drop. After that moment of looking at his blood, Sebastianus then raised his sword. He saw the creature coming. Then, at the last second, Sebastianus thrashed the sword into the beast's face and it didn't bleed. Then it disappeared and intro the foggy air.

Sebastianus was out of breath as he remembered the beast coming right at him. Then a little rumble shook the ground. A piece of the wall lifted itself. Sebastianus looked to see lights. And people.

Chapter Eighteen:

The Fountain of Youth

L ittle houses made of hay and sticks were all over the muddy
surface of the ground. Torches were lit and lanterns were
hung. People were running all over with wagons of hay,
food, wood and all sorts of stuff. Children were playing with
sticks and balls. A giant sign made of stone was stiffly stuck into
the ground. The same odd writing was there. Sebastianus saw the
letters: □□□□□□□□□□□□□

The city stretched on forever. The horizon was smeared with
little houses and peoples all working. Sebastianus saw right in
front of him, a red river. As he stared at it, Apollo told him about
the red river. "When you enter the world of the dead, you must
throw your blood into the river. It's believed one the blood will
turn blue and the people of the dead will return to earth and unite
with their family. It has happened once", said Apollo.

"When was that?" asked Sebastianus.

"When Atra Erus died", said Apollo.

Then Sebastianus saw a little bridge that went over to the
sign then formed a path that lead through the city. Sebastianus
stood in the middle of the line the hunters made. Everyone's faces
were pale. Their eyes all seemed to point Sebastianus forward.

"Sebastianus, we must find a place before dawn. We will camp there and then find the Fountain of Youth. If we can find that, Sebastianus, drink from it', said Apollo.

"Will you guys drink from it?"

"Sebastianus, the Hunters of Azell are met to be born, fight, be honored, be famous, and be dead. If we do not die, then the Hunters will never be replaced and we would disgrace our clan. All of the other hunters would be forgotten and no other hunters could join us. We have sworn an oath to fight til death", said Medsus.

Icarus then looked around. Then he let out a sigh and screamed. All of a sudden, a carriage came up. A skeleton with a cloak rode it.

"Ducis?" said Sebastianus.

"I'm Sicud", he said.

Then they jumped into the carriage. Sicud's black horses galloped fast on the muddy ground. After a couple of minutes, Sicud stopped. "We're here", said the skeleton.

Sebastianus jumped out of the carriage to see a giant, rectangular, black and gold tower about five hundred feet tall with silver designs. Sicud took out a little book from his cloak. It was as thick as the carriages wheels. It was green with black edges. On it, it read Book of the Dead. Sicud looked at them and then whispered their names as he wrote them. "You're on the top floor. All of you on the left, now", he said.

So Sebastianus and the hunters walked up to the tower and knocked on the massive, thick, fifteen foot tall doors. "Does he know we're not dead?" whispered Sebastianus to Gabriel.

"Of course he knows we're not dead!" yelled Gabriel. "If we were dead, we'd be paler than the color white itself."

"Oh", said Sebastianus.

Then the door slowly opened. A man in silver robes stood in front of them. His face was pale and white. "Hello, my name is Monus. If I'm correct, you are the Hunters of Azell. Come with me. Let us see. Ah yes, Apollo, Artemis, Leonidas, Gabriel, Hector,

Minos, Medsus, Icarus, Mathias, and Bartholomew, I have stories to tell you", he said as he shook each one's hand. "Sebastianus, you did a brilliant job defeating Atra Erus. The curse will lift soon. I can sense it. Now, you better find the Fountain of Youth. Here's a map. Find it before the Warrgons do." He smiled and then gave Sebastianus a rolled up map he found in a cabinet. He waved politely and then shut the door behind him. Sebastianus could tell the hunters were amazed to see Monus.

After a couple of minutes of walking, Sebastianus saw on the map that he was getting near the fountain. After a couple more minutes, Sebastianus saw a giant hole in the ground. He looked down to see water. He saw in the water that a massive stick touched the top. It was lit with fire. "The Fountain of Youth?" asked Sebastianus to himself. Then the blue water was shook as the ground did too. A loud stomp was heard in the distance. Sebastianus quickly took a wine glass Monus gave him and then filled it up with water. He then gulped it all down. "Eternal life', said Sebastianus.

BOOM! A giant foot hit Sebastianus map and crushed it into the mud. It was a yellowish foot with long, disgusting toe nails. "Warrgon!" it shouted. It looked down at Sebastianus. It was bald with one giant eye on his forehead. He had a long black beard. He looked at Sebastianus. He didn't blink or move at all. Then his mouth dropped open. "F...F...Family...of...Dark...Darkness!" the beast yelled. Then it ran away in fear. Sebastianus was shocked for a moment.

Then he walked back to Monus' tower. He was silent for hours. Then he went to his room on the top floor and slept til the morning came.

Chapter Nineteen:

The Parasite

Monus said goodbye as the hunters and Sebastianus left. He gave them a carriage to take. It was pulled by two white horses. He gave them a map of the City of Souls. "There will be tasks", he said before they left.

The hunters and their companion, Sebastianus, road for hours until, finally, the carriage stopped. Apollo led the hunters out. Before them was a giant mountain. On the top was a cave. A tunnel went through both sides. A river went through and off into the distance. But it wasn't a river of shining blue water, but a river of orange and red flames that raised almost the mountain's height. "Well, we certainly can't go around it", said Sebastianus. "We could hike over it and down. But we would have to leave our carriage around either way."

"Well, it's the only way we can go", said Minos.

Then the eleven men went up the mountain. It was silent the whole time. It was hard to keep finding rocks that poked out so you could grab it with your hand or lift yourself on it with your feet. But soon enough, everyone managed to the cave. "I say we rest here for a little bit", said Apollo. Then everyone went a little deeper in the cave.

After a couple of minutes of walking down into the cave, Sebastianus tripped in some sort of gooey, wet silk. "What is this?!" yelled Sebastianus as he cleaned the gunk of his pants. Then something poked his shoulder. "Stop it. I get annoyed really easily!" Sebastianus looked up to see which hunter was poking at him. When he looked up, he saw no hand of a man, but a disgusting sLosury green tentacle. Then a larger tentacle popped out of the darkness. Then another five tentacles shown themselves, til finally their were around fifty tentacles. Then four pinchers came out, then a scorpion like tail. In the center of the monstrous creature was a mouth. It had teeth all around, forming a circle. Behind those teeth was another row that formed a circle. The pattern repeated itself until a small hole was all but left. It had another, smaller tentacle coming out of it.

"The Parasite!" yelled the hunters and they all ran away. Sebastianus followed. So did the beast. Its tentacles grabbed onto rocks on the sides of the cave and it pushed itself forward. It spat gooey, wet, silky globs from its mouth. It hissed and then one of its tentacles grabbed Sebastianus' ankle and pulled him back.

Literally, when Sebastianus was seconds away from being eaten by the parasite, the tentacle fell with the silk flying all over. Sebastianus was covered in the goop and pits of silk. Sebastianus looked back to see what had happened. Bartholomew was struggling to fight. His sword was covered in goop. Then as soon as Sebastianus got up and pulled the Sword of Vinco, the Parasite took hold of Bartholomew. Little strings attached themselves on Bartholomew. He got paler and his muscular arms began to get a little skinnier. Drool dropped from his lips. His eyes got bigger and bigger. A little bit of his hair turned grey and some strands fell off. Soon enough, Bartholomew looked like an old man. He was thin, pale, bald, and then he died. The Parasite roared and then stuffed Bartholomew into the mouth. Sebastianus couldn't bare the sight.

"It's how the Parasite kills. It feeds off the victim, becomes more powerful and then eats", said Minos. Then he and Medsus went up for the attack. "It's horrible, really", said Medsus. Then they each tore through tentacles. Goop and silk went everywhere. Sebastianus joined Minos and Medsus. Apollo, Icarus, Mathias, Leonidas, Artemis, Gabriel and Hector joined and the tentacles kept falling everywhere. The Parasite simply grew another smaller tentacle each time. But when Sebastianus chopped off a tentacle, it stayed off. No tentacles grew back when the Sword of Vinco struck. Sebastianus then went up to strike the mouth. But two tentacles grabbed him! The little strings attached themselves. Sebastianus saw everything a little blurry. He felt himself getting weaker. He had to breathe heavier. Then, all of a sudden, someone chopped the little strings and the tentacles. Sebastianus' sight seemed better. He saw Medsus. "Thank you very much", said Sebastianus.

Medsus nodded and then he ran up to the parasite. Sebastianus did the same.

Then he realized that the tentacles were growing back, but maybe if he stabbed the mouth…?

Then Sebastianus charged for the beast and raised his sword with both hands on the hilt. He then let his sword down. Silk and goop literally covered the ceiling, walls, and floors. The Parasite was dead. "Sebastianus!" the Hunters cheered. Then they went out of the cave and up the top of the mountain and down. They continued their journey.

Chapter Twenty:

The Living Forest

Right at the bottom of the Parasite's mountain was a forest. Everything from trees to bushes was dead. Rotted fruits were on the ground and hanging from the leafless, grey, dead trees. "Shall we rest here? It's getting darker", said Sebastianus, looking at the black sky.

"There will be no resting here, Sebastianus. This is the Living Forest", said Medsus.

"You mean this forest is actually *alive*?" asked Sebastianus, looking at Medsus like he was psychotic.

"Sebastianus, Medsus tells no lie", said Icarus.

Sebastianus looked a little surprised. Then a growl like sound was heard. "That would be the trees", said Minos.

"Everybody, hide!" yelled Artemis.

"Artemis, there is nowhere to hide!" yelled Hector.

The ten stood there, not knowing what to do. Then Sebastianus blinked, and when his eyes opened, Hector was high on a tree with two branches holding him like hands. Besides Hector in the tree, something was going for him! Sebastianus, as fast as he could, took out the Sword of Vinco and chopped the branches off. Then the branches went for Minos and Leonidas. They both ran, but Minos wasn't fast enough. The branches scraped Leonidas and picked up Minos. He and Hector screamed for help. "I'll get you down!" yelled Sebastianus up to them. Then a branch went for him. Sebastianus tried to run, but the mud trapped his feet and crawled up to his thighs. The branch went down and then everything was black. Sebastianus felt the blood squirting on him. The branch stabbed andr Sebastianus through the chest. Sebastianus saw Raphael, his turkey friend who was killed by the Atra Erus. Then the blackness turned into the image of Hector and Minos trapped in a tree, the other hunters fighting off the trees and a branch right in the center of Sebastianus' chest. He saw the blood and how sharp the point of the branch was, but felt no pain. "The Fountain of Youth!" yelled Sebastianus. "I can't die!" Then he smiled as he pulled away the branch.

He then took the Sword of Vinco. He decided that first of all, he would kill the first couple of trees that were attacking the other hunters. He ran up to a large tree that was fighting Apollo and Medsus. Then, he took out the Sword of Vinco. The tree swung a branch at Sebastianus. Sebastianus ducked and then swung the Sword of Vinco. It cut off one of the branches. Then Sebastianus cut off another couple of branches. Then he stabbed the tree on one of the thick roots. Then the tree fell to the ground.

Sebastianus went for the tree that Artemis and Mathias were fighting. As the tree was so concentrated on them, Sebastianus went for the back. As soon as Sebastianus was going to stab the tree in the roots, it turned around and scratched Sebastianus' forehead. Then Sebastianus swung with the Sword of Vinco. It chopped off a couple of branches. The tree nearly fell. Then Sebastianus stabbed the roots. The tree fell.

Sebastianus then went up to the tree that was fighting Leonidas, Gabriel and Icarus. They fended pretty well. But then the tree swatted Leonidas and Gabriel aside. "Sebastianus, get away well you can!" yelled Icarus as he chopped off the top of the trunk then stab the roots.

"Icarus, I must help you!" yelled Sebastianus as ten trees detached them selves from the ground. They went for Icarus. Sebastianus took one tree out when he chopped off the bottom and thrashed his sword into the roots. Icarus took out five. Three trees stood on the right and two on the left. Icarus slid on his stomach and cut the roots on the way. Then he threw a dagger right at the roots of one tree sending it on the ground. Icarus was insane in the battle. He threw six more daggers. Two daggers ended up in each tree's roots.

Sebastianus stabbed every tree that came in his way and ones that weren't even alive yet. He just thrashed the sword into the roots. He tried to do some crazy stunts like Icarus would do. Some of them ended up kind of sloppy, but they worked. After a while, almost every tree in the area was gone.

Then Apollo decided to stab the tree that Hector and Minos were hanging on. He stabbed the roots and they fell. A little puddle of mud was below them. Then Sebastianus remembered what the mud did to him. It was alive too! "Minos, Hector – no!" yelled Sebastianus as the two fell into the mud. Sebastianus saw some heads and legs poking out along with arms. But seconds after, Sebastianus saw that the two wer dead. Soon enough, they'd all be dead.

Chapter Twenty-one:

The Water's Kings

Everyone was there waiting for Sebastianus at the end of the forest. They all greeted Novan. Then they walked off.

After a little bit, the same writing was there on a giant sign. It was the language of the Labyrinth. This time it said: ❑❑❑❑❑❑❑❑❑❑❑❑❑

"The Dwarfen Territory", said Novan.

Then Sebastianus noticed that there were fresh plants and clear andls of water and grassy grounds. There were huts and caves everywhere. Sebastianus saw that people about three or so feet tall were walking around, politely greeting each other with barrels, wagons and wheelbarrows full of stuff like vegetables, hay, fruit, brick, stone and wood. They each had little robes, red pointy hats, and long grey beards. They were the dwarfs. "Hello fellow humans", they said in funny high-pitched voices.

"Hello", answered Sebastianus.

Finally, after walking through a small city, the hunters and Sebastianus came to the water. The coast was a giant beach where several dwarfs seemed to enjoy. A small dwarf there came up and looked Apollo in the eye for a couple of minutes. "Apollo, it's been years! How is it up in Hestour? Any sort of wars or problems?

Why, it's been four hundred twenty two years since I was there", he said in a jolly, high-pitched voice.

"Hello Creer", said Apollo.

Novan stared at Creer for a moment. "Creer, is that you?" asked Novan.

"So, you've met Creer, too", said Apollo.

Then Creer laughed. He walked over to a giant boat. *Princess Alreida* it read on the side.

"Hunters, Novan, Sebastianus, the Water's Kings demand to see you", said Creer.

"What are the Water's Kings?" asked Sebastianus.

"Once, the water was of the Dwarfen Territory used to be run by sea monsters. There were thousands of them. You wouldn't find any fish unless it was horrifying and giant. It was the Sea of Demons", said Creer. "But the race of giant Sea Turtles conquered the monsters and they became the Water's Kings. They are ruled and lead by Drawde. He has a mission for you. I'm sorry, but even I don't know what this task will be. Lasciare Morto Devoto Sperare!"

Everybody looked at Creer weirdly.

"It's what the Dwarfs say", he said.

After a couple hours of eating, pranks, talking and playing some card games Novan had brought, Creer yelled out "The waters of our Water's Kings!"

The boat stopped. Sebastianus saw Mathias and Gabriel looked a little nervous. He himself was incredibly nervous. Then a small wave rocked the boat. Sebastianus blinked. When his eyes opened, the boat was half under water! Then the whole thing was down in seconds. It sunk and sunk and soon enough, it hit the bottom with a thump. Fourteen Giant Sea Turtles around the size of three of four Icarus' (Who is massive and the biggest of the hunters) put together. They carried the boat with no trouble. After a couple a minutes, the boat was in front of a giant temple that had walls and towers and smaller parts of the temple that stretched beyond the end of the sea.

Then Sebastianus noticed something. "Creer, how come we're breathing fine and we're underwater?!"

"Magical waters it is", he said.

Then a giant golden door creaked open. Several giant sea turtles stood along the sides. Then the other sea turtles dropped the *Princess Alreida*. It didn't make much of a sound but it hurled water away into darkness.

Then several of the sea turtles lead Sebastianus, Novan and the hunters into the door and through giant and long halls. They twisted and turned. There was a door about every three or so meters. Finally, there was a giant golden door at the very end of one hall. There were no doors aside it. Above it read: ␣␣␣␣␣␣␣␣.

When the doors opened, there were giant sea turtles bigger than the other ones. They wore fancy robes and stood. They sat in thrones that were in rows and faced a giant throne that was surrounded by five other thrones. Everyone bowed, so Sebastianus did the same.

"Lord Drawde, we bring you King Azell's hunters, Novan the great one with eternal life, Sebastianus, the most famous of men in history and Dwarfen Prince Creer", said a deep, stiff voice that seemed to be coming from a giant sea turtle with green and red robes.

"Excellent!" bellowed a jolly, deep voice. It was coming from the giant sea turtle. Lord Drawde.

"Take a seat", he said.

Sebastianus and the others did what told.

"Peoples and Dwarfs, I would like to ask you a favor. There are small problems in this sea. Small problems only turn into bigger ones. So I need you to defeat our biggest problem. He traveled from Formighte to the Sea of Fire, which only leads to the Underground City. A river from the Sea of Fire leads to here. According to Formighte, he is known as the Ship Crusher, the Sea King, Water's Worst Nightmare, Sea's Living Hell, and the Formightan Pirate's Fear. But his real name is the Kraken.

Chapter Twenty-two:

The Kraken

Ten sea turtles were ordered to carry Sebastianus, Creer, Novan and the hunters. They were each green with a shining brown and grey coloring on their shell. The carrying Sebastianus said that his name was Transporto III. They traveled fast through the water. After a couple of hours had passed, they stopped. There was a giant mountain that went out of the water and up into the skies. A giant tunnel that seemed to drop hundreds and hundreds of feet was at the bottom of the mountain and surrounded by big, sharp, pointy rocks. "This is as far as we can go. This is the Moloana side of the sea."

Then Novan and Apollo lead the way through an opening in the rocks. Then Apollo stopped everyone so he could make an announcement. "We shall jump to the Kraken's lair. Beware men; take your weapons with you down the tunnel."

Everyone drew their weapons. Sebastianus pulled out the Sword of Vinco and looked at Mathias who was breathing gust of wind around a stick that looked a little more like a sword every second and then became one.

Then the Hunters of Azell jumped down the hole. The water carried them down fast but safely. Sebastianus and Novan jumped after. Then Creer jumped.

Several minutes after, they landed like they had a parachute. Everything was mossy and dark.

"Don't worry. I'll give you some light", said Mathias as he clapped his hands together and made a fire. Then Sebastianus saw a couple steps ahead of him were a giant pit. He stepped forward and took a small look down and saw thousands of bones: Skulls, arms, legs, and all other bones.

"The Kraken's scraps", said Creer.

Then the hunters looked down. A rather large tunnel was on the other side. "I'm guessing that would be the living quarters of the beast", said Novan.

Then Leonidas and Apollo looked at each other. "I say we go in right now and murder the beast with your sword, Sebastianus. Then we go out and tell Drawde that we murdered the beast. Then we go to land and face our next task then look for Liberius", said Leonidas.

"Easy to remember and will probably work", said Icarus. Then he sliced some bones away and cut down some moss and then they were at the lair.

Leonidas looked inside and then out. His eyes were big and he was shaking. "Leonidas, what's wrong?" asked Sebastianus.

"That's not normal", said Icarus as blood dripped from the back of his head and down his chest. Then an octopus' tentacle moved from behind his head and Leonidas fell into the pit. He was covered in blood.

"Another down!" yelled Icarus. Then he jumped in the tunnel of the Kraken. Sebastianus and Apollo went with him.

Before themselves was a horrid creature. Each of his tentacles was soaking in black, inky water.

"The Kraken!" yelled Icarus in a crazy, blood thirsty voice. Its eyes were black with small white dots floating in the center. It had a mouth that was just like the Parasite's. Then he threw a spear. It hit the Kraken in the eye. SLosure spilled out as it screamed and screamed. Then it went for Icarus. The hunter laughed and then threw another spear. It hit one of the tentacles and sent it flying. It hit a wall and then dropped and floated like driftwood on the black water. "The Kraken shall not touch such a glorious warrior. For I, Icarus, will not be defeated by such a freak!" yelled Icarus. Then he laughed and laughed. "It's as simple as 1, 2, and 3!"

Then the Kraken screamed and hit Apollo. He went about ten feet back and then hit the wall.

Then Mathias came in, leading Gabriel, Artemis, Medsus, Novan and Creer. Creer's war cry was hilarious. Imagine a three foot dwarf. His face covered with a beard and him screaming with the most high-pitched voice known to man.

Then Mathias made a fire and sent it right at the Kraken. It screamed and then several of the tentacles fell off.

Each man took turns and nearly destroyed it. Finally, when the giant creature was barely breathing, Sebastianus went up and thrashed the Sword of Vinco into the Kraken's face. It screamed until death.

As the ten men walked away, Sebastianus saw something. Something was on Artemis' back. "Art…Artemis, what's that on your back?"

Artemis then looked at his back and fell to the ground. Blood was all over him. Then Sebastianus saw what was on him: a tentacle.

"The Kraken's not dead!" yelled Sebastianus.

Icarus was the first to respond. He immediately ran back to the beast. He dodged tentacles and stabbed plenty of them, too. Then he thrashed his sword and a couple of daggers and spears into the mouth. The beast then squirted blood from its tentacles. Sharp weapons poked from his skin and blood came out of his mouth. Then he took a spear. "Mathias, make some fire!" he ordered.

Then Mathias made some fire and tossed it over to Icarus. Icarus put the flames on his spear and wrote on the Kraken's skin: ICARUS.

The men went back to the top of the tunnel and road the sea turtles back to Lord Drawde. The told him what happened. He thanked them and then ordered some sea turtles to carry the bunch to the Territory of Chaos. That was where the next task for them was. They had to Defeat the Troll of Chaos.

Chapter Twenty-three:

The Troll of Chaos

The land was cold and the ground was muddy again. "Myth has it that the Troll of Chaos lives within the Territory of Chaos. I believe it lives on Three Mouthed Mountain", said Icarus.

Then Apollo said, "I believe Three Mouthed is right over there, Icarus." Apollo pointed to a large mountain in the distance. Three large caves were on it. There was one above them all, one in the middle, and on below them all. They were all in a straight row.

"We must travel to it", said Gabriel. "The river from the Sea of Fire is right behind it. If we go around, we'll be ash by the time we reach Timos."

"Then we shall hike up and down the mountain", said Apollo.

Then the bunch walked at the mountain.

After several hours, Sebastianus, Creer, Novan, Apollo, Gabriel, Icarus, Medsus, and Mathias were on the other side of the mountain. In the distance they saw a temple and volcano. It was Liberius' palace and Timos' volcano.

"What happened to the troll?" asked Medsus.

"Well, we should have faced him about two or three hours back", said Icarus. Then he mumbled something under his breath and smiled.

Just then, the mountain shook a little and chunks of rock began to fall off. Then a large crack that went all the way around the mountain started to spill green goop. Then the goop began to catch smoke. It burned the rock and slowly melted it down. When it was inches from the bottom, it hardened. Then there was only a little left of the top of the mountain.

"The Troll of Chaos!" yelled Gabriel as a giant arm swung out from the top of the mountain. Then another arm sprang out. Then came a giant head. It was a brown shade of green like the arms and had glowing yellow eyes. It was a chubby beast but very muscular. It had a mouth full of the goop and its nostrils shot flames of fire. Then a body jumped out. It was naked except for a cloth that hung from a belt and covered up his from one crotch to the other.

"Trespassers?!" it roared in a deep, deep voice. "I like the meat on that one. He'll be good to eat!" it roared again looking at Gabriel.

"Troll of Chaos, we demand a battle. You can eat us if you can defeat us. But if we defeat you, we can go on with our quest to defeat Liberius and Timos", said Icarus with a grin.

"Alright, then; you realize trespassers that you're basically committed suicide", he said with a grin.

Then Novan pulled out a sword. Creer took out arrows. The hunters took out swords, arrows, daggers, knives, and some small bag that Sebastianus didn't know about. Then Sebastianus pulled out the Sword of Vinco.

The beast smiled and took out a thick, long stick that was strapped to his belt. He pointed one end by sharpening it with his long nails and shot the other end with fire from his flaming nostrils.

"For Darkness!" the beast shouted. Then he slapped his stick -like weapon right by Gabriel.

"Dodged it easily!" he yelled over to Sebastianus.

"Yeah right, Gabriel. The thing was literally a good two inches away from you. So much for that *close call*. Ha!" said Sebastianus. Then Gabriel smiled at him and put his fists up jokingly.

"Straight line!" shouted Apollo. The five hunters then took out their bow and arrows and formed a straight line.

"Aim for target!" yelled Apollo. The hunters then did so.

"Neal and fire!" he yelled. The Hunters did so. Mathias lit each one in the air with fire and blew them farther and harder with wind. They each landed on the troll's chest. The goop spilled instead of blood. He screamed in pain and terror.

"Ready men!? Bows ready! Arrows loaded! Position yourself! Fire!" yelled Apollo. The hunters did exactly what they had done before.

Mathias lit them with flaming orange fire and pushed them farther. They hit the same spots as before. The beast roared and tried to react, but the hunters were already letting go of the arrows.

Novan, Creer, and Sebastianus threw spears at the arms. Creer – every couple of minutes after throwing numerous spears – used his own arrows.

The routine was used for nearly a half hour. After at least the thirtieth shot, the troll finally lifted his stick and hit it with the side that was on fire.

Mathias was the first to react and blasted the fire away and turned it into water. Mathias hit wind at the water and it spilled and hit the troll. The water – which was steaming – hit several of the wounds. The beast screamed more.

After a small recovery, it took the other side of its stick (the pointed side) and then swung. Gabriel and Apollo then tried to stop it with some sort of force that was in between the stick and them. After a couple of minutes, Gabriel' nose began to bleed. His arms were quaking. Then he fell. Apollo ran. The Troll of Chaos swung. It hit Gabriel and sent him flying back into the river of lava that was a little by the horizon. The sixth hunter was dead.

Then Sebastianus and Icarus seemed to be thinking the same thing: vengeance.

Sebastianus had the Sword of Vinco by the hilt as Icarus had a giant black, blood stained sword. "DIE!" yelled Icarus. Then he threw his spear and it hit the Troll of Chaos in the mouth. "AHHH!!!" the troll yelled. It screamed so loud, the earth literally shook.

"Finish the thing", said Icarus with a blood thirsty, psychotic look.

Then Sebastianus ran up to the troll. He threw the Sword of Vinco at the chest. Then goop went everywhere. Apollo created a force field around everybody. Sebastianus ran to the troll and took his sword. Then Sebastianus looked over at Icarus. The troll had swallowed Icarus' sword. And even if he didn't, Icarus hadn't even been to get his sword back.

Chapter Twenty-four:

The Great Timos

After hours, the men reached the volcano of Timos.

"Creer, please..." said Apollo without finishing his sentence.

"Sure, Apollo", said Creer.

Then he pulled out a little horn from his green robe. It was brown and covered in designs. When he blew in it, it sounded like *boo ooh-ooh-ooh!* It was silent for a minute or two. Creer and Apollo waited patiently for whatever they were waiting for.

Then, in the distance, a dwarf on a white horse came.

"A single dwarf?" said Icarus.

"Not even close", said Creer.

Then a bunch of other dwarfs on horses appeared. Then thousands and thousands of other dwarfs on foot appeared behind them. A massive flag was carried by each dwarf on a horse. It had a crown in the center and was red all around.

"Dwarfen Territory!" they all yelled. Then they all ran to the hunters, Novan, Creer, and Sebastianus.

Then Apollo, Sebastianus, Creer and Novan lead the army of dwarfs to the volcano.

After they reached Timos' lair, they saw before them a massive brass door with the same writing on it: ◻◻◻◻◻◻ ◻◻◻◻◻◻ ◻◻◻◻ ◻◻◻◻◻

"We shall go inside and fight like men!" yelled one of the dwarfs carrying the flag and riding the horse.

Then everyone pushed the doors til they finally opened. Even with an army of dwarfs, it took about twenty minutes for the brass entrance to open.

The inside of the place was a small chunk of land surrounding the door and a massive staircase that went up to the top of the volcano. All around that was lava.

"Fight like men. Fight like men", mumbled Creer to himself as he took giant breaths.

Then Apollo looked around. "We go up the stairs!" he yelled.

Then everyone grabbed their weapons and ran up to the stairs, chanting and howling. "May the best dwarf win!" yelled a dwarf that was dressed up like a midget barbarian. Then he pulled a hammer and ax from his belt. "Liberius and Timos shall die as the Dwarfen Territory takes place as best!" he yelled.

"When I see Liberius, I'm going to –", said Icarus. But no one should be hearing the rest of his words.

Then after about a half hour, everyone was up the stairs. There was a huge cave. It had pillars around it.

"I say we go in", said Novan.

"I agree", said Mathias.

"I also say so", said Icarus.

"I agree with Novan. We must fight", said Sebastianus.

"I don't care what we're doing as long as Timos and Liberius die!" yelled some dwarf from the army. Then they ran in the cave.

After some time of walking, the cave ended as a giant room. In the center was a huge abyss.

A young man in a cloak with the helmet of a gladiator and a staff with skulls on it chanted something on the other side of the abyss. "Oh, Timos, rise. Oh, Timos rise", he chanted.

Sebastianus took a closer look at the man. His green eyes were so bright, they were barely visible. "Liberius is here!" yelled Sebastianus. Then everyone looked at the young man. He chanted about three more times, laughed and then disappeared in a puff of black smoke. Right where he was standing was the mark of the Family of Darkness. It was the black triangle with a triangle inside that was red.

Then the ground shook. Everyone stared at the abyss. Sparks rose from it. Then gallons by gallons of lava came from it. Then a chunk of rock came out of the abyss. It was cracked. In the cracks was lava. Then a hand that looked the same as the big, circular rock came out. Then four arms immerged. They were all the same rock with crack filled with lava. Then legs the same as the arms came out along with feet. Then some cracks that weren't filled with lava opened. Soon enough, forty-nine faces appeared all over his body. There was a giant one on his chest. Then fifty giant snakes all green, black, brown or blue sprouted from his back. Then a head came from his shoulders. At first, the monster was lifeless. But then, a black mist went through the mouths, filling it with lava. Then the beast awoke. "**RAOR!!!**" it yelled.

Then a voice from the abyss bellowed, "All hail my creation or die!"

Then everyone was silent.

"DIE!" yelled Icarus as he sent a blade hurling to his face. Then it melted to the lava.

Then, immediately, the dwarfs fired thousands of arrows at once. Spears were thrown and also swords. Finally, a couple of snake heads fell off. Then Timos began to fight. He stomped on about ten dwarfs at once.

"Retreat!" yelled one of the dwarfs. Before he could even get to the stairs, he and a couple other dwarfs were shoved into the abyss. Then flames from it rose.

Sebastianus and Apollo worked together, throwing spears and firing arrows from one direction, then running to the other side of the room.

After hours of fighting, only about two hundred or so dwarfs were left. Creer was lucky to be alive. He had been firing arrows the whole time and Timos hadn't even noticed it was him. Creer had already chopped off fourteen of his snakes.

"I have an idea", said Mathias. "If I can get anywhere of five feet from Timos, I can turn his lava into cold water, which would probably kill him because the arrows wouldn't melt."

"Maybe that would work", said Sebastianus.

Then Mathias ran behind Timos. Sebastianus waited to see water from his cracks. But after a couple of minutes, Sebastianus realized that wasn't working.

Then Sebastianus saw the faces of lava. Maybe if he could...? Then Sebastianus realized it would be too much of a risk. But when he saw the head of Mathias flying through the air and then into the abyss, he knew he had to do it.

Sebastianus ran over to Timos. He dodged the fists and stomps and swings of the monster and then he looked at the giant face on the chest. He drew the Sword of Vinco from his belt and then he leaped up and into the monsters chest. Since he had eternal youth, he couldn't die. The temperature was unbelievable. Sebastianus sweated and sweated. He tried to find the center.

Finally, after about three or so minutes, he saw what looked like a heart. It was black and beat slowly like: thump... thump... thump...thump. Sebastianus then looked at it for a second. There was some sort of image on the heart. Maybe it was inside. It was some sort of skull with a beard of snakes. It was Latorin. Then Sebastianus quickly stabbed the heart. From it spilled green goop.

After a moment or so, Sebastianus felt nothing. Then the beast fell forward. Then it exploded! Sebastianus felt no pain to the explosion or lava.

When Sebastianus was out, several hundred dwarfs were there. Creer, Novan, Apollo and Icarus were also there.

"Sebastianus!" yelled everyone. They cheered and cheered; every single on of them. Everyone except Icarus.

Chapter Twenty-five:

Liberius

The remaining army went back down the staircase and through the brass doors. A couple feet away from them were Liberius' palace.

"Only the immortals of this group shall fight. For Liberius can kill the simple human with the rise of a finger. But, for him to kill an immortal means he actually has to fight them. So Sebastianus and Novan, please step up and fight", said Apollo.

As soon as the two were about to go in, a voice called to them. "Wait for the rest." It Icarus with his sword. Behind him was Apollo and some sort of dwarf getting of his horse and giving his flag to Creer.

"Sebastianus, meet Lord Krodd. He's the king of Dwarfen Territory. He has drunken from the Fountain of Youth. Me and Icarus are hunters. Hunters are immortal", said Apollo.

Then Novan and Sebastianus shook hands with Lord Krodd. He was a kind guy. He was kind of chubby, but he looked powerful. He held the hilt of his sword so steadily, it looked like he could easily take Liberius out with sword skills.

Then Apollo used some kind of force that blew the doors of Liberius' palace open.

The immortals walked down a long, empty, grey hall for about a half hour and then they walked up a spiraled staircase for another hour or so.

At the top of the stair case was a door. Sebastianus opened it to find himself on the roof of the palace. "Liberius, show yourself, you coward!" yelled Icarus, eyeing every spot of the empty roof.

"Liberius, where are you?!" yelled Sebastianus.

"In the name of Dwarfen Territory, show yourself!" yelled Lord Krodd.

"Patience all", said Novan. Then he smiled as he threw a stick that he grabbed from his cloak at a random spot. The stick then froze in the air and then fell.

"So, Novan, Lord Krodd, Apollo, Icarus and Sebastianus, how did you defeat my creatures?" asked a voice that came from nowhere.

"So, are you going to go for the sneak attack and stay invisible, or are you too much of a softy to show yourself, Liberius?" asked Novan.

Then a figure appeared. It was about seven feet tall with a dark cloak and a gladiator helmet. He was about twenty or so. His green eyes were as bright as the sun.

Then Liberius pulled out a golden sword from his belt. "How **dare** you make fun of the Royal Destroyer!" yelled Liberius.

"Liberius, you almost conquered Atra Erus seventy years ago and now you are the face of evil! Why?" asked Sebastianus.

"Sebastianus, I can see into the future. The dark one, Latorin shall rise once more with an ultimate empire. In fact, his empire shall rise in exactly one year from now. The Spargerian Empire will show itself", said Liberius.

Then, all of a sudden, a golden arrow whistled past Liberius' face. "Who dare –" Liberius was cut off.

"Shut up! Three years I have waited for this. Liberius, give me what I desire!"

"Icarus, we made a deal. Once I kill them, you get what you want", said Liberius.

"No, Liberius! Give me it!" yelled Icarus.

"Fine", said Liberius. Then he pulled a bag from his cloak. He handed it to Icarus.

"Fools, you believed me. You honestly think I was trying to help you defeat Liberius. Why would I kill him. Why would I kill my father?" then he jumped off the palace.

Within the blink of an eye, Liberius had his sword through the chest of Lord Krodd!

"You're cruel!" yelled Sebastianus.

"Life is cruel", said Liberius.

Then he ran with his sword over to Novan.

Sebastianus drew the Sword of Vinco and then blocked Liberius' blade from Novan's chest.

Then Apollo took the hilt of his sword and stabbed Liberius in the chest. Liberius didn't mind. Black blood dripped from his chest.

Then he took a shot for Apollo's throat. Sebastianus used the Sword of Vinco and once again blocked Liberius' sword.

Then Sebastianus took the Sword of Vinco and stabbed Liberius in the throat. This time Liberius screamed in pain. Then Sebastianus stabbed Liberius again in the chest. He screamed more and more. Then Sebastianus stabbed him again in the face. He bleed black blood all over which stuck out a tone on the golden floor. Then Sebastianus took another hit. It jammed Liberius in the face. Well, that was what was supposed to happen.

Liberius then took his own sword and swung. It was literally seconds away from slicing Sebastianus head off. Then someone jumped in front of the blade and took the fall. Then Sebastianus saw beside him the dead body of Novan.

Then Sebastianus quickly jammed the Sword of Vinco into Liberius' wrist. Liberius screamed in pain and then let his golden blade go.

Sebastianus, obviously, picked it up. He pointed it to Liberius' throat. "Liberius, die. Die right here, right now."

"Sebastianus, you honestly think if you stab me with my own sword, I'll die", said Liberius. Then he laughed.

Sebastianus started to sweat. Was Liberius just trying to mess with him or would a stab from his own sword make him more powerful? A cold stone formed in Sebastianus stomach. He took a gulp and then held the hilt as tight as possible. He closed his eyes and turned his head away to the left and then he just thrashed the sword into Liberius. Before Sebastianus did that, Liberius said, "The Prince Alexander awaits."

He didn't take the sword out. When he opened his eyes, his head was still turned. When he looked at Liberius, there the sword was, in his mouth. He was nearly black with blood (his weird black blood). His lifeless green eyes turned black. Then his soft, tan skin turned pale and wrinkly. He went from young to old. At least eighty or so. Apollo stood there, shocked at the scene. Then, he opened his mouth but no words came out. Finally, he managed, "Liberius is dead?"

"He's dead", said Sebastianus, taking big, big breaths. "Hopefully."

Then the two walked through the doors and on the spiral staircase and the grey hall and threw the doors. As Apollo and Sebastianus came out, the dwarfs all cheered. They all cheered to the sight of Liberius' head in Sebastianus' hands. They were sad to hear what became of Krodd and Novan, though.

Chapter Twenty-six:

The Vikings Invade

The dwarfs showed Sebastianus and Apollo the way back to Hestour. Exactly three weeks had passed since they started the quest. But anyway, the way up to the Hestour was a staircase that went way up but only took about, literally, a second. Like Creer had said, the City of Souls was magic.

After the really short walk up the stairs, they found themselves right by the Northern Forest Bay. There was a ship in the distance. Since it was about six in the morning, Sebastianus could barely see it because of the fog. But he did see one clear thing. The Formightan flag. It was red with a Viking helmet in the middle and a sword and shield right by it. Then he heard a horn blow.

"We have to tell Lord Titus!" yelled Sebastianus.

Then Apollo said, "I shall hold them off with another force field."

So Sebastianus ran for the kingdom.

After about ten or so minutes, he came to the kingdom doors. The knights stood there. "Sebastianus, why are you rushing and where have you been the last three weeks?"

"I can't talk to you now. I have to speak to Titus. Then the guards opened the doors. Sebastianus rushed in. He ran through the Royal Hall, the Royal Dining Room, the Royal Garden and then he finally reached the throne of Lord Titus.

"Titus, the Formightans, Apoalans and Musans are invading. Prepare your army. Apollo, the last of the Ten Hunters of Azell is fending us from them at the bay."

"Sebastianus, what do you mean the last hunter?"

"It was a quest I went on with them. I'll tell you about later... if we live."

Then Sebastianus took out the Sword of Vinco.

About ten minutes later, Sebastianus and the rest of Titus's army were all ready. When they ran out, all of the teenager knights in training from the Knight Camp were getting ready. Every man from the Royal Court were getting ready.

When they reached the village of the kingdom, Apollo was the only one fighting as several thousand Formightan Vikings were murdering villagers and burning down houses. They all were around seven or eight feet tall and dressed up in animal clothing and had at least four weapons each. They were all very muscular and had crazy looks on their faces. But the one who looked craziest, about eight feet tall with long blond hair and a long blond beard that was braded on each side and in the middle was the king.

"Lord Huvaudrull", said a voice behind Sebastianus. It was Lord Titus.

"I kind of thought he may have been king", said Sebastianus in a sarcastic voice.

Then the Hestourns fought.

Sebastianus had killed around twenty or so Vikings with the Sword of Vinco.

At one point, Sebastianus saw Huvaudrull fighting. He was killing about five people at the same time. He had every weapon Sebastianus had ever heard of in his hands, strapped to his belt back.

Then another horn blew. It froze almost everyone. Then, Sebastianus saw gladiators and samurais fighting and running for the village. Muse and Apoalan arrived.

Chapter Twenty-seven:

The Battle

Sebastianus and Apollo fought side by side and made sure to stay close to Lord Titus. Apollo would make a force field any time someone tried to come up and kill him. Sebastianus didn't mind if he got stabbed or shot with an arrow. He would live forever. So Sebastianus had incidents were he should had died about nine or so times.

It looked as if Formighte were winning. But Hestour were doing okay.

Sebastianus was doing well. But he was kind of hoping to kill Huvaudrull.

After hours of fighting, Sebastianus saw one of the samurais was coming toward him. He looked like the king of Apoalan.

"That's Lord Mikato", said Apollo.

Then Sebastianus took the Sword of Vinco and fought for about ten minutes. Mikato was very skilled using a sword. He did all of these tricks and stuff like that. When Sebastianus finally stabbed him in the arm. He bleed a little. Then he gave a angry look at Sebastianus. He licked the blood and then spat it Sebastianus.

Sebastianus pointed the Sword of Vinco at Mikato. When he saw what the sword was, his tan skin went white.

"The Sword of Vinco!" he yelled. Sebastianus did have the Sword of Vinco, but no one he'd ever faced had flipped out like that, especially a king. Well then again, Sebastianus had never fought a mortal. But still.

Then every Apoalan around Sebastianus scattered away.

Sebastianus then killed a couple of Musans and Formightans. Then he and Lord Titus went up and fought side by side.

But after a couple of hours, they split up.

Soon enough, Sebastianus found himself face to face with Muse Territory's king. Lord Titus had once told Sebastianus of him. He was the most clever king known. His name was Callius.

Sebastianus took the Sword of Vinco by the hilt and then thrashed into air. Callius dodged it. Then Sebastianus thought to himself, *If he's the most clever king known to time, then I shouldn't just thrash the blade into the air!*

Then Callius took out a bow and arrows from his belt and shot them at Sebastianus. He fired about seven or so before realizing Sebastianus wasn't hurting at all. So then he took out his sword. It was blue with stripes of black. "Do you think they shall defeat thee? For I am the smartest man alive!"

Sebastianus then laughed.

"Why would thy be laughing at I?"

"Sorry Callius, you had the pretty breath-taking speech and everything, but, I kind of stabbed you in the thigh. It's bleeding super bad. And about three or so seconds, the pain will be unbelievable."

Then Callius looked at his thigh. It was completely red with blood. The cut was so deep, it nearly went through Callius' leg. "AHHHH!" yelled Callius. Then Sebastianus stabbed him in the thigh again. He screamed once more. Then he Losurped as fast as he could over to some other Musans.

"That was pretty pathetic", said Sebastianus to himself.

Then a sword went through his stomach. He turned around to see some samurai. Then Sebastianus pulled the sword from his stomach and thrashed it through the Apoalan's chest. "How…?", he asked. Then he died.

After another half hour or so, he saw Huvaudrull running straight for him. He gutted every man in his way. He looked even more insane and scarier from a closer view. "So, I suspect you're the big hero who defeated Lord Atra Erus!" he said. He was so tall, he to crouch down and say it. When he said it, Sebastianus' face was soaked with spit.

He laughed unstably and then he thrashed his giant, black, rusty sword through Sebastianus. Sebastianus didn't even flinch. He looked at the Formightan king oddly and then laughed. "I drank from the Fountain of Youth", said Sebastianus, casually.

"Aye, but can things still hurt?" asked Huvaudrull. Then jabbed a dagger through Sebastianus' throat.

It hurt so bad, Sebastianus wished that he could die. "Now tell me, do you feel dead?" he whispered to Sebastianus' ear. Then Sebastianus looked at him. He tried to reach for his dagger, but couldn't.

Then something in the sky appeared. It was a giant animal like thing. Huvaudrull took the dagger out of Sebastianus' throat when he saw the sight. Then he spit some more into Sebastianus' face. "I don't suspect you know Lord Bruno?"

Chapter Twenty-eight:

The Meeting of Truce

Lord Bruno landed. He looked more horrifying than normal. "Attention warriors!" he yelled. Everyone stopped.

"Does anyone actually know the point of this war?" Everyone was silent.

Some Apoalan man then spoke. "I heard Hestour were trying to kill Formighte. So my nation and Formighte came here to kill Lord Titus and his country."

"So you honestly think that was the point of this war? So how are Muse here?" asked Bruno, sounding drunk.

A man from Muse raised his hand and then lowered it when Bruno looked at him.

"I heard that Hestour and Apoalan were teaming up to invade Muse Territory."

"So that's what everyone thinks this war is about. Well, actually, I told a couple of dirty lies. I like death."

Then he kill a couple of people. Then Callius, Lord Titus, Apollo and Lord Mikato all seemed to running the same way towards one of the Apoalan ships.

When they entered it, they saw Huvaudrull on it.

Then the Formightan king stood up from his chair. "So what is this? King vs. king with a hunter and a pest?" Then as soon as Huvaudrull was about to stab Apollo, Callius stopped him.

"Bruno is one of the most powerful beings known to life and history. We have to work together to defeat Bruno. At the end, we go back to our own tribes and live at peace til the next war. Does it sound okay?"

"Aye, it's alright", said Lord Titus.

"I personally think as the Formightan lord, that's absolutely, breath-taking, impressively a **horrid** idea! The traditional Formightan fighting style be a solo!" yelled Huvaudrull.

Then Apollo came back. "So, are Apoalan not included in this tradition to work alone. Wouldn't teaming up with the Four United Seas of Apoalan be a duet. I'm nearly positive that that is not a solo. Nothing near it, Warlord Huvaudrull.

"Shut up, Azellian", yelled Huvaudrull in a deep, deep voice.

"Huvaudrull is right. It's been over one thousand years that more than two nations out of the 99 have ever joined forces. Three would be just –" Titus was cut short in his speech.

"If we join forces with one that can't die and contains the Sword of Vinco and four nations, we'll have plenty of power to over throw Bruno", said Mikato.

"Fine, I'll join forces", said Lord Titus.

Then everyone looked over at Huvaudrull.

"Alright, I'm in. But only if the pest gives up immortality", said Huvaudrull. He didn't even look at Sebastianus when he said it.

It was silent for a minute, which seemed like hours. "Fine", said Sebastianus.

Everyone was shocked.

"So, how do I give up my eternal youth?"

"That's an easy one, pest", said Huvaudrull.

Then he showed Sebastianus. "Well, look up at the sky and hold the Sword of Vinco."

"Okay", said Sebastianus as he did just that.

"Now close your eyes and say: I pray to thee to except my offering. I give to you my immortality. The immortality from the Fountain of Youth."

Sebastianus closed his eyes and said, "I pray to thee to except my offering. I give immortality. Immortality from the Fountain of Youth", then a large pain hit Sebastianus. It hurt way more than when Huvaudrull had stabbed him in the throat. Then water went up his throat and into the air. Then it vanished.

"You made a bad mistake", said Apollo.

Chapter Twenty-nine:

The Fight of Bruno

Sebastianus, Callius, Huvaudrull, Mikato, Lord Titus and Apollo told their armies.

Immediately, everyone fought Bruno.

Mikato, Sebastianus, Lord Titus and Apollo all went up to fight Bruno. He looked so hideous and horrifying, Sebastianus vomitted.

"I see that we have three kings, a hunter and a warrior", said Bruno. Then he drew a sword from his belt. He took the hilt by both hands and then swung at Apollo. Apollo – obviously – dodged it.

"It seems the swamp lord is drunk again. You're always drunk before fighting, aren't you?"

"That may be true, hunter. But it doesn't mean I can rip you Losurb from Losurb along with your other little cowards!" yelled Bruno at Apollo.

Then Sebastianus stabbed Bruno in the arm. The king howled and howled.

"Who just stabbed me?! Was it you?" Then Bruno began beating a tree. He chopped off one of the branches. "I got your arm! I got your arm!"

"Bruno, this is truly the most ridiculous thing I've ever seen", mumbled Sebastianus, almost laughing at the pathetic creature, still attacking the tree with his sword..

"At least I'm not drunk!" he yelled across the air, which formed a large amount of laughter from numerous people.

Then Apollo fired a couple of arrows at him. He screamed in pain as blood fell down his fury chest.

Then he took his sword and he thrashed it in air. It hit Mikato in the neck. Blood poured and poured. He was dead.

From behind ten arrows shot through Bruno's spine and legs. Callius and Apollo had been firing as much as they could. Then Lord Titus was given a bag full of spears from one of the Royal Court members, who had been collecting them, Sebastianus had seen, from the non-dangerous areas (not there there were many). He threw each one, missing many as he was clearly a sword fighter. Sebastianus kept stabbing Bruno's arms. Finally, he dropped dead.

"That was easy", said Apollo.

Then as they were about to scream out Bruno was dead, a spear went flying right through Apollo's neck.

"Sebastianus, kill the swamp lord", the hunter struggled. But then, he died.

Sebastianus turned around to see Bruno standing straight and tall. His sword was pointed towards Sebastianus.

"Let us battle...for real!"

Then he sliced a cut on Sebastianus' chest.

"Ahhh!" yelled Sebastianus. Then he took the hilt of the Sword of Vinco with both hands and he thrashed the sword through his chest.

"Sebastianus!" he roared and then he swung and hit Sebastianus' arm. Then he swung again and hit the same wound.

Sebastianus bleed horribly. Then Bruno swung at the legs. Sebastianus was then stabbed in the knee cap.

Then Bruno threw a spear at Callius' head while Sebastianus was down.

"Three and a half down, one and a half to go", said Bruno.

Then he stabbed Sebastianus in the chest. Sebastianus felt that several ribs were broken. Then he tried to get back up, but Bruno shoved him back down to the ground.

Then, as Bruno took the swing for the face, Sebastianus ducked. He took the Sword of Vinco and thrashed it through Bruno's knee cap. Then Bruno fell.

Sebastianus finally had the strength to get up. He took his sword and jammed it into Bruno's neck.

Bruno screamed, but he didn't die.

"How come you can't die?!" yelled Sebastianus at him.

"You know, I still haven't figured that one out yet", said Bruno, still incredibly drunk.

Then Sebastianus told Titus to keep firing arrows and throwing spears. Titus did so.

Sebastianus had the answer why Bruno wasn't dying. A couple of meters away was a small swamp. So Sebastianus tried to think and then he had it.

"I bet you can't catch me, Bruno!" yelled Sebastianus.

"I bet I can", said Bruno. Then Sebastianus ran as fast as he could away from the swamp. Bruno followed.

Finally, when the kingdom was almost out of sight, Sebastianus stopped. He held the Sword of Vinco in front of him. Bruno couldn't stop at the pace he was going. So, he ran right into the blade's tip. It went all the way through his body.

Then Sebastianus saw Huvaudrull. He threw a sword, but missed.

"I also like death", he said.

Chapter Thirty:

The Vikings Betray

Sebastianus ran for his life back to Titus. But when Sebastianus got there, the Formightans were dominating. Sebastianus then thrashed the Sword of Vinco through a couple of Formightans.

When he got to Titus, Huvaudrull was there, too.

"So pest, we settle this like men. If I murder you, then you're dead and I win the war. But it could be the other way around. Now let's fight", he said.

Then he swung at Sebastianus. Sebastianus dodged it and then he thrashed the Sword of Vinco at Huvaudrull's thigh. It bleed, but he didn't mind.

Then he took a swing at Sebastianus. It skinned his chest.

Then Sebastianus thrashed his own sword at Huvaudrull's wrist, like he did to Liberius. Huvaudrull dropped the sword. Then Sebastianus stabbed him in the back as he bent over to get it.

Huvaudrull then fell. Sebastianus stabbed him in the back again. Then he got back up and thrashed his sword into Sebastianus' stomach. It bleed like crazy. Then Sebastianus vomitted.

Then Sebastianus banged his sword on Huvaudrull's. They each held the hilt by both hands. Sparks flew on their faces and all over. They used all of the force they could to push one another back and go for the kill. But they were pretty even.

Sebastianus then thought of an idea. He took off the hilt and punched Huvaudrull in the stomach as hard as he could.

Huvaudrull vomitted after getting the wind knocked out of him like that.

As Huvaudrull vomitted, Sebastianus took an ax from his belt and hacked the Viking's back four times. Huvaudrull then vomitted up blood.

Sebastianus took another hit with the Sword of Vinco. Huvaudrull blocked it at the last second. Then he stuck a spear that he found on the ground through Sebastianus' shoulder. Then he hit again at Sebastianus' neck.

Sebastianus dodged it and then threw the ax at Huvaudrull's chest. Huvaudrull almost dodged it, but it hit his ribs.

Then Sebastianus took the Sword of Vinco with both hands on the hilt. He swung and it skinned Huvaudrull's face.

Huvaudrull then took another ax from his belt and hacked Sebastianus' leg once.

Sebastianus screamed and then fell. Huvaudrull then tossed the ax and grabbed his hammer. He smashed it into the ground. Sebastianus rolled out of the way and then tripped Huvaudrull by kicking his feet.

Then Sebastianus got up and took the hammer. He smashed it on Huvaudrull's hand.

Then as Huvaudrull got up, Sebastianus swung the Sword of Vinco and it hit Huvaudrull's sword. They pressured each other with their swords again. Sparks flew everywhere.

Then Sebastianus moved his sword and stabbed Huvaudrull's side.

Huvaudrull screamed and then kicked Sebastianus' arm. He let go of the Sword of Vinco. It then stabbed the ground. And when it did, a huge crack formed. It spread the land in two. In between the land was lava.

Then Sebastianus blinked and the sword was no longer in between the two parts of the land. It was in his hand.

Then he thrashed the sword into Huvaudrull's arm. It went all the way through. Huvaudrull's respond was to stab his sword right where Sebastianus had hit his. Then Sebastianus came from behind Huvaudrull and kicked him in the back. Huvaudrull fell to the ground. Then Sebastianus dug the Sword of Vinco into Huvaudrull's back. The Formightan dictator screamed in agony. After a moment's hesitation, he rose from the battlefield and swung at the slightly unprepared Sebastianus. The two warriors swords clashed as Sebastianus had made the right move at the very last second. The swords created sparks, which flew into the two's eyes and eventually, Huvaudrull backed down for a moment and Sebastianus saw his chance. He swung low at Huvaudrull, but again, the Formightan dodged it by surprising Sebastianus with a very large leap and again, clashed his sword with his opponent.

Sebastianus kicked Huvaudrull in the upper leg . The Viking king fell. He was yelling and screaming. But he knew that he would die. Sebastianus then lifted the Sword of Vinco by the hilt and then thrashed it into Huvaudrull's chest. Then Sebastianus cut off Huvaudrull's head. He shoved the body in the lava.

"Peoples of the Hestour, Apoalan Seas, Muse Territory and Formighte Islands", everyone froze and looked at Sebastianus "this is Huvaudrull's head!" then he threw it in the lava.

The earth closed and Sebastianus collapsed.

PART THREE:

THE NINE RIDDLES
OF THE SLEEPING GIANT

Chapter Thirty-one:

The Nine Riddles

Blood spattered across a broken bed as Sebastianus was laid down in a hurry by several hooded, ominous men. Quickly, the men retreated and immediately were on their way back to their leader and own lives. Sebastianus barely was breathing but could only be kept alive by his desire to win the war that was being fought. His mind was scrambling and he needed to fight. "I have to go help!" demanded Sebastianus to no particular being. There were many in the room of his filled with rubble.

"You *don't* need to, Sebastianus. You won the war. You did it. You defeated Huvaudrull and won!" said the calm voice of Lord Titus. "Just rest now. You've saved nearly a hundred thousand citizens of our nation. So relax and enjoy the rest of the day."

"Liberius?" the ill and injured soldier asked.

A different voice aided to his question this time. It was the voice of an unknown figure to Sebastianus. "He's dead for now. But Latorin can just as easily resurrect him. In fact, we'll most likely be seeing Crusak and, if he chooses to form an alliance with him, Bruno as well in a short time."

"Yes, indeed", mumbled Titus. "Azell, you should be on your way. The hunters will be eager to see your wellness and I'm sure you, theirs. Goodbye for now."

"It was a pleasure to see you once more, Titus", said the man whose name was Azell, a famous and familiar name. He was the lord of his own nation and an 'immortal'. He fought with Vinco against Latorin in the period so long ago. He was the head of the hunters and also practiced magic. He was an idol all around but, besides Sebastianus, definitely the most wanted man of Latorin.

A quietness fell upon Sebastianus and he sensed the presence in the room disappear, one by one. Struggling, Sebastianus was no realizing how dehydrated he was. He had not drunk anything in days, let alone water. His lips were as dry as the deserts. His throat was almost in pain due to the incredible amount of dryness. Quickly, his eyes focused on what appeared to be a cup of water by his bed. Immediately he grabbed it, only to find it empty. With dissatisfactory, he threw it downward and pouted. His lack of fluids was enough to kill him, but his own body was torturing him. He was positive that his head was knocked so hard he would always feel like there a brick being forced against his forehead. The insides of his mouth were stained with blood and his arms were what he suspected to be a break.

Now Sebastianus's mind was flashing. His memories of pain and horror came back to him and this only added to his current hurting. He moaned like a tired and ill elderly man. The bed was of discomfort, his body was more physically harmed that it had ever been, he was so dehydrated it almost deadly, and his mind was flashing with images that had left marks upon his brain, etching the horror and pain into his thoughts. Sebastianus shivered. He wanted to sleep, but was unable to. His mind was a prison. It was controlling his body's miserable stature. It was the very prison that held the memory's of the deaths of Raphael and the hunters. His open and aching hands formed fists, which caused him pain. It was a good pain, drowning his sorrows of the deaths that were, as he believed, his fault. These were the very things holding him back from his true stature as the champion, the king, of the battlefields. Titus has told him this once.

"Sleep, Sebastianus. Just sleep", was what the fictional voice said in a calm and comforting voice that almost made one slightly sleepy. Sebastianus shuddered, his eyes widening. It was fictional, but real. It wasn't there, but it seemed as though the words were like an indelible mark that reminded him that he was so alone and so surrounded. He was surrounded by the evil spirits that lurked along the edges of the room. They were unable to physically destroy. Liberius, Bruno, Crusak. The darkest spirits watched over him, waiting to crush him. It was unexplainable, the feeling that Sebastianus had.

"Just sleep", the voice came now almost surprisingly, angered, and even aggressive. It demanded it this time. It was a scratchy voice, like the dead. It was similar to Krausin's, but yet the voice was different completely with a personality of its own. It was frightening, but calming and put Sebastianus into a trance as he followed the orders of the voice and within moments, the prison of his mind was temporarily demolished and he could relax and rest his eyes...

There was truly no way to describe what Sebastianus was seeing. There was fire devouring what he could scarcely make out as the world. He was standing on top of a high cliff, watching the destruction of the world. He heard screams and roars. The screams belong to the humans engulfed in fire and the roars came from the beasts from below. The fire cleared and there, standing over their dead human bodies were creatures of the vilest variety. They scared Sebastianus almost to wake. One was what he believed to be a troll, though it had spikes coming from one of his arms and his face was arranged differently so that his eyes sat underneath his mouth and fur grew on his back and legs. He had teeth that dropped to his chest, stained with human blood.

The next beast was worse. He had eyes covering his whole entire body completely, besides his mouth which was twice the size of which it should have been. He had four arms and crawled along the edges of the rubble. There were hundreds much more creatures, but one caught the attention of Sebastianus the most. It was a creature barely visible in the clouds. It was bigger than anything Sebastianus had ever seen. It was as large as an island. The ungodly beast seemed to have an octopus head and tentacles, each the distance of the Larkon Lake. Crab pinchers appeared from beneath the tentacles. Roaring, the demon placed his eyes upon Sebastianus and yelled an ear-scratching noise that nearly shattered his eardrums. To a human, the roar was a very demonic and unpleasant noise, but to others, it was a summoning.

Stones rose from the earth and lightning struck only inches from Sebastianus. The ground shook ferociously and large cracks formed that led down to the center of the earth. The sea's waves powered to five hundred feet high and fell on the ground, destroying any surviving humans. And in front of Sebastianus, a perfectly proportioned and shaped rectangular formed from swirling dust in the air. Another formed behind it, slightly higher. More and more came until steps to the clouds formed. It was the staircase leading to the very throne of the one that all feared.

Latorin walked down the steps. He didn't walk, but slightly hovered above the staircase at an incredible speed. His crimson red cape was glorious, better than a king's robe. He wore the ancient combat clothing: nothing to cover his bare chest, which was bulging with muscles and red veins, and royal brass belt with a thick leather apron hanging all around it. His face was grim. His eyes sunk in the back of his head, black and non-human like. His face was as though the very signs of life had been taken out. The skin was a light grey color that would scare anyone. His short and bushy black hair and beard was the only normal feature. And as he finally appeared to Sebastianus, his thin and colorless lips produced the words that always remained in both of their brains. What he said destroyed confidence and hope, but yet motivated,

Sebastianus. The words were like those spoken in his bedroom. It was fictional, his mind tricking him, but so real. This was a real vision that was false. But when Sebastianus thought this, only the word 'real' was thought properly and clearly.

Latorin began the sentence. He stared at Sebastianus and then at the destroyed rubble of humanity. "This is your world..." he said calmly, now smiling, "...in six months to the day."

And as Latorin and the staircase vanished, a new creature appeared from what Sebastianus recognized as a sand-filled beach. He was figured exactly like a man. The creature had the same muscles and features, but all were made from sand. It was a giant made from sand! Sebastianus could not believe the image, but soon did when the creature now moved its humungous body towards Sebastianus, dragging along the aftermath of the death of humanity. He was now towering over the cliff that Sebastianus was standing on, his head being the same size of a mountain. His body was in the skies he was so large. As he prepared to grab and destroy Sebastianus, the dreamer awoke and lay awestruck in his bed.

The simple small timing of his nap had nearly completely rearranged the way of thinking for Sebastianus. His new ideas were much different. And now he now longed for the presence of the wise Raphael, who always seemed to know the tales and what to do in a situation like so. And he felt the same for Titus. He remained lonely though. Sebastianus looked aside now, eager to see his surroundings in which he had not even given the slightest attention before. Around the bed was a small hole leading to the battlefield created from a Formightan cannonball's attack. From there he could make out a hint of the aftermath of the war.

"Sebastianus!" called Titus, coming from nowhere to Sebastianus. His voice appeared at the right and left, but eventually Titus revealed his face. Sebastianus smiled now. He was enjoying the feeling of seeing a face that was legitimately real. There were no tricks. But Titus's face was grim and this frightened him.

"I can only assume that you saw the vision as well?" Titus asked.

"Latorin…?" Sebastianus said, almost stating the question, as his voice trailed off into space.

"Did you see the giant?" Titus asked as he showed no hint of attention to what Sebastianus had just said.

Sebastianus nodded.

"Then it is true. And we are all condemned to death. For the Giant was possibly the strongest creature that Latorin ever…" Titus looked for the right word, "…forged. His blood, fire, and sand from the hottest of deserts formed a sand giant that could not die. The giant caused chaos for eighteen years during the twenty year war of Vinco and Latorin. Vinco fought the giant for nearly a month straight. They camped in the desert to defeat it. In the end, he finally was victorious. He didn't kill the giant, but merely imprisoned it in the…catacombs of the desert, where the giant has been condemned to sleeping forever. And that vision, I know, was a sign from Latorin that the giant is coming back."

"Who would even think about resurrecting that fowl beast?" demanded Sebastianus.

"Liberius couldn't be back alive by now…Crusak is rebuilding his forgeries and kingdom. Icarus…?" Titus mumbled.

"Icarus Brunecelli, the hunter? We would need some special skills if we're tracking him."

"Yes, well we're not even sure that's the man we're tracking."

"Who else would it be?"

"Then how *would* we track him. He's a monstrous man and has more tactics and skills than almost anyone in this world."

"Well obviously the very teacher of Icarus and the hunters has more skills. I am guessing you are still in contact Lord Azell."

"Yes, yes I am. And he also was there the day the giant was taken down. So he would be clearly the most knowledgeable of such an event."

"Then we shall travel to the nation Azell."

✦   ✦   ✦

For a very small time, a group of the most skillful soldiers in all of Hestour assembled together. There were almost five-hundred all together. It was very much enough. It was separated in two different groups: one hundred-fifty archers and three hundred-fifty knights. They all lined before Titus's four finest wooden ships, styled to look like different animals. They were each named *The Lion*, *The Eagle*, *The Tiger*, and *The Bird*. They were brilliantly constructed and always amazed Sebastianus when he saw them, even though he had seen hundreds of times.

"Come, Sebastianus", Titus began. "Follow me. We're boarding *The Lion*."

Titus was wearing full armored gear, which was only half covered by a magnificent violet robe. "Now, this voyage is of great magnitude, so please, we must succeed." Sebastianus could tell that Titus was deathly worried, which was unusual as he was often the calmest in the kingdom.

Stepping into the damp, wooden dock sent an odd chill through Sebastianus. The ship had an amazing capacity of fifty rooms, each holding up to four soldiers, with ten rooms of storage. They were all luxury rooms, each fit for a king. Titus had his own room, which was the equivalent of two of the knight's rooms. He stayed there almost the whole voyage. Sebastianus was having an unexpected time in his place with his three new roommates.

There nearly one hundred knights shuffling around the hall on the second floor, where Sebastianus was sent. He found himself in his decided room with three other familiar faces. One was elderly, whom Sebastianus did not recognize. But the other two, he could barely make out.

"Sebastianus?" asked a man the same age with curly brown hair and a muscular build, sharpening his arrows with a thin rock.

"Is that you, Johann?" Sebastianus asked, dumbstruck. When he was only a little boy of five years of age, he had always had fun with a boy named Johann van Hersits, who had immigrated to Hestour as a boy. The two had been the best of friends and had for years, had a great time. Then Sebastianus was condemned to live with Titus as Johann went back to his homeland for a time. Sebastianus had never known of his arrival.

"I can't believe it!" began Johann, his bright blue eyes brightening the dark room. "I thought you left Hestour when I left. So, what have you been up to the last couple of years?"

Sebastianus told his long, depressing, unexpected and very adventurous tale to the interested and eager Johann. "You're *that* Sebastianus? The one who has now saved the world…" he hesitated to figure out the number, "…three times?"

"I never thought I would be seeing your face again", Sebastianus chuckled while he spoke.

Delighted, he decided to converse with the other two people in the room. "Hello, I'm Sebastianus."

The elderly man snorted. "I know who you are", he said in a nasally voice. "My name is Rusol."

The other man was a lot friendlier. "Hello, Sir Sebastianus. My name is Sir John Hemming. You are my idol and I'm honored to meet you. Is there anything at all that I can get you?" he said, hyperventilating.

"Just take it easy", Sebastianus said, laughing a little. "It's great to meet you too." John stopped talking, feeling embarrassed. Sebastianus examined him. He had bright red hair and was very tall, with a thin body.

Now *The Lion* was beginning to slowly saunter off to a new direction. It was coming to the Great Wall of Azell. The ship stopped for security before the wall's brilliant golden doors opened, letting *The Lion* into one of the world's wonders. As the voyage came to a complete stop, *The Lion* opened and Sebastianus came to the dock, seeing the kingdom of Azell for the very first time. There were magnificent gardens with plants never seen by the world outside of the kingdom. There were temples and glass domes with lakes with structures beneath their waters. It was an unbelievable sight. Every building was even better than the glorious palace at Hestour. The people were equally brilliant, with fine clothes that almost made Sebastianus look bad.

The group of knights and archers were welcomed by the kind citizens and shown the way to the grand castle of Lord Reabius Azell himself.

The Grand Castle of Azell was the greatest building Sebastianus had ever seen. There was a giant wall that surrounded the area of the kingdom of Hestour. Inside the wall were different towers and domes with ponds and gardens and statues, all of brilliance.

"Please, enter", said a voice from the shadows. Blended into the dark, the Hunters of Azell were now guiding the soldiers into the wall's entrance. There, they entered the largest of the domes, where Azell sat in his throne.

Lord Azell sat on his throne. He was about six feet ten inches tall, towering over the six feet tall Sebastianus. He was tan and wore a green robe. Beside him, the Hunters were swarming, protecting him.

"You wish to see my garden, don't you? I know that the giant is awaking. My hunters and I have sensed you arrival and search for the answers to the Nine Riddles Come Titus. Bring your men."

All of the soldiers walked to a giant room where a green tile rested in the floor. Azell lifted a key from his pocket and struck it into the tile, which opened like a hatch. He sent his Hunters down to retrieve a large chest. Azell opened it with the same key and there, he pulled out a very old scroll written in fine handwriting. He handed the scroll to Titus, who read it aloud.

"The First Riddle of the Garden of Azell:
Find the only plant that is dead and conquer the beast. Search for your prize inside its feast.

The Second Riddle of the Formightan Statue:
Get through the guard and retrieve the cup of the king. And win the battle of the guard's ring.

The Third Riddle of the Palace of Bruno:
Unlock the Three Minions from their rest, they'll tell you what you need to know and guide you west.

The Fourth Riddle of the Ship-Wreck Sea of Plundorios:
Don't let the sea take advantage of your ship. Find the sea king and receive his tip.

The Fifth Riddle of the Rebucian Jungle:
Watch out for the monkeys. Watch out for the tigers. Do your best to find the Flyers.

The Sixth Riddle of the Apoalan Chest:
In the depths of the temple, unlock the chest. Take a bite and leave the rest.

The Seventh Riddle of the Driban Staircase:
Walk up the stairs and use the map. Go for the Lair and don't fall in the Gap.

The Eighth Riddle of the Musan Fountain:
There is no water, but only dust. Drink from the fountain of it you must.

The Ninth Riddle of the Grean Valley:
Look at the tree and upon the gate. Look at the boat, there the Prince Awaits.

Signed Hestour Vinco II."

"So, those are the Nine Riddles of the Sleeping Giant. If we figure those out and follow the steps, we are able to track the giant and defeat it. Now follow", Azell said, putting the scrolls back in their place, leading

Behind the doors was a giant garden. It went way beyond the horizon. It was really wide, too. But Sebastianus could see the golden walls.

"Come, Sir Sebastianus, Sir Johann, Sir John, Sir Rusol and of course, Lord Titus", said Lord Azell. He then shrugged and pointed to a knight in the middle of the clump of soldiers. "You come, too."

After signaling them to follow behind, Azell led them through his grand halls and magnificent rooms. "I would prefer your company rather than others. I have seen great skills in your ways", he mumbled.

The six, all quite curious on why they were chosen, merely walked on. Johann was a good fighter, but not the best. And John was a good archer, but there were better. And Rusol remained mysterious, not revealing a thing. All the same, Azell seemed to know every little fact about him. Not to mention the fact that Sebastianus had no clue who the knight Azell selected was. All the same, following Lord Azell and his wisdom, they soon came to his garden. Every plant was larger than a man and more exotic than any plant than Sebastianus had ever seen. Eventually, Azell came to a small fountain in the very center of the complex outdoor wonder.

"This fountain", Azell explained, "is the heart of this nation. The water goes down into the underground pipes. There are hundreds of pipes. Everyone has a reason. The most feed the plants, support buildings, provide drinking water, and filter lakes and other bodies of water. Also, my biggest secret lies below. That's where we're going."

Sebastianus saw how Azell and Titus were friends. They were the same in every way: secretive, talkative, storytellers, born-leaders, and soldiers.

Azell removed something from his pocket. At first, Sebastianus thought it was just a very large key, but as he looked closer, he saw what it truly was. Only seeing illustrations of it, Sebastianus was amazed. It was a wand. Azell was a sorcerer. Quickly, with the large white utensil, he lifted the fountain off the ground. Sebastianus was awestruck. Underneath the hovering structure was a large pit filled with water. Over the water, though, was a thin metal bridge, only big enough for one person at a time.

"Knights first, lords after", said Azell with a smile.

Johann crawled downward onto the bridge, which he passed, leading him to a tunnel. Following was Sebastianus, then John, Rusol, and the unknown knight, and then Titus, and last Azell, who closed the fountain, but lit a torch.

At the bottom were three tunnels. One had giant brass doors. Another had doors that were metallic silver. The last one was grey.

"First thing is first", said Azell, removing a sword from his belt. He, there on the spot, murdered the unknown knight with a sword through the neck. He then removed the armor on the back of the knight, revealing a snake tattooed up and down the spine, with the Symbol of Darkness branded hard on the back of his neck. Underneath it were the words:

Servant, Spy, Soldier: Hecen of Latorin

"Just as I thought", mumbled Azell. "There goes a spy. We're safe from Latorin, just not what you're about to see. We go in the grey door."

"What do the doors even lead to?" asked Sebastianus.

"The brass leads to my finest couple of plants. The silver leads to my most exotic and living and wild and one-of-a-kind plants. The grey leads to the only beast in the nation that was untamable", said Azell. "He feeds on small animals that live there. So I assume that those animals would be his feast."

Then he took out a key that was grey, matching the door and slowly opened it...

There was a staircase in a damp cave that led slowly downward to a large cave with water dripping from the sides. Hanging from the edges were rotting human bodies, with the arms eaten clean off, with only few bones. Inside the cave were torches with a thin path along the side of the cave. This led to an underground swamp and a drop-off that led nearly one-hundred yards down into darkness. The men climbed down while Azell floated down magically with a torch in his hand. The bottom was an endless pit, with all sorts of caves and tunnels, the surface completely hidden by bones, rotting flesh, fur, and the aftermath of the Scorpia's meals.

Then a sound of twisting, scurrying and running through bones was heard. Johann looked at the pile of skulls... and one of them moved. Immediately, John shot a dozen arrows at the . This only resulted in

"Die!" yelled Sebastianus. Then he stabbed the scorpion in the chest. It throbbed on the ground and then it raised its venomous tail. It tried to hit Azell, but the king dodged it and then through a spear from his belt at Scorpia.

Then Sebastianus went a little closer to the monster and used the Sword of Vinco and chopped off the pincher.

Then the other pincher tried to take hold of Sebastianus. But it only cut him. Then Sebastianus cut it on the side.

Then it clawed Sebastianus in the side. Sebastianus then took the hilt of the Sword of Vinco and swung with his eyes closed.

As Sebastianus opened his eyes he saw the scorpion dying. It backed up and up til he hit the giant dead tree. And from a hole

"I saw that the giant hates water!" said Sebastianus.

"For what I did for you, Sebastianus and the rest of you, you will not tell anyone of Scorpia. She is an illegal beast that I bought from Eboue Monreilia, a dealer. It was only to protect the mushroom. If anyone lets out the secret, I – the most trusted lord of history – will charge you for false things. There fourth, you would be sent to the Prison of Idanlesh. May I remind you that that is on the edge of Torninoa. You will – on behalf of me – be sharing a cell with Atra Erus. That will happen if anything of Scorpia will be mentioned", said Azell.

"How can you share a cell with a dead man?" asked Sebastianus remembering how he killed the Atra Erus.

"Idanleh is met for souls in the section of the Dead, the first six-hundred forty two floors. Then the other nine-hundred fifty eight floors are for the real-living. But I can make an arrangement."

"I'm not sure that would be possible!" yelled Lord Titus.

"On behalf of King Mogrod, Prince Tirmius, Prince Zan and King Osmani, that's possible!" yelled Azell.

"Wait, I know of Mogrod, king of the ninety nine nations and Tirmius, Prince of the ninety nine nations and Zan, the other prince of the ninety nine nations but when was Prince Osmani crowned king?" asked Sebastianus. "And besides, wouldn't Tirmius get crowned and then Zan?"

"King Mogrod and his two sons were out hunting. They were attacked and killed", said Azell.

"By what?" asked Lord Titus.

"Yeah, no beast could kill Mogrod, he's Formightan, the strongest human beings alive!" exclaimed Johann.

"I know. I know what really happened. Latorin's becoming more powerful by the second. His minions are returning. There are crawling back from the Torninoa. They are slowly breaking out from Idanleh. Some are being persuaded by Liberius, Icarus, Cassius, Morfore, Oall, Rimac, Lotten, Benatrize, The Black Knight, and Ebal and much more!"

"Who are those people?" asked Sebastianus. "I've never heard of them.

"They come from different places. Cassius and a bunch of others come from Idanleh. Some – as I told you before – crawl up Torninoa. Some come from the Mouth of Latorin. Some find their way –"

"What's the mouth of Latorin?" asked Sebastianus.

"Yeah, what is it?" asked Johann.

"I don't know!" said Titus.

"I'm not good with history", said John.

"No one of this world knows to be exact", said Azell. "People think it is a hole in the ground that demons come through. Some think that it actually is Latorin's mouth and that he spits monsters that are formed from little chips of his teeth."

"I know what it is", said Rusol with his head down in a low voice.

"What's your name again?" asked Azell.

"My name is Rusol."

"That name, there's something..."

"Anyway..." continued Rusol

Chapter Thirty-two:

Losur, the One from Latorin's Mouth

"When Latorin ruled the world, he formed a crater in the earth. It was more like a bottomless pit. He said that if someone were to kill him, his minions would go down the pit. They would have to fly back up when the Latorin Rege would ache."

"And the Latorin Rege is...?" asked Sebastianus.

"It is a symbol carved into your back. It is a picture of a skull with a snake going through the mouth and out the eyes. Then there is a sword that goes through the skull's side."

"Rusol", said Sebastianus",I read somewhere in the Book of Evils – a history book that was a gift from Titus – that there was a man named Losur. He was a man who did nothing but kill and murder. Rusol, take off your shirt and show me your back... NOW!"

"That wouldn't be too comfortable for me, Sebastianus."

"Rusol, on the behalf of me and Titus, you must do as we say! Take off your shirt and show us your back!" yelled Titus.

Rusol hesitated with a frown and then smirked. He removed his shirt. He turned around. The symbol sat on his back. It pumped like a heart. It was red and almost stuck out.

"It's aching. The moving Mountain is already in Formighte. In a year, King Latorin will rise."

"Losur, you horrible…!" shouted Sebastianus.

Then Losur started to glow red. His eyes shined. His skin fell off into the skulls along with blood and everything else. He had purple muscle under his bones. It was thin. But it bulged and his bones grew bigger too. Soon he was as big as Lord Huvadrull had been. Then Losur's eyes turned black and he sprouted leathery blue wings from his spine. He grew tow little horns on his chin, two huge horns where his ears should have been and goat horns.

"Yes, I am part of the Ater Latorin. Each of the Fifty of us has our part. The Ater Latorin also has people to kill!"

Then Losur was about to jump on Sebastianus.

Sebastianus then put his sword up, Losur fell upon it, but, surprising, it did not go through him.

"Why didn't my sword go through you?" asked Sebastianus puzzled when Losur got down.

"Latorin Rege protects me. Only Vinco can truly use the Blade the right way unless you're a relative of that man, there is no way you can harm by Rege!"

Then Losur's hand turned into a pointed end of a sword and then his other hand turned into another sword. "Prepare to die!" he shouted and then he aimed for Sebastianus with his hand. He charged for Sebastianus. Sebastianus jumped four feet in the air because of the Sword of Vinco and then he landed and then stabbed his sword through Losur's mouth. It went through his skull-like head and then began to drip some sort of blue liquid. It almost looked like ice, except it wasn't still.

"What in Heaven is coming from your head?" asked Sebastianus.

"It's called Henu, the blood of the Fifty. But sometimes its black!" shouted Losur. He was quite weird. He explained things which seemed odd.

Then he turned his hand into an axe. He charged at Sebastianus.

Sebastianus – because of the powers of the Sword of Vinco – leaped about six feet in the air. When he landed, he turned around. Losur was right behind him!

Losur raised his sword arms and then ran. Sebastianus dodged the one on the right. But, he couldn't dodge to the left arm. It went through his stomach. Sebastianus fell and put his hand over the wound. John ran up to Sebastianus and he knelt next to him. Johann and Lord Titus did the same. Azell was in shock and couldn't move.

Losur smiled and took the Sword of Vinco off the ground. Azell ran for him. But Losur said the words 'Nagareth' and then he vanished. Azell missed. The Sword of Vinco was gone.

Sebastianus' mouth filled with blood. He nearly choked on it. His stomach swelled with pain that hurt so much, he was blinded by it for moments. Every muscle ached and ached til Sebastianus finally spoke. "I'm dying."

Then Lord Azell tried to think up a plan, but he couldn't. "Maybe I and Risa could find a medical spell! No...no that would take too long. But if I disappear with someone, we could catch up to Losur and maybe.... No! That will never work. I have no clue where he is!" Azell thought to himself for what seemed like hours. "The Moving Mountain", he finally said. "But that is sacred ground so he would have had to teleport somewhere near it, but not directly on it or the area. We have to beat him to it...or else he will kill us all. The Mountain will move to Allias if he stabs it. It will take seconds. But if it gets to Allias, then Pravus the giant has the power to push it all the way to the desert once more. Once it reaches the desert, Liberius, who has control of Pravus, can make him push about ten times to its original spot in Hestour...and then, Latorin would be back."

"Doesn't sound good", Sebastianus struggled.

Sebastianus felt his consciousness pass, but within moments, was being what seemed like electrocuted by the power of Azell. He felt his wounds and sores disappear and the blood seep back into his body.

"I know a spell that can get us there", Azell immediately said as Sebastianus hopped back on his feet. "Drema Transpo Bermot!"

Then they were all going through a black tunnel. They were floating in the air and going at the speed of light because after no more than a second had they appeared in the center of the famous city, Bermot, Formighte. "The mountain isn't here", said Sebastianus.

"No, it isn't. I understand that. But we have been back in time twelve minutes, which is all we have to complete the first riddle. That means Losur just left for the mountain. He could have only come outside around one hundred miles. It will be a while until he breaks the mountain's defenses. So, we actually have the upper hand right now."

Bermot was the largest city in the world, seven times larger than Hestour city. It included magnificent churches, palaces, libraries, and a fifteen foot thick, fifty foot tall wall surrounding all of it. Though it possibly the most beautiful city, it also the most dangerous. The Formightans swarmed like bees and flies. Many were armed, many drunken. A murder occurred on the main street and yet it was normal behavior and unnoticed by the vile citizens.

"Here", Azell pointed to a cathedral beside the main palace, "is what we are looking for. Look at the front of the building."

A brilliantly formed clay sculpture stood in place, resembling Lord Huvadrull IV of Formighte, the one Sebastianus had killed.

"Get Through the Guard and Retrieve the Cup of the King. Win The Battle of the Guard's ring", Azell said to the cathedral doors. Immediately they opened, revealing a weary old man with a cloak, bald and miniature in stature. "Hello", said the man softly but in an annoyed manner. "What do you want?"

"You know what we seek, old man." Azell said firmly, pushing the man out of the way and stepping into the cathedral. "The cup and the ring...", he said, staring at the old building. The seats had been half destroyed as well as shattered glass, holes in the ceilings and walls, and scurrying animals.

Azell had found what he had been looking for. A statue of Bermot Formighte in his traditional robes was at the altar. Pointing his wand, Azell shot a beam of light, which removed the statue, revealing

Then there were lights all over. Everything became a seeable and Sebastianus could see. He was standing in front of a Formightan in a toga. His helmet had golden wings on them instead of grey horns. He had a long golden beard that stretched to his waist and his hair that went down to his shoulders. He had a thick, thick book. Behind him was a black gate.

"Purpose for visit?" he said.

"Of...?"

"The Formightan Burial Ground, of course."

"Um...oh yes. I kind of just spaced out", Sebastianus lied.

"Well, why are you here? Visiting friends or relatives? Are you paying respect to random people?"

"Paying respect to random people", said Sebastianus.

"You may go in and pay respect. But you may not go into the Tomb of King Formighte."

"King who?"

"King Formighte, the first king of the Nation!"

"Oh, sorry, I've never been in here before and I just spaced out again."

The Viking stared at him for what seemed like hours.

"I guess you can go in", he finally said.

"Um...thanks."

"Have a good time at the Burial Ground."

"Wait", said Sebastianus. "I have a question. What's your name?"

"Lord Huvadrull", he said.

Sebastianus looked at him.

"Senior", he said.

Then Sebastianus walked into the black gates. Hundreds of thousands of Vikings of old and young roamed the golden sand below them. They were not bones or half eaten, they were the exact same as they were when they died.

Sebastianus followed the path on the golden sand that lead to a huge city. Sebastianus got to it to find it exactly like Bermot. In the distance of Bermot was another city. Then also on the other side of Bermot was a town. Sebastianus was in a replica of Formighte.

Sebastianus saw a great temple a little farther into to the ghost's replica of Bermot.

"Excuse me?" Sebastianus asked a man.

"What?" growled the Formightan.

"How do I get in the castle?"

"Oh, so ya just died, did ya? First couple of minutes here, I suppose?"

"Yeah, it is", said Sebastianus.

"Try just walking through the wall", he said. Sebastianus could tell behind his giant orange beard he was grinning and chuckling.

Sebastianus went up to the golden stone wall that's color matched the sand. Then he took a long breath and walked through the wall.

He found himself in front of a staircase. Sebastianus walked up and then walked through a locked door. Inside were several other Formightans all guarding the room. They were guarding a large coffin. On it were the letters:

KINGFORMIGTE

The guards were huge Vikings. Also, on the tomb was a small telescope. Sebastianus remembered what the riddle said.

"Are you here to take the Ralscon to Lord Huvadrull's grave?"

"Um...yes I am", said Sebastianus.

Then one guard put it on a pillow and gave it to Sebastianus. Immediately, Sebastianus saw the giant sinking into the orange sand of the desert and into a cave. Then it showed a small cave that lead to the giant's underground lair.

"Take care of it. If you break it..." said one of the guards.

"The other guard, who was bigger than the rest, finished the sentence. "...We'll have your head instead of that Ralscon!" He boomed in a deep voice. His voice was from his giant gold beard.

Sebastianus walked through the door and went down the stairs through the wall. He hid the Ralscon under his shirt and then walked through Bermot. No one thought that he had the Ralscon, but they did stare at the lump on his stomach.

Finally, Sebastianus reached the black gate. The doors opened for him.

"Done paying your respects?" asked Huvadrull Sr.

"Yes I am", said Sebastianus, nervously.

"Well, so you stole the Ralscon?"

"What?"

"Sebastianus, I'm not stupid."

"Who's Sebastianus?"

"You killed my son and now you're stealing the Formightan treasure. My son cannot go to the Heavens until the custom is complete! The Ralscon leads to the Afterlife! You are taking that chance away from the greatest king of Formighte, my son!"

Then Sebastianus dropped the Ralscon as Huvadrull Sr. got up and took a sword and shield from the air. His shining white toga turned black. His beard became dusty blond and the wings on his helmet turned to grey horns.

"Please, Lord Huvadrull, I will set the Ralscon on the grave of your son. Let me go and I will never disturb Formighte again!"

"Will it make up for theft and murder?"

"Well..."

"Please, Huvadrull let me go!"

"Well, as a Formightan, I must show mercy for those who beg for it. But, since you murdered my son, I'll make a deal instead. If you can defeat me, I'll let you out of here, but if I defeat you, you're my slave til the end of time."

"Sounds good enough", said Sebastianus.

"But I have no sword."

"Fine", he said.

Then from the air, a grey sword appeared from the air.

"Alright, lets have a go then!" said Sebastianus.

Then he went up to Huvadrull Sr. and rammed the sword through his stomach.

For a moment, he screamed in pain. Sebastianus stabbed him three more times as he screamed.

As Sebastianus went for the face, Huvadrull Sr. raised his shield and stabbed Sebastianus in the leg.

Sebastianus did not go down. He found little strength to stand, though.

Sebastianus then backed up three or four feet and then charged at Huvadrull Sr. He thrashed his sword into Huvadrull Sr.'s chest.

Huvadrull Sr. screamed in pain. Sebastianus took advantage of his screams and stabbed his face and his back.

Huvadrull Sr. fell back to the ground. Sebastianus slit his wrist and took Huvadrull Sr.'s sword.

"You…you have defeated me. Jump in my book. Please take the Ralscon and put it on my son's grave."

Sebastianus took the Ralscon off the ground. He went to Huvadrull Sr.'s desk and opened the book. There was a portal in it. Sebastianus jumped in where he found himself back where he started, staring at the statue of Huvadrull. He had the Ralscon in his hands and apparently not even a second had passed. Sebastianus set the Ralscon on the statue without answering any of the questions of everyone about the Ralscon and what happened.

Sebastianus finally spoke. "The Moving Mountain is three miles from here. If I'm correct, we'll arrive there when Losur does."

Sebastianus stared at the mountain in the distance.

Chapter Thirty-three:

Secrets

Sebastianus and the others, with Azell's spell, were at the Moving Mountain in seconds. On the very top of the mountain, there was the simple of darkness imprinted on the rock: the triangle with another triangle inside. When they got there, Losur was running up the mountain with a case shaped like a sword.

"So, Dramilius, we meet once more", said Losur once he reached the mountain top.

"My name is Sebast –"

"Only the Latorin Ater and the Dark Lord know of your name, Dramilius!"

"But..."

"I believe Titus knows it as well", he said in a cruel voice with a grin that made the corners of lip touch his cheeks.

"No! My history is a bit of a secret and a shock, I know. But Titus is my king. I am his warrior. He would tell me if he knew anything about me. Plus, my birth name was Sebastianus."

"If you are not going to believe me, let us not argue...Let us fight!"

Losur took the Sword of Vinco and mumbled *Albunus Quandias!* Then some sort of force field blocked Losur and Sebastianus from John, Johann, Titus and Azell.

Sebastianus then raised his hand and showed Losur that he was unarmed.

"I would not want to go down in shame and no honor. I would rather that you were killed and that I was to stand up with shame and no honor."

Sebastianus didn't know what to do. When Losur raised the Sword of Vinco, Sebastianus saw that the end was near. He saw that it was his time to die.

Losur looked satisfied with himself when he could use the sword to kill.

"Please, don't, Losur!" shouted Sebastianus.

"Why?"

"Would you want to live with...?"

"Yes, I would want to live with the fact that I killed Sebastianus, the only thing in the king's way?"

Then Losur swung for Sebastianus. But when the Sword of Vinco was no less than an inch from Sebastianus' face, it stopped.

"I can't move it!" shouted Losur in disbelief, tugging the hilt.

Sebastianus was shocked.

"I guess I'll blast you into thousands of bits!" shouted Losur. He put his hands out and shouted *Ebalia!* But nothing happened.

"This can't be happening! My powers! Latorin, I don't deserve to serve you!"

Sebastianus' vision went black. He had no idea what was happening.

"If it's your request", boomed a deep voice from the sky, "then so be it!"

Purple lighting came from the sky and struck Losur.

"How, Dramilius?" asked Losur as Sebastianus could see again. Then Losur died.

Everyone stood in shock.

"What?" asked Sebastianus.

"Sebastianus how did you...?" asked all of them at the same time.

"What?" cried Sebastianus.

"Sebastianus, the lightning!" cried Johann.

"What about it?" asked Sebastianus.

"Sebastianus, you...!" cried John.

"The Family of Darkness!" yelled Titus. "The powers that you inherit, Sebastianus. You shot that lightning. That voice, Sebastianus was you!"

"What?"

Chapter Thirty-four:

The Palace of Bruno

Sebastianus felt horrible for the rest of the day. He had the Sword of Vinco inside a case. The group camped in a forest near the Moving Mountain. Azell had used a spell that formed a huge tent. Inside were five beds and a fire place. There was food on a desk and a cauldron of cold, clear, ice water.

Sebastianus went to bed immediately and drifted off to sleep. The next morning, he awoke at six in the morning and then cooked breakfast for himself: a piece of chicken and eggs.

As Sebastianus ate his breakfast, he heard a voice from behind him. "Good morning, Sebastianus", said John.

"Yeah, good morning", said Sebastianus, shoving boiled eggs down his throat.

"Hey, John", said Johann at the same time he yawned. "Sebastianus, how's it going?"

"Good, thanks", said Sebastianus piling up chicken in his mouth and then swallowing it.

"Alright", said Azell, "finish up your breakfast quick. We're going to the Ruins of Lord Bruno's castle. We'll find the Minions there!"

"The what?" asked Sebastianus, who could not here Azell over his and John's loud chewing.

Azell did not answer.

After everyone finished breakfast, Azell said the words *Drema Transpo Bruno!* Then, they all found themselves in the city of Bruno. The buildings were not gold like the last time Sebastianus had been there. They were grey. But there were still hundreds, possibly thousands of people, animals and monsters walking on the streets. Sebastianus saw all of the people selling stuff. There was a group of old women that almost looked like toads they were so plump and small selling old clothes. There were andr people that wore grey rags that sold old papers and food. Also there was a bunch of Arabic fellows. They had large turbans, red vest, huge thick mustaches and beards and huge pants. They sold jewelry. But there were more.

In the center of the city was a worn out grey castle. There were huge chunks that had fallen to the ground and boarded up windows and doors. It had sunken about ten feet in black, bubbling mud. There Sebastianus realized that it had been pouring.

"Follow me!" yelled Azell. He was barely heard from the storming wind and the pounding rain.

Once Azell had gotten the others inside, the sound wasn't so bad. But the castle was wet, smelly, full of spider webs. Old paintings had been worn out. There was at least an inch of dust on the floor.

"This place is in horrible condition", said Titus looking around.

"Yeah, I know", said Sebastianus, wiping a spider off his forearm.

John and Johann both vomitted at the sight of a dead, rotting body, with rusted armor and a half sword. It sat in front of a door.

"We go in that door", said Azell.

"I'm not moving that body", said John.

"I'm not!" said Johann.

"Not…not me", said Titus. Then he gulped.

Azell gave a look that basically said what he was thinking.

Sebastianus got on his knees. He rolled down his sleeves over his hands. He slid the body out of the way with his knuckles, which were covered up by his sleeves. Sebastianus then vomitted.

Azell opened the door just by brushing it. Inside was a room that was entirely gold. The floor, ceiling, walls. There was buckets, chests, bags and piles of treasure. There was a golden throne at the back of the room. There were huge golden pillars that surrounded it.

"Drumaniomus!" shouted Azell.

All of a sudden, the throne moved. There was a little hatch under it.

"How did you know?" Sebastianus asked Azell.

"I know much. Also remember that Bruno was my arch rival. I knew many secrets about him as he knew none of me", said Azell, looking quite satisfied with himself.

Then Azell said *Meendoma Derosse!* Then the hatch opened.

There was a dusty, grey stone staircase that went about twenty feet down. Azell, once again, led the way down.

At the bottom of the staircase was a huge swamp. But the swamp was kind of nice. It had huge white pillars that stuck out of the water, a small garden beside it, the room was as bright and hot as ever.

"Is this where *the Minions* are?" asked Sebastianus.

"Yes", said Titus and Azell at the same time.

"What are the Minions?" asked Johann.

"They are –"Azell was cut short.

A huge, moss colored snake about fifty feet long jumped out from the water and snatched Johann in with him.

"That's a Minion!" yelled Azell.

They all too out there weapons. Blood was on the surface of the water: Johann's blood.

Sebastianus, John, Azell and Titus jumped in the chest-high water. They saw long, snake-like shadows in the water.

After about ten minutes which seemed like hours, they decided it would be impossible to find the Minions.

"Wait", said Sebastianus, "Azell, didn't Apollo once catch a Minion for you?"

"It escaped", said Azell.

Then, all of a sudden, three huge snake heads appeared around the group. They formed a triangle.

"Why do you intrude?" asked an odd , high pitched scratchy voice.

"We come as the Nine Riddles foretold us. Pravus is awakening as I expected", said Azell.

"Liessssss!" shouted a different voice.

"I speak the truth. We have went through my garden, and the city of Bermot", said Azell.

"I would to believe thisssssss", said another snake.

"Yesssssss. Assssssss would I", said one of the snakes.

"I come from Hestour", said Sebastianus. "So does John and Lord Titus. Lord Azell comes from Azell."

"Ah, yesssssss, well, I guess we can let you go."

"Ablerant", said a snake. "They look for knowledge. As we agreed, they must battle that from ussssss!"

"True, the agreement will not be disturbed."

Then the Minions spoke snake. "Hiss! Hiss! Hiss, Hiss!" They went on for about twenty minutes. Finally they came to a stop.

"You must battle us to get what you need. Azell, your powers do not work here", said one of the snakes.

Then Sebastianus took out the Sword of Vinco. Titus took out his sword along with Azell. John had a bag full of arrows and a bow.

They all then began to fight.

Sebastianus slashed one of the snakes' back. Blood fell from under his scales. Then he swung his head and took a bite for Sebastianus, but he missed. Then Sebastianus stabbed it in the face. It screamed in agony.

As it was in the water, cursing and swearing, another snake went behind Sebastianus.

Sebastianus heard it slithering from behind. Sebastianus took the Sword of Vinco, turned around, and thrashed the sword into the snake's back, from the tip of the sword to the hilt.

Sebastianus then saw that both snakes were raising there heads. They were soaked in blood and water.

Sebastianus stabbed one in the face as he had done to it before. It screamed. Then it raised it's head.

Sebastianus saw that the other snake was ready to bite. Sebastianus stood in between them til the very last second. Sebastianus ducked under the water for about a minute. When Sebastianus raised his head, he saw the image of one huge snake dying with another huge snake's fangs deep in it's head and through his mouth.

Almost the whole swamp was red with blood, now.

As one snake was dead, one alive and one still trying to get the other off his teeth.

Sebastianus stabbed the one with the snake on his fangs and John shot it with five arrows to make sure it was dead.

Finally, there was only one snake left. The one called Ablerant.

"Do you honessstly think you can defeat me, the King of Snakessssss?" asked Ablerant. Then he hissed several times and went for Azell.

Azell through his sword and waited for the snake to come to him. At the last second, Azell made a fist and nailed Ablerant in the face.

Then John shot it seven times with his arrows. The snake was turning more green than ever.

"What's happening?" asked Titus.

"I put the snake's venom on the arrows", said John.

Then Sebastianus slashed Ablerant in the face and it died right after it said "go that way", his tongue pointed west. "The giant has breath unbelievable strength. The only thing that can stop its strength is venom of myself." Then it died.

Sebastianus collected venom and then they left Bruno.

Chapter Thirty-five:

The Mealins of Bruno

Sebastianus and the others paid their respect to Johann when they were nearing the beach of Bruno where they would go to Plundorios.

"We should set camp", said Titus.

"Why?" asked John.

"Yeah, it's the middle of the day", Sebastianus exclaimed

"But the boat to Plundorios doesn't come til tomorrow night. We didn't think Azell would join us on our journey", said Titus.

"Magic is something you can never have to much of", said Azell with a grin, looking proud of himself.

"Magic is something I wish I didn't have", Sebastianus mumbled to himself.

No one heard him.

"Wait!" yelled Sebastianus. "Azell, why can't you just transport us to Plundorios?"

"Plundorios have certain laws. Twenty three years ago, Lord Tumis Kirkon Garew of the Nation of Garew invaded Plundorios. Plundorios, who live with no magic nor laws were nearly defenseless as Tumis Kirkon Garew, with the help of Nilrem Brigo, the third greatest wizard of all time, used an army of magic. But when

Nilrem died, the magic no longer worked. The Plundoriosns raided the Garewans out of their country. Ever since magic has been forbidden in Western Bruno, Plundorios. So I forbid myself to break an important law. I am loyal to each country and their rules", said Azell.

"Stupid", muttered John.

"I would blast you in bits", said Azell.

"But you can't!" said John with a howl of laughter.

"I'll beat you", said Azell.

Then the laughter stopped. Azell smirked and then used the same tent they used before in Formighte.

"Oy, Titus, I need something to drink!" exclaimed John.

"Alright, fine", said Titus. "Sebastianus, go to the second door on the left and get a couple of bottles of wine from the cellar."

"Sure", said Sebastianus.

"Great, thanks", said Titus.

"Yeah, welcome", mumbled Sebastianus.

Then he went in the tent and saw that on the lion skin chair was Azell. He was reading a book called *A History of A King*.

"What's it about?" asked Sebastianus.

"A king", replied Azell as he took off his spectacles and took his head off the book.

"What about a king?" asked Sebastianus.

"A king in the middle of a war", said Azell, this time putting his spectacles back on and looking towards the book.

"See ya", said Sebastianus.

"Good bye, Sebastianus", said Azell.

Then Sebastianus went to the door of the wine cellar and got eight bottles of wine and three wine glasses that were laying on a desk.

Sebastianus went outside thee door with the bottles and glasses and then out of the tent and poured the wine.

"Thanks", said John, gulping his wine down within seconds.

"Welcome", muttered Sebastianus.

Lord Titus didn't talk.

The three of them sat and told stories for an hour or so.

"Titus, pass the wine", said John, now drunk.

"It's gone", said Titus.

"I saw a bottle there a second ago that was full", said John. Then he burped.

"That's because you have drank five bottles of wine!" said Titus.

"Titus, there was another full bottle of wine there", said Sebastianus.

"Impossible!" yelled Titus.

"Maybe it was theft", said a familiar voice.

Azell walked out the tent. "The Mealins are all over eastern Bruno at this time of the year."

"I doubt it was a Mealin", said John. "I bet that", he hiccupped "you stole the wine!" yelled John. Then he coughed and hiccupped and passed out.

"Alcohol is like a transformation", said Azell. "Too bad."

"So Mealins you say", said Sebastianus after a moment of silence and hesitation.

"Mealins, yes", said Azell.

Sebastianus then thought of his best friend who had suffered to Atra Erus, Raphael. Raphael was a Mealin.

"Mealins are fascinating creatures, like the one stealing the wine glass of yours, Sebastianus", said Azell.

Sebastianus looked behind him and saw a giant, fat turkey with black feathers stealing the small wine glass.

"Mifriocro!" yelled Azell.

Then the Mealin dropped the wine glass. It shattered. Then it fell to the ground.

"I thought magic wasn't aloud?" asked Titus.

"Yeah, I thought you were loyal to the laws of the other nations", said Sebastianus.

"As a well known and responsible king, I and Lord Lobret are aloud to do", said Azell.

"And you didn't transport us into Plundorios?" asked Sebastianus.

"Well, in the day it is illegal to use magic", said Azell.

There was a moment of hesitation.

"It the Mealin dead?" asked Sebastianus.

"Of course not. Killing a creature would be fowl. It's just knocked out!"

Then Sebastianus took the Sword of Vinco out of the case beside him.

"What are you doing?" asked Titus.

"Shhhh!" said Sebastianus.

Then he went up to a log. He stared at it was a second and repeated Azell's words. "Mifriocro!"

Then Sebastianus saw behind the log were three knocked out Mealins.

For about ten minutes, Sebastianus yelled the spell at places where he thought there might be hiding Mealins.

Sebastianus found himself surrounded by about twenty knocked out Mealins.

"Abrifico!" yelled Azell. Then a small force field appeared over the area.

"We should bring in John", said Sebastianus.

"Melico!" shouted Azell.

Then John was soaring through the air into the tent and into a bed.

Sebastianus also went immediately to sleep along with Titus. Azell, on the other hand was up all night reading his book.

Chapter Thirty-six:

Plundorios

A brown worn out ship came to the beach that morning. A small plump man was driving the ship.

"Yer names please", he said in an Irish accent.

"Lord Azell is my name", said Azell.

"Sebastianus is my name", said Sebastianus.

"John."

"Lord Titus."

"I be Niccelsent. You should know me. I am the son of Jonathon Read who was indeed on Davy Jones' crew."

"Interesting", said Azell.

"Oy, you going to Plundorios or Manifus?" asked Niccelsent.

"Jones City, Plundorios", said Titus.

"I thought we were going to Malchest", said Sebastianus. "Jones City is a horrible place."

"May be so", said Azell, "but it's the only city that will lead to the Ship-Wreck Sea."

"Jones City...Jones...Jones City", mumbled Niccelsent. "Ah yes, right ahead. We'll be there in twenty minutes!"

"You, Niccelsent, anything to eat on this ship?" asked John.

"There's some food in the bottom!"

"What kind?" asked Titus.

Niccelsent didn't answer.

After around twenty five minutes, the boat stopped on a beach with several ships lined up by the water.

"Enjoy yer stay. Hopefully, you won't be robbed or...Well, hope you live on yer journey to the Ship-Wreck Sea. No one has ever lived through that sea!" cried Niccelsent.

"That's not to good to know", muttered Sebastianus.

"We must find the Andrey, the Sea Keeper", said Azell, once they were off the boat.

"Andrey, ey", said a deep, scratched voice.

"Who are you?" asked Sebastianus.

"Deeby Kingston. Anyway, ya think ya can find Andrey? No one ever has. They say that his ship, the Golden King, turns invisible every time someone gets near it. They say that he is the greatest pirate ever to live right after Davy Jones. They say he calls himself the Sea Keeper."

"Excuse Kingston", said a deep, deep voice. "Gets drunk every day! I'm Edward Thomas."

"Did you escape Jones' crew?" asked Titus.

"My grandfather did that", said Thomas.

"I was named after him."

"Interesting", said Titus.

"Very", said Sebastianus.

"Um...you can rent a boat. Take a sack of gold and buy a good one", said Thomas.

"Where do you get a sack of gold?" asked Sebastianus.

"Me, of course!" yelled Thomas.

"Where did you get the gold?" asked John.

"Nowhere!" he said with a wink. Then he squinted his eyes towards a man looking through his pockets and on the floor for something.

As Thomas walked away, Sebastianus took the gold from John's hands and went over to a small boat. It was brown with wood that seemed new and had white sails that looked like they weren't ripped.

"We should get this boat", said Sebastianus.

"Looks damn lot nicer than mine", said Kingston with a hiccup.

"We not?" said John.

"Looks alright", said Titus really slowly.

"We should get it then", said Azell.

"Alright", said Sebastianus. "I'll go give the sack to that guy selling the boat and we'll be off."

Then the three waited as Sebastianus took about twenty minutes to bargain the cheapest price with the man who sold the boats called David Crouch. His nickname was Lowlife Crouch. Sebastianus had realized why. The man seemed as lazy as possible. He didn't care or listen to what Sebastianus said til he heard a good deal.

"I'll give three coins and the deal is settled", said Sebastianus.

"Mmm", mumbled Lowlife.

"Then it's a deal!" said Sebastianus.

He took three coins from the bag (which would be the equivalent to a penny) and then ran off and too the boat.

"How much was it, Sebastianus?" asked Titus.

"Yeah!" said John. "Bloody hell, the bag's still full!"

"All he charged was three coins", said Sebastianus with a grin.

They all got on quick. Sebastianus laughed. By the time they were pretty far in the sea, Lowlife realized that Sebastianus had actually left and a huge commotion in Jones City went on for a couple of hours.

"Once", said Azell after a little bit "we get through the Transeriq Island, we'll be in the Ship-Wreck Sea."

"You do realize we'll probably going to die a horrible brutal death", said John.

"We don't need your damn negativity!" yelled Titus. "Go get drunk and enjoy yourself, John!"

"I don't need you, you son of a…" John's voice faded.

Three huge rocks appeared. Each of them one hundred feet tall. But they weren't rocks, they were sculptures. The one in the middle was the Dark Lord, Latorin. The one beside him, a man slightly taller. He was normal, but he was extremely muscular with a beard that went down to stomach. The beard was made of fire along with his tall, flaming hair. The one beside the both was a man shorter than the other two. He had tattoos that covered his body. He was naked, except the small piece of cloth over his crotch that fell down to his knees.

"Cassius, Latorin and Ebal, the worst bunch alive", said Azell.

"Those freaks!" said John.

"Why do those statues stand there?" asked Sebastianus.

"A warning to not enter what is beyond them", said Titus. "The Ship-Wreck Sea."

"The…those swords look familiar", said Sebastianus staring at the sword in Latorin's hand and then Ebal's and then to Cassius'.

"Why is my sword glowing around the statues?" asked Sebastianus looking at his sword that glowed blue.

"The Four Swords of the Elements", said Azell.

"What are those?" asked Sebastianus.

"The Four Elements", said Titus "are Fire, Darkness, pain, and light. The swords belonged to Minicus, the creator. Of course, Ebal, Latorin, Cassius and Morfore went to steal them. When Vinco, Reabius, Sobalus and Liberius – who used to be good – found out, they went to save them.

"Vinco, Liberius, Reabius, Sobalus, Latorin, Cassius, Morfore and Ebal lived through the fight between them. Minicus died. Latorin took off with darkness, Ebal with fire, Vinco with light and Liberius with pain.

"Liberius was overwhelmed by his sword. Evil ran through his veins, so he tossed it away. Cassius killed twenty three monsters that were on his side for the sword.

"Sebastianus, each of the swords are placed under these statues. But Vinco's was placed under his statue. It was blown to bits hundreds of years after the statues were built. The Sword of Vinco was stolen, stolen by Cato. The sword was taken by me as I found it strapped to you when Mogrod asked me to take care of you, Sebastianus."

Sebastianus was silent as he saw the seas getting darker along with the sky, the waves getting bigger as they banged the boat.

Sebastianus was shocked at first about the statues and all, but once he realized that the Transeriq island had passed, there was only one thought rushing through his mind.

"The Ship-Wreck Sea", he muttered to himself.

Chapter Thirty-seven:

The Ship-Wreck Sea

"Sebastianus, pull down the sails! Titus, steer the boat! John, stop downing that damn wine and get a bucket!" yelled Azell through the storm and the fierce, mighty sea.

"Why would I need a bucket?" asked John.

"To get the flipp'in water out of the boat!" yelled Azell.

Sebastianus looked at the sea and then onto the boat. There was no difference. They were both filled with green water.

Sebastianus pulled the sails down. He saw Titus struggling to steer. He could barely pull it to the left.

John, clueless and drunk, was using his wine bottle to get the water out. Azell was yelling at him and began doing it himself.

"Titus, do you need any help?" yelled Sebastianus through the pounding rain, howling wind, crashing waves and booming thunder.

"What?" Titus yelled back.

"Do you need help?" yelled Sebastianus at the top of his lungs.

Sebastianus struggled to pull and pull to the left. Then he pulled to the right, then the left. For almost an hour, Sebastianus and Titus steered.

The waves clashed and clanged on the boat. After a while, the water was over flowing on the boat and up to Sebastianus' waste. It was up to John's knees.

"What's that?" asked Sebastianus in shock.

"Great God in heaven…", said Titus.

"I can't believe…", said John.

"The middle of the sea", said Azell.

Sebastianus, Azell, John and Titus were steering and steering as hard a they could, as hard as possible.

The whirlandl was only hundreds of feet in front of them.

"Steer to the left and maybe we'll be able to go around it!" yelled Sebastianus.

"*Maybe*!" yelled John. "Well if it's a *maybe*, then *maybe* we'll die!"

"I don't control the sea, John!" yelled Sebastianus.

Only thirty feet away from the whirlandl now, Sebastianus was almost forced by something in his mind to draw the Sword of Vinco and stab the steering wheel.

"What the hell was that, Sebastianus?" asked Titus.

"I don't know", mumbled Sebastianus.

Then, all of a sudden, the boat began steering itself!

It was strong enough to get around the whirlandl!

Then, as they were safely on the other side of the whirlandl, Sebastianus was shocked and didn't know what to do or say. Everyone else was the same, too.

"How did you know to stab your sword into the…", said Azell.

"Something in my mind told me to", said Sebastianus.

Everyone stared at him for a moment with a half frown, half smile.

"I believe that a sea serpent lives in the Ship-Wreck Sea", said Azell. "Dramanus is the name I believe."

"I thought the excitement would have stopped by now", said Sebastianus sarcastically.

"A sea serpent?" John asked.

"Yes", said Azell.

"I fought one once", said Sebastianus, "with Liberius, Titus and my best friend who suffered to the Atra Erus."

Azell smirked. "My beautiful beasts can achieve much greatness", he said.

"What was that?" asked Sebastianus after he saw some sort of a black figure swim quickly under the water.

"What was what?" asked Titus.

"Did anyone not see what was in the water? I think it may be…what was its name?" Sebastianus asked himself.

"Dramanus", whispered John.

"Yeah that was it", said Sebastianus. Then he turned around as he realized John was staring at something behind him.

As he turned, he saw greenish, brownish scales and clear fins. Dramanus stood about seven feet above the water. Sebastianus was guessing that there was a lot more of its body in the water.

Sebastianus drew the Sword of Vinco and stabbed the monster. It howled and howled. Sebastianus stabbed it four times til it went back under the water.

"That was kind of easy actually", said Sebastianus with a grin.

Then the boat rocked. Sebastianus was worried at first and then realized it was probably just the waves.

He *realized* it was the waves and then he *realized* that he was wrong. A large head of a fish attached to what seemed to be a snake like body with fins broke through the ship and roared. Sebastianus drew his sword, but Dramanus swatted it away with its huge fin.

Sebastianus ran to grab it, but a large tentacle wrapped around his foot.

Dramanus' tentacle pulled Sebastianus fast, but when Sebastianus was close enough, he took his hand and made a fist and took a swing for the serpent. The beast howled and dropped Sebastianus. Sebastianus ran for the Sword of Vinco and then he clutched the hilt with both hands. He ran up to Dramanus and stabbed it in the face.

John took his poison arrows and shot as many as he could, but the beast could not go down.

Titus was throwing spears that Azell had bought in Plundorios just in case Dramanus would attack.

Azell used his sword and his fists. Sebastianus did the same.

Sebastianus took a mighty swing at the beast's head and finally it was dead. It's head flew off.

"Glad that's over with", said Sebastianus. Then he grinned.

"Hey", said Azell, "over there is Monol Island. That's means once we get passed the actual Ship-Wreck part, we'll reach the island and we can continue our journey."

Sebastianus felt a cold chill run down his neck. He turned to look behind him and saw a tentacle rising. Where Sebastianus had cut off the head, two heads were growing.

"Sebastianus, you need fire!" panicked Azell. "I didn't realize it before, but this is a Sea Hydra. Fire is the only thing that can kill it!"

Sebastianus then thought of where to get a fire. Then he yelled to John, "Find some fire and give it to me fast!"

Then Sebastianus raised the Sword of Vinco and stabbed the Sea Hydra's neck. Immediately, the beast began to burn to a crisp. Sebastianus took his sword out of the beast's neck and saw that the tip of the Sword of Vinco was on fire.

Sebastianus and the others celebrated their defeat until Sebastianus realized something.

"Azell, what are we going to do about the massive hole in the ship with a huge dead Sea Hydra poking out of it."

"Nothing I can do", said Azell. "Well, we got two choices: sink and die or swim to shore and die on the way."

"I got a third one for ya", said a deep voice.

Sebastianus, John, Azell, and Titus all turned around slowly to see a huge, huge boat that was completely golden with black letters on the side that read: The Golden King.

A rather tall, muscular pirate with a brown, beard that dropped to his chest, a black pirate hat, four swords strapped to his belt, a long black jacket with a grey shirt underneath, and a load of jewelry on him stood on it.

"Who are you?" asked Sebastianus.

"Andrey", he said. "Now, do you need a ride to Rebucia, it's only a half hour away?"

"Um, yes we do", said Titus.

"We need some information, Andrey", said Azell.

"I can help you there", he said. "Know everything there is, will and has", he said.

"Interesting", Sebastianus said.

"Very", said Azell.

"Now get on", said Andrey.

Chapter Thirty-eight:

Andrey and the Golden King

Andrey seemed like a pretty friendly guy, but he was tough. He bought them down to his room, which was as big as a house.

"Where are you taking us?" asked Azell. "You're supposed to be telling us what we need to know."

"I'll tell ya what I know once we get to the Ship-Wreck of the sea", said Andrey.

"How long will that take?" asked Sebastianus.

"About twenty minutes", he said. "Why don't ya have a look around. You look like a guy who'd very much enjoy my treasures and possessions. They can be pretty interesting", he said with a wink.

"Um, thanks", said Sebastianus, nodding his head and walking backwards.

Sebastianus looked around for about ten minutes. Within that time he saw several pieces of jewelry, an eye ball in a glass jar, a locked chest, a bookshelf of books that were so old and dusty, Sebastianus didn't dare looking at them, a huge painting of Davy Jones, a telescope, a pile of books that all read: *The Journal of*

Captain Andrey – by Andrey, a small tub full of fish, rocks, water and plants, a jar of toads and fireplace full of…something.

Sebastianus decided he would look around the bookshelf.

"Captain Andrey, do you mind if I look at a book or two on this shelf?" asked Sebastianus.

"Please do", he said.

"Thanks", muttered Sebastianus.

Sebastianus took one book at a time. The first was *Jones: A Pirate's Life*. Sebastianus looked through that. He read the first five chapters and very much enjoyed it.

Then he took *Garew and the Fight of Plundorios*. Sebastianus liked that one, too. He read the first three chapters and decided he'd take another as the book was a gruesome as could be.

The next one was *Sebastianus: The Heir to Vinco*. Sebastianus looked shocked and stared at the book for a short period. But to Sebastianus, the short period was hours.

"It can't mean me", said Sebastianus. Sebastianus opened the book.

Chapter One

Sebastianus' Birth

Sebastianus was the son of Cato and Medra. Sebastianus was born on the twenty-first day of the fox. He lives to this very day.

His father was a horrible man. He destroyed the great statue of Vinco and stole his sword. It was not long til King Mogrod found out and retrieved the sword. Cato and Medra were executed and there three year old child was brought to live with Lord Titus.

He worked as the Royal Court Artist.

Sebastianus shut the book. "Wait", he said before he put it back into the shelf, "I can find out if I am supposed to kill Latorin, when I die, what my future will be like", whispered Sebastianus to himself.

Sebastianus flipped to the end. No words were there. There were no words as Sebastianus flipped through the pages. Finally, when he came to chapter twenty, there were words.

Chapter Thirty-nine:

The Ship-Wreck Sea of Plundorios

Sebastianus saw that the book was writing itself. Everything that Sebastianus did was written.

"I'm the error to Vinco", he mumbled to himself.

Sebastianus put the book in his sack and looked back to Andrey and smiled.

Then Sebastianus looked at another book that said: *For Sebastianus, from Andrey.*

Sebastianus opened the book and saw that there were all blank pages. But, the last page had the image of a huge desert with a huge sun in the background. There was also a huge giant who was falling apart from rocks hitting it. Then it regenerated itself. Then a sword hit the giant and a huge clump of it disappeared and didn't regenerate. Sebastianus looked closely at the sword and saw that it was his, the Sword of Vinco.

Sebastianus smiled and turned to Andrey. He gave a dirty grin revealing his yellow and brown teeth. Somehow, Sebastianus knew that that meant he didn't want anyone to know what he had just saw.

"Thanks", said Sebastianus once they came to a stop at the Ship-Wreck of the sea.

Sebastianus walked out of the boat onto a bridge that lead to about one hundred ships all piled up on each other. Except there were sidewalks, statues, a small hotel that was made out of a ship, rivers and small boats that were tied to a dock, there were people all over, people were selling stuff, their were little places to eat. Then there was a huge cave in a huge hill in the water by the sea where the *Golden King* was supposed to be parked, there were bridges and towers, and a huge castle in on the top of the ships. There was also construction all over. There was a huge gate being built around the Ship-Wreck. Also, a huge stadium was being built (half of it being a ship).

"What do ya think of Ship-Wreck City?" asked Andrey.

"Who are all of these people?" asked Sebastianus. "People say you're the only pirate to survive this sea."

"I believe in my city, nine hundred and eighty three now live here. They come to see my city and me and to live here. Besides, how could I be *Captain* Andrey if no one lived here or was on my crew. I like to call myself: *The Other Lord of Plundorios.*"

"It's impressive", said Azell. "Is it a law to use magic here? If I can, I could help your city out and make construction go much faster and everything more firm and nicer."

"Than its not a law anymore", said Andrey, chuckling to himself. "Azell, could me and you go for a walk and I'll show you the flaws of the city and you can fix them how you want. Titus, John, Sebastianus, go and explore the city. Here's a bag of gold, get some things", he said, taking a black bag out of his pocket on his jacket. "If ya get into trouble, say yer a friend of me", said Andrey, disappearing behind all of the pirates with Azell.

No more than thirty seconds after they were gone, three huge pirates came to John, Sebastianus and Titus. One was Apoalan and bald with only a black ponytail for hair. He had a snake tattoo on his bare chest. The other guy was Rebucian. He had a tall, square orange hat with a tail hanging off it. He was black with a shaved head and a blue and red vest. He had a tattoo of a lion and ape fighting on his cheek. The next man was Plundoriosn.

He was hundreds of pounds overweight and didn't look to bright at all. He had just a tight, small pants on him.

"Give me the damn money", said the Rebucian in a deep, deep, deep voice.

"I'm a friend of Andrey", said Sebastianus.

"You ain't even a pirate!" yelled the Apoalan man.

"I have the Sword of Vinco!" warned Sebastianus.

"It was stolen and never found again!" yelled the Rebucian man.

Sebastianus drew the blade an showed it to the three men.

"Edwards", said the Rebucian man.

"Yeah", said a mentally handicapped voice which belonged to the huge Plundoriosn.

"Grab the sword and give it to me!" yelled the Rebucian man.

"Okay Koalaps", said Edwards.

Then the Edwards ran and placed his huge hands on the Sword of Vinco and flew back ten feet.

"If you have the blade, you must be somewhat important", said the Rebucian man, "meaning you probably are a friend of Andrey."

"Yes, did it take that damn long to figure that out?" yelled John.

Then the three pirates ran away.

Sebastianus and the others got soup and wine to drink at *Thomas Black's*. Then they went to a store called *Jones*. They each bought a Skull, which could drive evil pirate spirits away.

After an hour or so, Sebastianus saw that the city looked a lot nicer and that Azell and Andrey were only a couple feet away.

"See ya", he said. "You're aloud to just transport yourself to Rebucia from here."

"Thanks for everything", said Sebastianus.

"Drema Transporto Rebucia!" yelled Azell.

Then, they found themselves on a beach that touched the jungle. A huge city was there.

Chapter Forty:

The Rebucian Jungle

The huge jungle spread far out past the horizon. The people wore exactly what the Rebucian pirate in Ship-Wreck City wore. They lived in huts on the ground and in tree houses. Around fifty of them were there.

"Sebastianus, this is Riddicaw", said Titus as a tall, muscular Rebucian walked up.

"Titus ow' is it goin", he said slowly, not knowing English very good at all. "An dis is Sebastianus", he said pointing to Sebastianus.

"Yeah", said Sebastianus.

"An ya are Gon Artha", he said pointing to John.

"Yeah, call me John", said John.

"Lord Azell, a pweasure ta met ya", said Riddicaw.

"As to you", said Azell.

They all shook hands with Riddicaw. Since Riddicaw was horrible at his English, Titus spoke Rebucian with him and then told the others what he was saying.

"Gar dak lawf ant?" asked Titus.

"Rubbic", said Riddicaw.

"We go east", said Titus.

Then they began going through the jungle. They passed tree houses and animals. The trees stood around fifteen feet tall.

Finally, after an hour or so, Riddicaw said, "Dramanicus drulu miniverio derepso okoso hert mek."

"He cannot help us from here", said Titus. "We must keep going east and find the owls."

"Why do we need to find owls?" asked Sebastianus.

Titus ignored Sebastianus.

Riddicaw rustled through the bushes as the group went east.

"What did the riddle say?" asked himself.

"Watch out for the monkeys. Um, watch out for the tigers. Do your best to find the flyers", said Sebastianus.

"Well, the flyers are the owls", said Titus.

"And it probably means avoiding the tigers", said John.

"But what harm could monkeys do?" asked Sebastianus.

"The Ecula are the protectors of the jungle. They are apes the size of houses", said Azell.

"That seems pretty bad", said Sebastianus.

"The tigers can't be that bad", said John. "We've fought much worse."

"Have you fought worse than tigers that are nearly the size of the apes and have teeth the size of a you. Also, their tails are snakes as they have horns on their backs and small wings that can't even carry them", said Azell.

"If you put it that way...", said John.

Then he looked up at a huge row of trees that went much further back.

"How come the trees just become suddenly taller?" asked Sebastianus.

"So the Ecula and tigers can hide within them. Do you see that small mountain way in the distance?" asked Azell.

"Yeah, why?" asked Sebastianus.

"Because that's where the edge of the jungle is", said Titus.

"Indeed", said Azell.

"So", said Sebastianus, "watch out for the monkeys and tigers, find the owls and make it to the edge of the jungle alive."

"That's it", said Azell.

"Alright", said Titus, "I know more about Rebucia than any of you do. As I lived in Rebucia for seven years in this very jungle. So I will lead the way."

"I've been around for seven centuries and you think you no more than me?" asked Azell.

"Name every Rebucian in that village", said Titus.

"I can't", muttered Azell.

"Well I can", said Titus.

"Fine", said Azell, "lead the way!"

Then they walked for another hour or so. Sebastianus heard the fluttering of wings on the way many times and figured it was the owls that Titus had mentioned earlier.

It was fairly quiet for a while til the huge stomping of an animal was heard to break the silence.

"It's the Ecula", said Azell.

"Most definitely", said Titus. "They'll be here in about five minutes."

Then the stomping got louder…and louder…and louder til a huge black figure that was covered in spiked armor. His face was swelled up. Behind him were several more. They looked the exact same and said, "Dora dom kark?"

"Neriiso", said Titus.

"Egrubie", said one of the Ecula.

"Neriiso!" yelled Titus.

Then the beast looked at each other and raised their arms and pounded their chest.

"Is that a good sign?" asked Sebastianus.

"Well", said Titus, "it just means they wants to eat us."

"Shall we run then?" asked John.

There was a long pause of silence as the Ecula stuck their face down at Sebastianus' face and they ran.

They ran for no more than a second had the Ecula already grabbed Azell with its fingers and started to look at him. He opened his mouth just as ten arrows went right onto his swollen lip.

He dropped Azell and then the gorilla died.

Sebastianus took the Sword of Vinco and stabbed another gorilla. It almost died. Sebastianus stabbed it once more in the waste and it died.

Sebastianus and John didn't have much trouble. But Titus and Azell did. The Ecula were apparently magic-proof and so Azell had to use the Sword of Minicris, his sword to fight. Titus and Azell were defending themselves more than fighting.

John had fired at least a thousand arrows. Sebastianus began to wonder how he got so many arrows. He didn't take the ones he had used and use them again.

"John", said Sebastianus stabbing an Ecula, "how do you", Sebastianus stopped to kill another Ecula, "have so many arrows?"

"I can't tell you that!" yelled John over the screaming Ecula.

"Why?!" yelled Sebastianus back as he stabbed another Ecula.

"I'm a hunter!" yelled John back. "Azell hates me because I'm an ex-hunter!"

"Then how do the arrows magically appear to you?!" yelled Sebastianus.

"I'm a hunter – magic!" yelled John with a howl as a huge, black fist went for him.

John and Sebastianus took down at least seven of the Ecula together and then helped Azell and Titus.

After an hour or so, the four were breathless. Still, at least twenty or thirty more Ecula remained, unharmed.

"We should give up", said John, "We're going to die!"

"We will win this fight", said Sebastianus.

Then the four of them went for an Ecula and killed it with one hit of what they each had.

They went for another, but were stopped by a different huge ape and killed the both of them. Sebastianus took three or four swings at each of them, John with only three of his arrows to each, Azell with a swing or two at the first and none at the second, Titus with one hit total.

They each worked together until finally, only four remained.

"Ecribindo!" yelled the biggest of the apes. Then, suddenly, there was a long pause of silence and confusion til about twenty huge, massive apes, all dressed with their red, spiked armor appeared and screamed. They charged for John, Azell, Titus and Sebastianus.

Everyone knew that it was the end for the small, bunch of four.

But then, as Sebastianus shielded his face, he heard the flapping of thousands of huge wings. Then the howls of the Ecula stretched far as thousands of owls each – unbelievably – killed the Ecula.

"The owls", said Titus with a shocked grin.

"Well, we'll thank them later", said Sebastianus.

"We will", muttered Titus.

"Let's continue", said John.

"Let's get this damn journey over", whispered Sebastianus.

Chapter Forty-one:

The Tigers of Rebucia

The small group of four walked for hours and hours til Sebastianus finally said, "Titus, why did those owls come and kill the Ecula?"

"I know them. They are sacred. Most people don't believe in them. Rebucians do, though. It's an old legend. It's believed that Vinco, Liberius, Sobalus, and Reabius once stumbled upon a dark cave. There was a huge black gate that sealed the entrance.

"Vinco decided that it would be good to open because the mark of Latorin was on the gate, meaning that Latorin imprisoned whatever was in there. It couldn't have been bad. When Vinco opened the doors. Rusolions of giant owls, the size of humans came rushing out. The smallest one said 'I am the Queen of owls. You have freed us and I will give you four of my owls for you to ride til death'. Vinco and the others rode the four owls. Vinco's was Grobas, Liberius' was Melindico, Sobalus' was Zobicask, and Reabius' was JosLosuran.

"Two years later when the war started, the owls bread and their were billions. Every male and some female owls fought in that war. Twenty two years late, when the war ended, the owls went to a great place, the Rebucian Jungle to live in Vinco Tree, the biggest tree ever", said Titus.

"That's an…odd story", said Sebastianus.

"History can be odd, Sebastianus", said Azell.

"John", said Sebastianus, "tell Titus your little secret."

"Fine", said John. "Titus, I'm an ex-hunter. I have magic to summon arrows any time I want."

"Really?"

"Ya", said John.

But Titus didn't think it was that cool or exciting.

For a little while, no one talked. They listened for the sounds of stomping to see if the tigers or the left over Ecula were coming.

"Wait, Azell, how come you didn't transport us to Rebucia?" asked Sebastianus.

"Because", said Azell, "Andrey offered a favor and I was polite."

"I guess that sounds like a decent thing to do", said Sebastianus.

Then Sebastianus was about to ask Azell how John was forced to leave the hunters til a loud stomping was heard.

The four ran as the knew that the tigers were coming.

There were growls and running and stomping til finally an orange, giant cat with black stripes, small little bird wings, two small horns that stuck out of his forehead.

"Run!" yelled Sebastianus.

The four ran for their lives til finally, they realized it was no use. They were cornered by the huge mountain.

The giant tiger roared.

Sebastianus raised his sword as did Titus and Azell. John took his bows and several arrows appeared in his hand.

John shot seven or eight arrows. The beast was now swollen in a bunch of different spots.

Sebastianus went up and stabbed the beast, but the tiger leaped up and grabbed Sebastianus. His claws were near his throat. The beast was about to scratch his throat and rip. But Azell stabbed the beast's foot and it let go of Sebastianus.

The tiger roared as John shot it again.

Sebastianus went for another stab and got the beast in the chest. Finally, the tiger fell with a loud thud. It was dead.

"I'm glad that's over with", said Sebastianus.

"It's not", said Titus, pointing to a herd of giant, orange and black beasts heading their way.

"We can take on thirty", said Sebastianus.

"Hopefully", muttered John.

Then they all raised their weapons.

Sebastianus split up from the bunch. He took the Sword of Vinco and swung at a tiger. He missed and then took another swing and slashed his face. The tiger then raised it claw and Sebastianus went for another chest swing. The beast died.

Sebastianus went for another one and stabbed it in the claw. It screamed and swatted for him. Sebastianus dodged. Then tiger killed the other beast behind Sebastianus.

Sebastianus stabbed another one in the leg. It fell and Sebastianus went for his face. It died.

Sebastianus looked for another tiger and found it. He chopped of its tail and then, as the beast screamed, Sebastianus got on its back and rode it.

He stabbed another tiger in the face, and another in the chest. He stabbed them for a while til there was only seven or eight tigers left.

One jumped for Sebastianus and his tiger. Sebastianus jumped off the beast and the other tiger killed it.

John shot arrows into the tiger that was on top of the other.

Sebastianus stabbed one in the leg, arm and then stomach.

Finally, there was only five.

Azell used his strength and banged two tigers together.

Sebastianus stabbed one in the face and stomach and it died. John shot one with his arrows and Titus stabbed one in the chest.

There was one left. It was the biggest one. It was bigger than three Ecula put together. Then it roared.

Sebastianus held the hilt of the Sword of Vinco with both hands and pointed it at the tiger.

Sebastianus closed his eyes and then looked at his sword. Blue and silver blinding light was shooting from the tip.

The tiger roared and then turned to dust.

"The sword surprises me sometimes", said Sebastianus, shocked from the miracle.

"No kidding", mumbled John.

Chapter Forty-two:

The Owls

Titus kept going on about owls as they hiked up the mountain. It was really getting annoying. It was always 'the owls once...' or 'The great Owls had once...'.

Finally, when they reached the top of the mountain. Titus took a deep breath and said, "Behold the kingdom of the Owls!"

There were huge trees that were each one hundred feet tall and as thick as a house.

Then they walked down to the kingdom. They were soon in front of the biggest of trees. There was a huge door in it. They walked in and saw that the inside was like a palace. Thick branch that stuck out of the wall formed stairs to the top.

Titus lead the three up the stairs. Two huge owls the size of chairs stood with spears and said, "Titus, prisoners or friends?"

"Friends", said Titus.

"What is your purpose to see the Queen?"

"We're on the quest and the chosen one is with us. We need an owl for him and one for us", said Titus, pointing to the others with his index finger.

The owls moved aside. Their was a woven, brown curtain behind them. The guards moved the curtain aside to show a golden, huge, completely circular room with branches and leaves coming out of the wall.

A golden nest sat on a branch. There was a white lump curled up in it. After a small pause. The lump popped a head up. It was a white, beautiful owl's head.

"Titus, how can I help you?", she said in a high-pitched voice.

"I need Almasic back and these people need some good owls. This is an ex-hunter", he said pointing to John. "This is Lord Azell, the immortal king", he said pointing to Azell. "This, my queen, is the Chosen One. It is Sebastianus in the flesh, the heir is in your presence."

"Thank you, Titus", said the Queen.

"Excuse me...um", said Sebastianus, "my queen –"

"Call me Elipsa", said the queen owl.

"Queen Elipsa, can I pick an owl as quick I as can. I really am excited the fact I get an owl and...", said Sebastianus.

"Cornelius!" called Elipsa. "Take these gentleman to the un-picked owls!"

Seconds after that, a grey owl appeared. "Yes, my queen", he said in a deep voice. He led the four down the stairs and out of the tree to another one.

There were at least a hundred owls. All of them. They all sat there and stared at Cornelius. "Line up!" he yelled and then they all flew outside in a line on the ground.

"Now everyone put out their hand and if the owl raises his wing and touches your hand, you are united with that owl", said Cornelius.

Titus already had an owl named Almasic. Then Sebastianus nodded his head. He started from the beginning of the line. There was a giant black owl. Sebastianus put his hand and the owl took no notice of him and Sebastianus figured it was a no.

Sebastianus went to the next, a big brown and white owl. Sebastianus lifted his hand towards the owl. The owl nearly bit his hand off, swearing and cursing at him. It was defiantly not the owl that he was supposed to have.

Sebastianus was nearing the end of the line and still didn't have an owl. He had went through brown, white, black, and all sorts of owls. John had already gotten his owl, it was the big black one that was Sebastianus' first try. Azell had a big brown one with grey speckles. John's owl's name was Cailsell, Azell's was Ramus.

When Sebastianus only had two to go, Cornelius appeared to him and whispered in his ear, "Don't even try the last owl. His name is Audax, he's a trouble-maker, a menace, no the brightest and an outcast that will remain forever an outcast."

"I'll give him a go", said Sebastianus aloud.

Finally, he had no owl and went to Audax, a dark grey owl with white feathers on his back that sort of made some sort of picture of a sword…The Sword of Vinco.

Sebastianus knew that Audax would be his owl. He raised his pail hand towards Audax. For about a minute, Sebastianus held it there. Audax was silent and motionless. But, just as Sebastianus was about to give up, the grey, scared, feathery wing of Audax raised and touch Sebastianus.

All of the owls looked shocked. Cornelius didn't know what was going on at first, but then he looked over to Audax's wing and Sebastianus' hand touching.

"Queen Elipsa!" screamed Cornelius as loud as he could. "Audax has been chosen by the heir!"

Then Cornelius fainted. Sebastianus laughed as he put his hand down.

"I need to know your name", said Audax in a deep voice.

"I'm Sebastianus", said Sebastianus. "Most people here call me the heir or the Chosen One here, though."

Audax couldn't build up his voice.

"Audax, right?" said Sebastianus.

Audax nodded his head. "Would you like to ride me to see if you really want to be with me?" Audax finally said.

251

"Is it scary?" asked Sebastianus nervously.

"Na", said Audax.

Sebastianus climb on his back. "On three", said Sebastianus. "One –"

Immediately Audax flew up a couple hundred feet in the air. Sebastianus' skin was being pulled back. The wind was blowing hard in his face. He going as fast as four hundred miles an hour. Audax was now flying around the kingdom and above the Rebucian Jungle and then the sea and then over Plundorios and then he went back to the kingdom of the owls and then to the mountains of Rebucia. Finally he went back to the owls and landed.

"That was more horrifying than Atra Erus!" yelled Sebastianus.

"So, do you want me?" asked Audax.

"Of course", said Sebastianus with a grin.

The four, with their owls, slept in a small tree that was for guests. The owls did not sleep. They guarded the four.

When they woke up, Azell didn't even bother casting a spell to get to Apoalan, they took the owls.

Before Sebastianus left, Elipsa gave Sebastianus a weird looking plant. He was supposed to eat it. He did and saw the giant was being hit by red beams. But Sebastianus noticed that the symbol of darkness was falling off him and he was screaming.

Chapter Forty-three:

The Apoalan Chest and the Golden Monkey

Audax was the fastest of the owls, but he had to go slower than usual. Ramus was an owl who was much like Azell: wise and nature loving. Cailsell was a boring owl. He was a lot tougher than Ramus, though, but Audax was more than him. Titus's owl, Almasic was kind of old. He had a white head and brown body covered with grey spots and white spots. He was six hundred forty nine years old.

"Audax", said Sebastianus when they were flying to Apoalan, "how old are you?"

"I'm twenty two now. In seven weeks, I'm turning twenty three."

"How long do you think you'll live?" asked Sebastianus.

"Most likely another a thousand or so more years", he said. "Don't human normally live around eighty?"

"Usually", said Sebastianus.

"You really live a short life!"

Sebastianus was silent for a moment. Then they landed on the warm dirt of Apoalan. Monks walked all over. They were going in and out of a huge, grey, stone temple.

A golden statue of a round man stood at each side of the door. On the walls were paintings of the man under a tree, beside a huge pillar, and a monkey somersaulting on his palm. There were a bunch more paintings.

Sebastianus, I have a feeling that that is where we want to go", said Titus.

"Can't be hard to get that Apoalan chest if it's in a small temple like that. If the monks are going to fight us, then let's go in!" said Sebastianus.

Then the eight went in. The temple was decorated with all sorts of statues and paintings. There was a locked door was locked and there were five monks guarding it. Sebastianus figured that the chest was in there.

Sebastianus, Audax and the others walked up to the door. "Do you hide the Apoalan chest in those doors?" asked Sebastianus. "We need to see it."

"Ecupata!" yelled one of the monks. Then every single monk in the temple began yelling one word, "Scara! Scara!"

Then the guards opened the door. "Muco desayo!" yelled a monk. They pushed the eight in and locked the door.

The room had a clear, even dirt path. Then there were completely fresh and living trees that produced golden fruits. Sebastianus realized that it was raining! Blue, warm drops of rain came from clouds that were where the ceiling was supposed to be. Sebastianus realized that there was no wall or ceiling. Sebastianus and Audax looked behind them and saw that the door was just standing there. There was no room behind it. Then Sebastianus heard a growl or two. He realized the other must've, too because they all started running on the muddy dirt path, trying to get the chest as fast as possible before whatever was coming didn't get the opportunity to get them.

After a couple of minutes the group of eight were stopped by a huge lump in the path.

"What's this damn thing?" asked Sebastianus.

"I think it's an...ant hill!" yelled Azell.

"What makes you so sure", said Sebastianus, not even looking at Azell, but trying out one of the golden fruits.

Then Sebastianus turned to see a red ant the size of a book crawling out of the lump of dirt. Sebastianus stabbed it with the Sword of Vinco. Then another ant popped up. Sebastianus stabbed that. Then about twenty or thirty came up. Sebastianus only managed to stab three before one bit his leg.

"Crukso!" yelled Azell. Then an ant blew up. He yelled this at least seven times til there were to many ants.

Sebastianus stepped on them all until he reached the ant hill. He took the Sword of Vinco and stabbed the entrance to the ant hill.

After a minute or two, Sebastianus took it out and then ran as did the rest. They hopped on their owls and flew in the rainy sky, just inches above the trees.

After a little bit, a bit of growling and rustling was heard in the trees.

"Azell", said Sebastianus, "is there more creatures?"

"Oh, Sebastianus, you thought that some red ants was supposed to be the big challenge? There are hundreds of creatures here."

"I most certainly was hoping that those ants were the only creatures", said Audax.

"I guess that's why they call you Audax the outcast", mumbled Azell.

Then, Audax began mumbling, "What just touched my chest?"

Then something jumped up near Sebastianus. It was a cheetah. Its claws were as big as its teeth, which were the size of Sebastianus' fingers.

John drew his bow as the beast jumped up again. As it jumped up once more, he shot three arrows at it. Then the beast went for Titus. Audax flew right by Titus, so Sebastianus could take the Sword of Vinco and the stab the beast. Sebastianus took a mighty swing and killed the beast.

Then Sebastianus looked down. Another cheetah was jumping up. Sebastianus took a swing and missed as the cheetah fell back down.

John took his bow and fired an arrow at the beast when it was on the ground. It died.

Sebastianus saw another ten cheetahs running. Two leaped up and Sebastianus managed to kill them both.

"John!" yelled Sebastianus.

"On it!" yelled John as he fired twenty arrows and only killing three. The rest leaped for Sebastianus. Sebastianus killed one and before he could take another swing, Azell yelled, "Crukso!" Several of the beasts were blown back, one killed.

The cheetahs ran away. Audax, who had never even given anyone a ride and never been the owl of a knight, was so excited, he did a loop in the air and Sebastianus nearly fell off.

"Sorry", said Audax as Sebastianus scooted himself tightly on Audax's grey back.

"It's fine. I know your excited to ride, but don't ever get too excited."

"I can't make a promise to that, Sebastianus", said Audax.

Sebastianus smiled and then he frowned once he heard Azell saying, "We must avoid the Golden Monkey."

"What's the Golden Monkey?" asked Sebastianus.

"A trickster, you could call him. He likes to challenge you at things that he knows he can win and that you can lose."

Then Sebastianus saw the chest.

"The chest!" yelled Sebastianus, pointing down to the blue and gold chest lying on a rock.

"But where's the key?" asked Titus.

Then a monkey, about the size of Sebastianus, went through the trees, swinging from branch to branch. His fur was literally gold. He wore a necklace around his golden neck. On it was a shiny, silver key.

"The Golden Monkey!" yelled Sebastianus.

Then Sebastianus yelled, "Audax, go for the monkey!" yelled Sebastianus.

Immediately Audax dove down for the monkey. Sebastianus was an inch away from the monkey. They were side to side.

"Give me the key!" demanded Sebastianus.

"If you can catch me", yelled the monkey in a high pitched voice, "I will give you the key!"

Then the monkey took off, going faster than ever.

Audax caught up with the monkey. Sebastianus raised the Sword of Vinco and took a swing. By the time Sebastianus had struck, the monkey had swung to another tree, leaving Sebastianus with a chopped leaf.

Sebastianus had caught up with monkey again. He took the Sword of Vinco out and then took a swing. But the monkey had mumbled some words and ran away. Sebastianus had found himself hitting a dozen monkeys, giant red ants, leopards, cheetahs, a couple of big, black bears, big birds with beaks that were as sharp as knives, and even a giant panda.

"What the...!" yelled Sebastianus. Then the birds started chasing him.

Sebastianus took the Sword of Vinco and stabbed two. There were still three left. One stabbed Sebastianus in the shoulder. Then Sebastianus killed it with the Sword of Vinco.

Sebastianus took down the rest in a single swing. Then Sebastianus saw that three monkeys were going at the same speed Sebastianus was. Sebastianus killed the first.

Then one was tugging on Audax. Then Sebastianus killed it with a strike and then killed it.

Sebastianus then saw that all of the leopards and cheetahs were jumping for him. As Sebastianus saw that Audax was about to be killed. About nine of the felines were killed by arrows.

"John!" yelled Sebastianus. "Thanks!"

"No worry, Sebastianus", said John. "Find the Golden Monkey and I'll get the rest of the animals. The panda is the slowest thing I've ever seen, so it can't be that hard to take him down."

"Thanks a lot!" called Sebastianus as his friend disappeared into the distance.

Sebastianus soon found the Golden Monkey laying asleep leaning on a tree. As Sebastianus tried to sneak up on the monkey, it awoke with a high pitched scream. It ran away and Sebastianus didn't even know what was happening. Everything disappeared from sight. It was black and Sebastianus heard a deep voice yelling unfamiliar words. "Trampsono!" yelled the voice.

Then Sebastianus could see his surroundings once more. He saw, behind a tree, a light brown monkey lay dead. He was bleeding from his mouth, ears and nose. The keys were laying beside him.

"No!" yelled Sebastianus. "Then he remembered what Icarus had said several months before. 'Sebastianus, promise me to never use this power. Tame it.' Sebastianus picked up the keys, looking worried and then he got on Audax and flew back to the Apoalan Chest with a straight face and a worried look.

He took the silver keys and slowly unlocked the chest. There was a golden fruit in the chest. He took a big bite and was about to take another bite til Titus said, "It is the Fruit of Knowledge. Knowledge is the key to power, but also the sickle of death."

Sebastianus then saw an image. The giant was roaring as hundreds of giant owls were breathing fire at it.

Then Sebastianus no longer saw the vision. He was in the Apoalan jungle.

"We have to transport ourselves to the nearest city and then we can fly", said Azell.

"Yeah", agreed the owls.

Then Azell said, "Drema Transporto Zangou!"

Then the group found themselves in a small village, quite like the town they had just been in. Then the flew to Driba.

Chapter Forty-four:

The Hidden History of Azell

After an hour or so of flying, the eight landed in a warm country. It was sandy and full with tents, a bunch of people in turbans and pointy shoes trying to sell stuff, and, at the end of the village. There was a white marble palace with a golden roof that twisted.

"This is Driba?" asked Sebastianus. "Everyone says that it's horrible."

"It is", muttered John.

"The palace would be our number one guess to find the... Driban Staircase", said Sebastianus.

"Oh, so ya think we have to go to that small tent over there and cLosurb a giant staircase and find out how to defeat a giant sand monster", said John.

Everyone laughed. Then they walked towards the palace.

The guards spoke terrible English. "Da ya ned ta ge' i'ta da pal'ce?"

"Yeah", said Sebastianus, after he finally he had figured out what he had just said.

"Only i' Hetlino les ya!"

"That's one hell of a joke, guys!" said John with a chuckle.

"Why?" asked one of the guards.

Then John shot an arrow at one. Then he shot another at the other guy.

They ran in the doors and then looked for anything that looked like a staircase.

"In here!" John finally called.

He pointed to a small door. It was only four feet tall. But when he lifted the red curtain that was draped over it, there was a staircase. It went down. It had no walls, nor end. But it got darker as it got deeper. There were black cliffs and mountains near the bottom. It formed a canyon and made the staircase twist sideways and up and down.

"You sure that's it?" asked Sebastianus.

Everyone laughed. Then there was a sudden creak and a squeak. "W-who's th-there? I-is tha-that you, Herbero?"

"It's the lord of Driba!" whispered Sebastianus. Then they all went down the stairs. The wall sealed behind them and screams of the lord filled the air. A couple steps in, a tablet stood before them written in Arabic:

Magic can not work here

Any sort of mystical creature will not work

No food or water of any sort will be provided

Sebastianus looked a little scared. But he kept walking down til it was hard to see. He saw that cliffs and canyons were surrounding the stairs and that he had to zigzag or curve or go up and then down every once and a while.

Then Sebastianus saw a small map on the cliff. He squinted to see and it had a map of the Driban Staircase. In some sort of Driban writing, there was a name and a note:

Βοηαμμαδ Δριβαэσ Χηανγινγ Μαπ
Τηε Σαχρεδ ιτεμ τηατ ωιλλ βε ηιδδεν τιλ Μαλυμ
Ρισεσ

Sebastianus leaned against the grey, pointing stone and grabbed the map. "Hey, guys, I found a map of the staircase!" yelled Sebastianus.

Azell turned around with sweat dripping down his forehead. His tan skin turned pale.

"Azell", said Sebastianus, "can you read this Driban writing?"

Azell shrugged and he took the map and slowly read, "Bohumed Driba's Changing Map: The Sacred item that will remain hidden til Latorin rises."

"Bohumed Driba was the first king of Driba, wasn't he", said Sebastianus.

"Yeah, he was", said Titus.

"Azell, why are ya looking so nervous?" John, Sebastianus and Titus asked at the same time.

"I'm not", said Azell.

"Yeah you are!" yelled John.

"Azell, come on", said Sebastianus. "You're drenched in sweat, shaking and…"

Azell was now muttering: *The secret will be hidden amongst the ninety-nine founders.*

"Azell, if this has to do with your past, I'm bloody-well the future savior of life. You can tell me", said Sebastianus, calmly.

Azell thought for a minute or so and then sighed. "Fine", he said. "Nine thousand, four hundred twelve years ago, Vinco fought Latorin with an army of three hundred twelve men. Ninety nine of those men were the founders of each nation –"

"Didn't your grandfather fight in that war as the founder of Azell?" asked Sebastianus.

"No", said Azell. "I did."

There was pause of silence and everyone was shocked.

"My full name is Lord Reabius Azell. I went by my last name and convinced everyone that my grandfather had fought in that war. Only me and my cousin, who is also immortal lived through the war. He goes by his last name as well. We have a…bit of a rivalry.

"After the war, the ninety nine founders took there most valuble items and gave them to Vinco. Vinco hid them and said that the true heir to him would find the Changing Map, which would lead them to the rest of the items.

"I don't know much of the items, but I can remember the Book of Life and Death. It was supposed to have powers unimagined. Only the true owner of the book could unlock its powers. But most people only saw that its power was that it could write itself. It wrote about the true owner. I can't remember the rest of its history, though."

"Azell", said Sebastianus, pulling the book about him out of his mail-coat, "I think that I have the book."

Azell looked at the book and said, "Only ninety seven more items to go."

"Ninety-eight, actually", said Titus.

"I'm sorry, I have forgotten Vinco's most valuble item. The Sword of God. But it has many nicknames: the Sword of Life, the Holy Sword, the Sword of Vinco…"

Sebastianus actually saw that coming.

"I knew something like that was going to happen", said Audax.

Sebastianus had almost forgotten that the owls were there.

"John", scowled Cailsell, "we need to hurry up."

"Yes, we do", said Azell. "Ramus", said Azell.

"Yeah", said Ramus.

"Do you mind waking Almasic up. He's getting old. Titus, you should have picked another owl", said Azell.

"One owl for me and that is Almasic", said Titus, grinning and looking proud.

"What's happening?" asked Almasic as Ramus woke him.

Sebastianus then thought of something. He thought of Apollo, who he had met and fought with a couple of months ago. He seemed like he had one of the ninety nine items. Also, Icarus

SEBASTIANUS: THE WAR BEGINS

had been handed a bag that Liberius gave him. Maybe that was an item. Maybe Lord Huvadrull had had an item. Maybe the Ralscon was an item. Maybe what he had seen in Azell, which magically healed him was an item. So many extraordinary items that could have been one of the ninety nine. Maybe under the water in the palace of Bruno, there could have been something. The Apoalan Chest could have been one. Maybe in Rebucia, there could have been one. He had already found one in Plundorios, but it's possible there could have been another or two.

"Azell", said Sebastianus, "you told us about Reabius, er, yourself and said that he, um I mean you, was one of Vinco's top servants."

"I was indeed one of Vinco's best men", said Azell.

"What was your item", asked Cailsell.

"The Wand of Azell", said Azell.

"What's that", asked Audax.

"A wand that is more powerful than any wand. It has more magic than the magic of the world put together. It only works for three people. Minicus and I made sure of that when he made it. Those people are myself, Vinco and his heir. Sebastianus, it would very much work for you."

"Do ya know where it is?" asked Sebastianus.

"In Azell, of course", said Azell. "I have hunted down each item and have only found thirty two. I would have never expected that Vinco knew about this staircase." "But", said Sebastianus, "it's Vinco, how could he have not known about the staircase!"

"Well, it has been a myth for a long time. People believed that some Driban man carved the stairs. Not even Bohumed Driba knew about it til…well minutes before his death", said Azell.

"Wow", said John, "I'm only twenty six and I already know."

Azell looked at him and then pretended it had never happened. "Anyway, the Changing Map shows you the map of anything you want, including hidden passage ways and where people are."

"So, why are these items so important?" asked Sebastianus.

"Because", said Azell with a pause and then a grin, "they are the only things that come close to defeating Latorin."

Chapter Forty-five:

The Beasts of the Staircase

Sebastianus walked until he was come to a stop by a small sign aside the stairs that said:

Βεωαρε: Τηε Μυχκ, τηε Βατσ, τηε Αλβιυσ, ανδ τηε Λαιρ οφ τηε Ιτ

"Beware: The Muck, the Bats, the Albius, and the Lair of the It", Azell translated.

"What's that supposed to mean? The 'Lair of the It'. That's just stupid!" yelled John.

The group didn't pay attention to John's yelling. They walked through the curving staircase, avoiding the rocks that pointed at them and the sharp cliffs. They tried to watch out for the muck, bats, anything strange that could be an Albius, or any sort of lair.

After a while. Sebastianus looked at his boots. They were covered in a half-liquid, black mud.

"Audax, do you recall seeing any mud. The cliffs don't look like they have any mud? Also the stairs are clean", said Sebastianus.

"Why are ya asking", asked Audax.

Sebastianus pointed to his shoe. But there was no mud.

"Yer point?" Audax asked.

Sebastianus was silent and then thought one word: Muck. Sebastianus looked at the bottom of his shoe, on the rocks, and in his hair.

"Hey", said Sebastianus, "have you guys seen the muck?"

"I have just now", said Almasic.

"Where?" asked Sebastianus.

"Turn around and I could tell you", said Titus.

Sebastianus knew that it was coming. As he turned around, a straight face, he saw a giant pile of black, half-liquid, mud. It stood around ten feet tall. It had mud arms and two big, green eyes.

Sebastianus raised the Sword of Vinco and stabbed the mud. It shrunk to only a foot tall and Sebastianus missed.

The mud traveled through Sebastianus' legs and went to John. John shot at it with his arrows and a puff of smoke came from it as the poison from his arrow hit it.

John was about to hit it again til some of the mud went on his boots and held his feet to the stairs. The other bit of mud formed an arm and a fist, which nailed John in the crotch.

As John screamed, Azell and Titus hit the mud with their blades. It did not mind and turned to nothing. The mud on John also turned to nothing in a flash.

Sebastianus didn't know what was going on. But, as he looked down at the staircase, he saw the smallest bit of mud going under his boot. Sebastianus lifted his boot and then scraped it off. The mud expanded on the ground and Sebastianus stabbed it. It screamed and then jumped back up, shaping itself into a man. It jumped on Sebastianus. Sebastianus struggled to get up. But Audax took a bite at the mud and it got up, going Audax.

Sebastianus stabbed it before it could get to Audax. The mud turned around and screamed right in front Sebastianus' face. Sebastianus stabbed the muck once more and then he noticed the symbol of darkness imprinted on his chest. It's red triangle shined and the mini black triangle inside the other was barely noticeable.

Sebastianus took a swing for the symbol, but the mud went to Titus. Titus stabbed the mud, but it did not mind. It crawled up his leg.

Sebastianus stabbed the mud. It squealed and slid for him. Sebastianus saw the symbol on his back. He aimed his sword and stabbed it. The mud then turned to sand. It fell through the small crack that separated the staircase and the cliff.

Sebastianus made sure it was gone. He looked under his boot, on his hair and a bunch of other places.

Then Sebastianus smiled and said, "It's gone!"

Everyone cheered til Audax spoke, "What the bloody-hell is that?"

Audax pointed to a flying figure. "A bat", said Sebastianus. "Just one, though.'

Then another two figures appeared at its side. Then more and more. Soon enough, there were at least a hundred giant, black bats. There wings were pale and pink with small veins.

Sebastianus raised the Sword of Vinco and stabbed the bat as it ran. It fell to the staircase, screaming. Azell finished it off with a thrash of his sword.

Another couple of bats came and Sebastianus stabbed them all and John shot some. Most died, but the ones who didn't, Azell and Titus finished off.

After nearly one hundred bats were killed, about five hundred more came. Azell shot about fifty down and Sebastianus killed around fifty or sixty and Azell and Titus each got about ten to finish off. There were to many of them.

One thousand bats were all flying all towards Sebastianus, John, Azell, Titus and the owls that cowered behind.

Sebastianus killed one hundred more, John got about eighty, Azell with fifty or so, Titus around twenty. But the bats were still too much. Nearly ten thousand were there.

"I have a plan!" yelled Azell over the sounds of wings and flapping and screeching.

Azell took a white, straight stick out of his belt and yelled, "SACANO!" Every bat turned to flames and blew up into ashes.

"Azell", said Sebastianus, "how did you do magic...Is that a wand?"

"Just as the Changing Map works and the Sword of Vinco work so does the Wand of Azell. Magic that is unexplainable it is", said Azell, stroking his wand. I've never had to use this wand, not since the war against Latorin."

Everyone had nothing to say. Titus finally spoke saying, "Well, we still have to face the Albius."

"I'm sorry", said Azell, shaking his head. "Did you say *Albius*?"

"Yes", said Audax, "He did. Your point?"

"Do you know what the Albius is?" Sebastianus asked.

"Yes. I do", said Azell, shaking he was so nervous. "I've been hunting that dreadful snake ever since Latorin spilled his last drop of blood, when Vinco killed him!

"When Latorin died, his blood happened to fall in ten places: On Vinco's sword, the sword of darkness, the sword of fire, the sword of pain and on Albius, the snake. The other five places are mysteries, though", said Azell. "Within his blood, his life remains. The blood of Latorin is in the Albius."

Then something began to make an odd noise and Sebastianus felt a small bump on his leg. He looked down and saw nothing but darkness and within it, a ten foot long green, scaly figure with yellow eyes. Within the Albius' eyes, there were no pupils. There were small triangles, the symbol of darkness.

Sebastianus pointed the Sword of Vinco at the snake. The snake stared at it and then a red spot popped up on the snake's back. It was a small patch of blood. Sebastianus looked at the tip of the Sword of Vinco and it was smeared in red blood. Azell pointed his white wand at the snake and it also showed a small spot of blood on it. Azell raised his wand and yelled, "CRUKSO!"

But when the red beam shot out of his wand, the Albius had disappeared.

"At least we don't have to fight it", said John.

Azell stared at John and said, "That's one of the reasons you were told to leave the hunters. I'm glad Apollo replaced you."

Sebastianus then saw that the staircase ended at a huge mountain. It leads right up to the cave. It was the Lair of the It. The eight went into the cave. It had white silk all over, which everyone avoided. Also, they saw bones and skulls all over.

The cave got so dark no one could see, so Azell said, "Litightam", and the tip of his wand became a glowing yellow light. Sebastianus then saw something move. Then he saw John look a little nervous as he must have seen the moving creature as well.

Sebastianus walked through the cave and then he felt that something was watching him. He turned around and saw eight fierce, hairy legs. It was a huge spider. But it had a scorpion tail. Also it had ten, yellow eyes. Its fangs looked like the ones on a basilisk. Also, on the back two legs, he had huge claws.

"No wonder they call it an *It*", mumbled Audax. Then the creature raised its hands as the eight ran. But it jumped onto the ceiling of the cave and clung to it. It ran ten times faster than anyone and when it was pretty well ahead of everyone, it jumped back onto the ground and blocked the owls, Sebastianus, Titus, Azell, and John.

It gave a howl unlike any howl Sebastianus had ever heard. "Also one of the reasons they cal it an *It*", said Audax.

Then Sebastianus took out the Sword of Vinco and noticed the blood stain was on it. But he lost interest in it and went for the It. He stabbed the creature and it howled again, but this time, producing a green gas that reeked beyond believe. Sebastianus almost passed out.

John shot several arrows at the creature. It screamed and then jumped on John. It raised its scorpion tail and injected the venom into his chest. John screamed and screamed. But when the creature stopped, John was silent. He was shaking and shaking. He was holding his chest until he stopped shaking. His eyes were wide as he stared into space. He sat still by the cave wall. He sat there, dead.

Sebastianus, Titus, and Azell pointed there swords (Azell pointed his wand).

The creature spoke in a familiar language with a soft, scratchy voice. Sebastianus had not heard the language spoken, but he had read it: The Language of the Labyrinth. "Hes day a tow cair ot amotow", said the creature.

Sebastianus then swung the Sword of Vinco, but missed the It.

Azell fired black beams from his wand, yelling, "DANICO MANTISTA!" But he missed every shot.

Titus took a swing, but missed and the It jumped on him. It was about to strike with its tail, but Sebastianus came, chopping it right off with the Sword of Vinco. Red poison fell from the It. The beast screamed and then jumped on Sebastianus. The creature tried to dig its basilisk fangs into Sebastianus, but Sebastianus chopped off one of the monster's legs and it fell of Sebastianus.

Azell yelled, "Fanto Demo!" and it missed the It.

It ran away for a crack in the cave, but Sebastianus took the Sword of Vinco and stabbed the beast. It was half dead. Then Sebastianus saw the giant. It was feeding off a bluish, whitish colored thing from a cup. Sebastianus saw a familiar face, but he did not see every detail. But it was obvious who it was: Liberius. Sebastianus stabbed it in the face and it died.

Sebastianus, Azell, and Titus took John's body. Sebastianus lifted the dead archer by his legs. In his pocket, there was a yellow piece of paper. Sebastianus took the note and read:

Sebastianus, in case I die, I wrote you this letter. My bow, I want you to know, is a special bow. It is one of the Ninety Nine Items. It is the Bow of Gale Daksor. I want you to have it. Use it well. It only works if you are confident. Please burry me in Muse. It's the only place

I've never been to and everyone says it's a pretty awesome place. See ya later, Sebastianus. Good luck and I hope ya defeat Latorin.

From John Spittorit

Sebastianus smiled and took the bow from John's back. He showed the letter to Titus and Azell.

They walked through the cave for twenty minutes or so and then found a small door. It was black. Azell opened it with a spell and they walked out. The owls felt a lot better now that they could fly. Cailsell went back to Rebucia after John died. He didn't even say by or stick around for John's funeral.

The three got on there owls and went to Ghaladar, Muse.

Chapter Forty-six:

The Funeral of John

The six went to a small store and got a coffin for John.

"We should burry him outside of the city", said Sebastianus.

"Yes", agreed Titus.

The three flew on there owls, the coffin strapped to Audax with John in it.

When the owls landed, Sebastianus took the coffin off of Audax and set it on the flat, dirt ground. Azell took his wand out and said, "Digitone!" The ground then shook and then formed a hole that was a perfect rectangle only a little bigger than John's coffin. The hole was about five to six feet deep.

"Sebastianus, could I get a little help, here?", said Titus, lifting the coffin up. Sebastianus and Titus lifted the coffin up above the hole and gently dropped it down. It landed with a small thud.

Sebastianus found a huge rock, about four feet tall and five feet wide. Azell lifted his wand. "Riteo Mantius!" Then the stone slowly carved itself into a cross. Azell then yelled, "Felino!" Then at the bottom of the cross, some sort of plaque appeared. It read:

John Spittorit,
Son of Hacket and Marriot Spittorit
Year of the First Raven to the Year of the Fourth Bear
A Brave Warrior, A Hunter, An Archer
May God Protect His Soul

"If I may", began Titus, "I would like to speak. "John, my friend's son, was a great archer. He saved each of our lives many times and indeed got us a couple of steps closer to the end of Latorin", said Titus, pointing to the bow of Gale Daksor. "He will not be forgotten. He will be loved and remembered. May God protect his soul. Now, we should all say something about John. Azell?"

"Mhmmh", Azell cleared his throat. "John may have been clumsy, but he was a brave soldier and the best archer I've ever seen. He fights like an animal and is a gentleman when he is not battling. He has always cheered us up. Also, I may have not told you this but John once saved my life from one thousand of Latorin's monsters. I was injured and he killed them all with his bow. I regret expelling him from the Hunters. He was a good lad, John was. May God protect his soul."

Sebastianus began to speak. "John saved my life countless times. He's an amazing archer. Funny lad also. I'm proud to say he was my friend. I'll remember him. May God protect his soul."

To Sebastianus' surprise, Audax began to speak about John. "Barely knew the flipp'in guy. He was an amazing, outstanding archer, though. May God protect his soul."

"Amen", said Sebastianus, Azell, Titus, Audax, Ramus and Almasic together in a soft tone.

"Fortois!" yelled Azell. Then an electric green shot from his wand. Above the tombstone was some sort of holographic picture of John, smiling with the Bow of Gale Daksor strapped to his back. He was nodding and smiling. It made no sound, but it seemed that John was laughing in the picture.

Sebastianus saw the picture of John and a couple of tears trickled down his cheek. Sebastianus then grinded his teeth together, not minding the pain. Finally, he managed to speak. His lungs ached and his jaws had never been opened so wide. "I WILL KILL YOU, LATORIN!" Sebastianus' face was red with rage as he yelled at the sky.

All was silent til a voice hissed in the sunny sky. "Do your worst. I'll crush you like your filthy little friend." Then the sky turned from a cloudless, blue sky with a blazing sun to a purple, very cloudy, windy, raining, and thundering sky.

Sebastianus raised the Sword of Vinco and yelled to the sky, "YOU CAN NOT KILL ME, LATORIN! I WILL KILL YOU!"

"Yes, Sebastianus. Let the darkness in you take over. Let it spread. 'Sebastianus, promise me to never use this power. Tame it'. Too bad Icarus is now working with Cassius to bring back the Spargerian Empire, you fool. If you try to kill me, Sebastianus, you will lose the ones you love most..."

"GET OUT OF MY HEAD!" yelled Sebastianus, now falling to his knees.

"I'm not in your head, Sebastianus", said Latorin with a small cackle. "I'm behind you."

Sebastianus got up to his feet. Everything was black and no one was there. Sebastianus was floating. Then he turned around and saw Latorin. He was nine feet tall with very muscular, purple skin. He had a skull for a head with huge, grey horns attached. He had a beard of ten snakes. He had five inch, yellow finger nails. His tail was long and green and apparently a living snake. The symbol of darkness was imprinted on his forehead and chest.

"Sebastianus", he said with something slithering around his legs that Sebastianus recognized as the Albius, "I...WILL... KILL!" Latorin took a five foot long sword from his belt. It was completely black except for swirling, glowing blue stripes and a blood stain at the tip. "MUST...KILL!" yelled Latorin. He struck with the sword and when the tip was brushing Sebastianus' mail coat, Sebastianus closed his eyes and then opened them. He was back in Muse with Azell, Titus, Audax, Ramus and Almasic. "Did you guys hear him? He's back."

Chapter Forty-seven:

The Basilisk and the Frog

"If Latorin truly is back, Sebastianus, then the world would be shattered to pieces by now", said Azell, later on.

Sebastianus had passed out but did not remember and was now by a fire in the middle of the night covered by covers. Azell was out there with him as the owls and Titus was sleeping.

"Azell, he's back. I saw him!" yelled Sebastianus.

"Sebastianus, Latorin is not back…at least not entirely."

"What do you mean?" Sebastianus asked.

"Latorin's blood. It's glowing. That means he is slowly returning, but ther would also be a potion that will be needed to bring Latorin back. But it has some of the most difficult ingredients in it."

Sebastianus didn't know what to say. It was all silent for a moment of two. Then he said good night to Azell, took his sleeping bag into the tent Azell had made and slept.

Azell woke up everyone early. It was barely dawn.

"The Musan Fountain", he said, "Is in a hidden location in Muse. Only Vinco knows where."

Sebastianus then took out the Changing Map. He looked on the map. Without even telling it where to show him, it showed the deserted map of the Sobalus Mountains. At the top of one mountain there was a small, very detailed illustration of a silver fountain producing silvery water. But Sebastianus noticed that there was a cave around the Fountain of Muse. But around the cave were three figures: A basilisk, a giant bullfrog, and a blue and gold figure. Beside them were small rectangles that said there names. Beside the basilisk ther was a name that said:

Taisor

Next to the giant bullfrog were letters that spelled out its name:

Crocktasar

Then next to the figure that Sebastianus did not recognize was the name:

Galideth the Death Soldier

Sebastianus looked a little shocked and then said to Azell, Titus, Audax, Ramus and Almasic, "I think I've found the Fountain."

The owls flew fast above a forest, a beach, a lake and then finally above giant black mountains.

Sebastianus looked on his map. "Audax, Almasic, Ramus, go for the really, really big mountain with a cave at the top."

"Alright!" called Audax, diving several feet and going for the tallest mountain.

"Interesting how it happens to be where everyone would think of", said Ramus, talking with a Azell about the location and how obvious it would be to find and following Audax.

Almasic scowled and then yawned and was half asleep. He dropped around ten feet almost landing on the mountain and then waking up and following Audax.

There indeed was a mountain that was much bigger than the others. It had a cave on top. There was a small sparkling inside the cave.

"Head straight for the cave!" Sebastianus yelled at the owls.

Then they all went straight for the cave and CRASH! Some sort of blue light showed and then the owls fell and Sebastianus' heart was racing. They had hit something. But there was nothing there. Then, seconds before everyone was falling, the owls caught the three. Well, Audax caught Almasic and Sebastianus.

"A force field!" yelled Azell. "How didn't we see that coming!"

Azell drew his wand and yelled, "SERPIO!" But nothing happened. A red beam hit the force field and then bounced off and hit one of the mountains which then disappeared. "Vinco's magic", said Azell. "No one could get past that, not even me."

Then Azell yelled one more time, "Binicoto!" Then a white beam shot out of his wand and then hit another mountain which turned to dust very slowly.

"Sebastianus", said Titus. "The Sword of Vinco."

"What about it", said Sebastianus.

"Great thinking, Titus!" said Azell. "Sebastianus, raise your sword to the force field. I bet something will happen."

"Alright", said Sebastianus as he raised the Sword of Vinco. Then the force field shined red.

"Sebastianus, walk through it", said Azell.

"Um...alright", said Sebastianus.

"Yeah, Seb, have a go!" yelled Audax.

"Audax", said Sebastianus, "never call me *Seb* again."

Audax nodded with a smile, but yet looking shot down. Sebastianus walked toward the force field and closed his eyes. He walked forward with his eyes closed. Then, when he hit a rock, he opened his yes. The rock he had hit was the mountain. Everyone cheered and then walked in there selves.

Sebastianus was only three feet up the mountain til something slithered from a door sized hole that no one had seen. It was green with two unbelievable, giant, white fangs. "The Basilisk!" yelled Sebastianus. Everyone got on their owls before the monster could strike. But there was a problem, the owls weren't flying. Everyone ran from the basilisk and as they ran, Audax yelled over to Sebastianus, "Almasic, Ramus and me will go out the force field and find a way around the mountain. We'll meet you there." Then the owls ran the other way.

Sebastianus took the Sword of Vinco and ran to his right while the Basilisk followed Azell and Titus. Then Sebastianus jumped on the Basilisk. He then jammed the Sword of Vinco into its back and it didn't mind. Sebastianus stabbed it again, it then howled as Sebastianus had stabbed some sort of pressure point. The Basilisk wiggled Sebastianus off and then went for him. It opened its mouth so wide, Sebastianus would have thought that the Basilisk's jaws would have completely been broken by then. It moved its head so quickly at Sebastianus, Sebastianus barely had time to duck.

Then the basilisk took another strike and this time, Azell shouted, "IPPIUS!" Then the basilisk shaking and shaking. Azell smirked. Sebastianus could tell it was about to explode, but it didn't. It simply vomitted up bones and green sLosure and then went for Sebastianus again.

"ZUKITOKS!" Azell yelled. But the beast did absolutely nothing this time. Sebastianus raised the Sword of Vinco and stabbed it again. It did nothing still. Then the basilisk did something. Sebastianus had finally noticed that the creature had its eyes closed the whole time. It opened its eyes just in time for Sebastianus to shut his own and stab the air randomly as the Basilisk had the power to kill with its eyes. But then, Sebastianus heard a scream of the basilisk and a roar of Titus, "Ya got the Basilisk's eye!" Then there was another scream and Azell had yelled, "Got it in the other eye! It's okay to look!"

Then Sebastianus took out the Sword of Vinco. He stabbed the basilisk, but it didn't mind once again. Then Sebastianus thought of one word that rushed through his head: *Pressure points.*

Then Sebastianus hid from the Basilisk, looking at so he could see its temple. When Sebastianus spotted it above his bloody eyes, he took the Sword of Vinco and charged at the snake. With a huge jab, the beast screamed and nearly made Sebastianus deaf, and then it died.

"Its croaks are believed to shake the earth", said Azell, as they walked up the mountain.

Sebastianus made sure nothing would pop out on him and eat him. He watched every direction and was well aware to try and see through the corner of his eyes. Nothing large or amphibian like was anywhere. But there were a couple of small snails that would occasionally come from under the dirt. That was the only sign of life they had seen besides the basilisk, though.

Sebastianus could barely see the cave from where he was. "Guys", said Sebastianus, "I can kinda see the –"

There was a large, horrible, insanely loud croak like sound and the mountain was splitting down the middle and rocks were falling. Pointing his wand at the rocks, Azell kept yelling and, "SERPIO!" The rocks disappeared into nowhere. Then there was a loud, booming thud on the ground and web like feet shoed themselves along with a ten foot tongue and green body. The Crocktasar was a very frightening creature. It was the size of a large house and a small castle.

Sebastianus pointed the Sword of Vinco at the giant frog and it croaked and a rock came hurtling down at Sebastianus. Azell drew his wand and yelled, "DISAPPEROT!" The rock caught fire and switched directions, heading for the frog. The frog merely opened its mouth wide and got the flaming rock on his tongue and rolled it back in his mouth and swallowed.

Sebastianus stabbed the Crocktasar's leg with the Sword of Vinco. The frog jumped up and down like a maniac and then croaked. Azell came prepared turning the balls into giant spiked things that went for the frog. They slightly penetrated the frog's skin.

Sebastianus stabbed the frog in the leg. The sword dug deep and went through his leg. Sebastianus cut it off and the frog howled. Rocks came flying down at everyone. Azell came prepared and froze the rocks in the air. Then they exploded into dust and landed on the ground. The frog, which had now stopped screaming, seemed to be growing its leg back!

Sebastianus was so furious, he held the Sword of Vinco, hoping that some sort of magical beam would come out and destroy the frog. Nothing happened, though. But it did give the frog time to charge at Sebastianus. The frog leaped a good four hundred feet behind Sebastianus on accident but then lightly leaped more towards Sebastianus. Sebastianus stabbed the frog and it croaked. Rocks fell, but Azell was once again prepared as he made the rocks float in the air and make a weird sound that made the frog look up at them. It was completely distracted. Then Sebastianus stabbed it in the stomach and the frog roared. Rocks again fell and Azell stopped them by yelling, "FREEZIOTIM!" The rocks then dug themselves back into the ground.

The frog was now croaking and screaming and Azell finally had enough. "REPITIOPTIN!" The frog began to scream, but it couldn't. Sebastianus was now feeling confident that the frog could no longer scream. Then Sebastianus thought: *Confident.*

Sebastianus took the Bow of Gale Daksor. There were no arrows. But Sebastianus was confident. Then, in the bow, arrows came out of the air. At the tip was the slightest bit of venom. Then Sebastianus aimed for the frog and pulled back the bow and he loosened his fingers and then...WOOSH! The bow went right for the frog's head. Then, as the bow pierced the frog's skin, something happened. A blinding light showed and a picture of a tall, red head man appeared and then went away.

Chapter Forty-eight:

Soldier of Death and the Fountain

Sebastianus walked up the mountain with Azell and Titus stumbling behind him. Azell was stroking his wand, saying how he had never used it so much in one day since the fight against Latorin.

Finally, Sebastianus came to the cave. "Shut by the Golden Gates", said Titus.

"Yeah", muttered Sebastianus. "Can't we just cLosurb over it?"

"Most certainly not", said Azell. "We don't know if it's cursed or not!"

"Well", said Sebastianus, "just, like, use your wand and find out of its cursed."

"My wand is completely worn out and I can't remember all of the spells. There are over a billion, Sebastianus. It took me four hundred six years to figure almost every spell. There are some I still do not understand!"

"Sorry", mumbled Sebastianus.

Then, all of a sudden, the earth shook and from the ground popped an eight foot figure. Golden armor shined upon him. His golden helmet shined but the grey horns that stuck out of the sides didn't. But only his arms, legs and face showed themselves. Blue, thin fur he had, but no regular skin. He had thick purple mustache.

"I, Galideth, the Soldier of Death, would like you to run now. You have thirty seconds to leave my presence or I'll slaughter you all!" Galideth boomed in a dark, deep voice, revealing his sharp, yellow and brown teeth. Then he pulled out a long, silver, blood stained sword, a huge, bloody axe and a blood splattered shield. Then he swung something which hit Titus and then made him fly back several feet. Then he looked at Sebastianus and said, "Dramilius, you and the dark lord, you have a connection. Everyone in the Ater Latorin is talking about it and..." he looked at Azell, "Azell! Been nine thousand, twelve years since we last fought ey?" Then his yellow eyes reached Titus. "How is Solomon, doing?"

"Who?" Sebastianus asked as he did not have a clue that Solomon was.

"Solomon Bruno", said Galideth.

"Bruno, I killed him", said Sebastianus.

"That's what everyone thinks. Anyway, back to your father, Titus. Cursed, right? Used to be *the most handsome man in the land!* Serves him right. He only works for Latorin 'cause he's afraid and wants power!"

Sebastianus didn't listen to what Galideth was saying. But he did listen to some of his words carefully as they came loud and clear to him. 'Anyway, back to your father, Titus.' Come to think about it, Sebastianus had never known who Titus's father was. But he would have never that that Bruno was his father. Wait, Bruno went by his last name and was immortal. He must have fought in the war with Azell. He must have been Azell's rival. He was Azell's cousin. He fought with Latorin. But Sebastianus thought, Galideth said that Bruno was still really out there.

It happened so fast. Galideth raised his axe, Azell drew his wand, Titus took out his sword and Sebastianus gripped the Sword of Vinco. Galideth charged and Sebastianus slashed his arm. Galideth – which sickened Sebastianus – did not mind the pain of his forearm bleeding black blood.

Galideth took another strike at Sebastianus. Sebastianus swung the sword and it was going right for Galideth's mouth. Galideth managed time to quickly smirk. He then turned his head and the Sword of Vinco hit his shining helmet and he then went for Sebastianus again. Azell yelled something odd and then Galideth was fired backward smashing into the golden gates.

Sebastianus charged at Galideth, but the Soldier of Death leaped about five feet above Sebastianus and landed behind everyone. He was running to the bottom of the mountain and Azell mumbled some fowl language and then yelled, "PELLATOS!" Galideth was being pulled back by a metallic gold beam.

He then stood in front of them. Sebastianus took a swing and hit his armor. There was a bang and Galideth laughed as he swung his sword at Titus. Titus just barely dodged it. Titus then stabbed Galideth and there was a metal crashing against metal sound again. Titus had stabbed Galideth's boots.

Sebastianus took a swing and hit Galideth in the chest. The sword bounced off his armor and Sebastianus was thrown back by a punch of Galideth. "Get up, scum!" yelled Galideth as he kicked Sebastianus in the face. Sebastianus' mouth was full of blood. Then Galideth raised his sword. Titus took a run for Galideth, but the mighty warrior tossed Titus aside with a howl of laughter. Azell was now firing at least twenty curses, spells, and jinxes at Galideth. But they all bounced off his armor. Then Azell yelled a spell. "REBITOK!" Then a horrible sight showed itself. First flames hit Galideth's bare fist. Then his hand melted off. It was quite revolting.

Then Sebastianus slowly drew the Sword of Vinco and stabbed Galideth's sword and it went flying ten to fifteen feet somewhere. Sebastianus then stabbed Galideth in the armor. The loud bang sound appeared.

"FELLONTIO!" Azell yelled. Then Galideth's armor turned to sand. Sebastianus stabbed Galideth and he fell to the ground, dead.

"Invincible armor", mumbled Azell. "Who would have thought?"

Then Sebastianus noticed something. The Golden Gates were opening. There was a fountain. Silver dust sprinkled from the mouth of the statue of Vinco into a small, bole. That bole was held up by a statue of Liberius which stood in a bole. A statue of Sobalus held up the bole Liberius was in. Sobalus was in bole that was held up by a statue of Azell. There was a bole under him. Dust sprinkled from bole to bole and also came from the mouths of each warrior.

There was a goblet beside the fountain. Azell picked it up, yelling with joy. "This", said Azell "is the Goblet of Sobalus Muse. If I can get my hands on the Crown of Liberius Volde, I will have the four most powerful of the ninety nine items!"

As Azell tucked away the Goblet in a bag, Sebastianus saw a plaque by the Musan Fountain. It showed golden letters. Sebastianus looked at them and read aloud:

"The Eighth of the Nine Riddles of the Sleeping Giant. To honor myself, my leader and his companions, I built the Musan Fountain. Once you get my Goblet, you must drink up the dust from the Fountain. You must drink every last bit of it in the Goblet. You will then see one of the Sleeping Giant's weaknesses. Have a good life and good luck in defeating Latorin. Cheers from Sobalus H. Xavittis Morto Muse III!"

Sebastianus then looked at Azell, who handed him the Goblet of Sobalus Muse. Sebastianus took a scoop of dust from the bottom bole and then the dust disappeared and turned into water. Sebastianus then gulped up a very unpleasant goblet of dust. He waited til every last bit of dust was in his mouth. Finally, he gave it to Azell.

Sebastianus felt sick but then felt amazing. He then spaced out. He saw an image of a clear blue sky and golden hills of sand. He saw the giant who was falling and falling til it sank into the sand. One thousand owls were in the sky. All of them were the size of humans, maybe a bit bigger. People from Rebucia, Formighte, Muse, Grea, Plundorios, Bruno, Hestour, Azell, Apoalan, Driba, and the rest of the nations were all on the owls throwing arrows, swords, spears and anything they could get there hands on. Sebastianus saw himself on Audax amongst the peoples. Azell was on Ramus, blasting spells at the giant and the sand around him.

Sebastianus then fell to the floor and then got up and told Titus and Azell about the vision and then they looked at each other. They all wondered the same question. How would they get out. Then, as they worried, trying to think of ideas, the fountain moved to the right. There was a staircase that led deep down and another plaque.

I, Sobalus H. Xavittis Morto Muse shows the way out to those who need to find their way out. It opens to those who wants to defeat the Sleeping Giant to rid evil, not for fame. I, once again, give you all of my luck on your quest. As, only the heir can be on this quest, Vinco is with you. Also, I, Reabius P. Robus Azell and Liberius S. Kart Volde will also be with you.

Then they went down the staircase til there was a light and an opening. There stood Audax, Ramus and half asleep Almasic who was barely flying in the sky.

Chapter Forty-nine:

The Grean Valley and the Prince Alexander

Sebastianus had never been so glad to see Audax. He and Audax talked for a while about what they had done in the time they were separated. Sebastianus told Audax about the basilisk, the bullfrog, Galideth and the Musan Fountain. Audax and Ramus fought off a wild back of giant vultures while Almasic slept in a cave. They basically just talked to escape the jumpy Azell talking about the powers the Goblet of Sobalus Muse possessed and how he and Sobalus Muse were best friends. 'The wisest, most knowledgeable man in the history and best friends', Azell had said with pride. He was also talking about how wondrous it would be if they got the Crown of Liberius.

Finally, after forty five minutes, the owls landed on the ground. It was a green bole. The valley was so nice. Many trees and bushes and plants were there. There were several pillars that formed a straight line at the end of the valley. There was a door in between the two biggest pillars in the center.

"Open!" yelled Azell as he pointed his wand at the golden door. It opened and then there was a completely different world. At the end of the door was a sandy beach. Beyond that was sparkling blue water. There was a huge brown ship. On the side were golden letters:

PRINCE ALEXANDER

"I have a feeling that we should go on the boat", said Sebastianus.

"Yeah", said Azell. "I got that same feeling."

"And we need to rest", Almasic put in with a yawn."

"That's True", said Audax.

"Very", put in Ramus.

"I think we should keep away from that boat. It belonged to Liberius! Its dark magic", said Titus.

"I'll search for every spell put on that boat", said Azell.

"It's magical and works by itself. Avoid the spell that makes it run by itself", said Sebastianus.

"I can do that", said Azell.

The six walked through the opened doors and shut them behind. They all walked on the boat. "FIGNINDOCRUSS!" yelled Azell.

There was a yellow beam of light that went over the ship. "Nothing evil", said Azell. "There is only one magical object on this ship, besides ours of course", said Azell. Then he walked into a room on the ship that Sebastianus remembered as Liberius' room.

Sebastianus was worried. But he was scared to death when he heard an "AHHHH!" Then Sebastianus went into Liberius' room, holding the Sword of Vinco with both hands.

"What is it?" Sebastianus yelled. Then he saw Azell unharmed with a small figure in his hand: A crown.

"Volde Liberius Crown of!" yelled Azell, who was nearly having a heart attack.

Sebastianus was excited. But nowhere near as excited as Azell. "You mean", said Sebastianus, "the Crown of Liberius Volde."

"Yeah", said Azell, keeping his eyes fixed on the crown, "That's what I said."

Sebastianus couldn't help but laugh. Azell then took his wand, the Goblet of Sobalus, and the Crown of Liberius. "Sebastianus, your sword", said Azell.

"Alright", said Sebastianus, giving Azell the Sword of Vinco.

He set the items in some sort of form. The crown stood above the goblet. Through the goblet's handles was the Sword of Vinco and straight across the bottom of the goblet. It formed some sort of person…in a way.

"Vinco! Sobalus! Liberius! I call upon you to show me the way!" yelled Azell. Then the boat began to run. Then the bloodstains on the items appeared.

"Why is there blood?" Sebastianus asked.

"The most powerful items are marked by the blood of their owners so only the owners of the heir of the owners may use the items. Only Icarus can use my wand."

"Not good", said Sebastianus.

Then, after twenty minutes, the *Prince Alexander* stopped. They were at the Desert of Allias. The Sleeping Giant waited.

Chapter Fifty:

The Sleeping Giant

They rode on their owls through the blazing desert. Sebastianus, Titus and Azell had token off their shirts. They were soaked in sweat. Sebastianus then realized something. He had heard stories about the Desert of Allias. It was nicknamed the Land of Ten Suns. They were not exaggerating at all. There were ten orange suns that stood still in the sky.

"Stop here!" yelled Azell.

The owls dove to the ground to where a rock stood. There was a black man. He was around six foot five inches. He was very muscular. He wore no shirt but cloth that hung around his waist to his knees. He was covered in tattoos all different colors. The one on his back was the Latorin Rege. "Cassius", said Azell with hatred in his voice. He grinded his teeth and Cassius gave a twisted smile that revealed rotten teeth.

"Reabius", said a deep voice. "So nice to see you again."

Sebastianus noticed he looked exactly like the statue of him. Then Sebastianus noticed he was holding something: The Sword of Pain. It was silver and was four feet long. He stabbed the ground with his sword and then yelled, "Latorin, with your power awake the beast! Upon these heads the Giant will feast!" Then, where he had stabbed the ground, there was a beam. It was ten beams all coming from the ten suns. Then, where the beam had hit, there was a hole that was as big as a house but as deep as the sea.

Cassius was ready to yell again. "Bring the monster from this lair! All because trespassers made a little dare!" Cassius stabbed the ground and then there was a moment of silence. But then, a hand the size a huge tree appeared. Cassius gave another twisted smile and then snapped his fingers and disappeared with a puff of smoke.

Another huge hand that was made of sand appeared. It was the size of half a house. He had no nose, no mouth. He just had two red eyes. Then he fully rose, looking like a giant man of sand.

"ABBERAT!" yelled Azell. Then red beams hit the giant and formed a hole in his stomach. But the sand came back and the giant looked fine.

Sebastianus ran up to the giant and took out the Sword of Vinco and stabbed it in his foot. The giant roared and the sand did not come back.

Then Azell got on Ramus, Sebastianus got on Audax and Titus on Almasic. Almasic didn't seem that sleepy anymore now that the giant was back.

Sebastianus took the Bow of Gale Daksor. He was so nervous. No arrows appeared. Sebastianus quickly tucked the bow back in his bag which was tied to Audax.

"DEMENTO!" Azell yelled. Then red beams shot at the giant's face. It knocked off his sand head. But then, his head reformed.

"Audax, get closer to the giant!" yelled Sebastianus.

Audax turned his head at Sebastianus.

"Audax!" yelled Sebastianus.

Then Audax looked forward. He was only thirty yards away from the giant. Audax was about to crash into the giant. But then, he dived down.

Then Audax flew around the giant. He was flying inches beside the giant's head. Sebastianus gripped the Sword of Vinco with both hands and then took a swing. The giant roared and then fell dead to the ground.

"He...He's dead!" yelled Sebastianus.

But then, Sebastianus looked at the sand. The giant was sinking into it. "What's happening?" Sebastianus asked himself.

Then the sand began rising and rising into a huge mountain of sand. There was a deep roar and the sand mountain shook as bunches of sand fell. A giant made of sand, no longer as big as before but now at least five hundred feet tall stood. There was a barely visible symbol on his chest. It was made of sand but sort of stuck out.

"The Sleeping Giant will not be destroyed that easily!" said Azell. "There's no way you can just stab it!"

"Then how do you kill it?" yelled Sebastianus.

"You know its weaknesses, Sebastianus!" yelled Titus.

Then Sebastianus thought. He knew how to destroy the giant. He was now confident.

He took the Bow of Gale Daksor and then hundreds of arrows appeared. Sebastianus took the arrows, which were each splattered with the venom of the Minions. He aimed the bow and...WOOM! It hit the giant and a whole the size of house appeared. Most of it reformed. But there was still a door sized hole in his chest. The giant sunk into the earth. Sebastianus hit the sand with dozens of arrows and by the time he was done with his arrows, there was a crater in the ground.

Then Sebastianus tried to think and then he remembered the plant he had eaten in Rebucia.

All of the sudden, the giant came from the ground. Sebastianus shot an arrow with the Bow of Gale Daksor and it went right into the very center of the symbol of darkness on his chest and it departed from his body. It was like a shield. The sand fell off it and Sebastianus saw the black and red symbol. Then Sebastianus yelled at Azell.

"Azell, cast a curse at him!" yelled Sebastianus.

"Why?" Azell called.

"Just do it!" yelled Sebastianus.

Azell pointed his wand at the giant and yelled, "DEMENTO!" The giant's arm blew off and it didn't grow back. "DEMENTO!" Azell cast the spell again and then red beams flew from the tip of his white wand. The giant's glowing red eye blew out of his head. It landed on the ground and Sebastianus saw that it was some sort of diamond or crystal.

The giant was slowly losing its power, very slowly. Sebastianus thought back to another time. Sebastianus then yelled at Azell, "Make some boulders and throw it at the giant!" Azell did it with some spells.

The giant went back into the sand before suffering anymore. Sebastianus saw that it was going into a small cave. It slowly fell into the cave which must have been a hundred feet deep.

Sebastianus went up to the cave on Audax and then flew in by stopped when who else but Liberius was in a tunnel. Sebastianus went out of sight before Liberius could look. Sebastianus took a peak. He was standing in front of a huge pile of sand. He was, just as Sebastianus had last seen him, young. He wore his cloak over his armor.

"How many times?" he yelled. Then he drew something out of his cloak. It was cup. "How many times can you get injured?" Then he breathed into the cup and a bluish whitish color came out and then he put a lid over it quick. Liberius then became paler and he face became something like five years older. He even had somewhat of a five o'clock shadow. His hair got a little greyer. Liberius then set the cup upside down and it faced the pile of sand. He took the lid off and the bluish, whitish color came out and went into the sand. The pile got bigger. "If I have to heal your injuries one more time with my own bit of soul, I'll run out of it!"

The sand slightly growled. Then the sand slid out of sight and somewhere out of sight. Sebastianus quickly flew out of the cave on Audax. Liberius didn't notice that Sebastianus was there.

When Sebastianus looked straight ahead of him, he saw a mountain size, human shaped sand creature. The giant had its arm and its eye. It was in perfect condition. It looked even better than before. Azell was firing curses; by they kept missing or just not affecting him.

Sebastianus shot arrows at the giant, but nothing happened. They were bouncing off his chest or any other part of his body. Titus was throwing spears at the giant which Azell made appear from the sky. But nothing was happening.

There was a weird noise. It was stomping. But there was also yelling. There were chants and familiar names. Everyone, including the giant, was feeling shocked when they saw at least a hundred thousand people. Sebastianus had seen it before. But they were owls, too in what he had seen.

"Get the giant!" Then, the giant hit about a hundred and they were thrown back fifty feet into other people.

Then there was something else. There was a screeching noise and flapping. There were thousands of owls. They all went by somebody and yelled 'Get on!' There was an owl for everybody. There were no extras. All of them went for the giant.

"Are you going?" Sebastianus asked Audax.

"Yeah!" yelled Audax as he swooped, biting the giant's forehead. "FOR THE OWLS!" Audax yelled.

"FOR THE OWLS!" every owl responded. Sebastianus couldn't help but laugh. Then the giant was being eaten to the ground. The owls were feasting upon him.

The Sleeping Giant then sunk into the ground and into the cave. Everyone cheered and cheered. "THE GIANT'S DEAD! THE GIANT'S GONE!" they yelled.

But Sebastianus knew it was fleeing for Liberius to give him his soul. Sebastianus and Audax then went into the cave. Sebastianus was hoping to sneak up on Liberius. But, as he dove down to the bottom of the cave, a voice said quietly and softly, "Sebastianus, you will only get to the giant if you get past me. *If* you can get past me, Cassius will already have given the giant some of his soul to revive its wounds. Then Liberius raised his golden sword. He was about to strike, but then...

"DEMENTO!" Beams shot from above and hit Liberius back twenty feet. He hit the wall and then rock landed on him.

Azell was on Ramus, flying above Sebastianus. "Sebastianus, only you can master the power of the Goblet of Sobalus Muse." He handed Sebastianus the goblet. Sebastianus held it in front of himself and waited for something to happen. Cassius was on his way. "Come on. Work!" whispered Sebastianus. Then some water trickled out of the goblet. Then more and more and soon enough, the goblet was pouring out hundreds of gallons a minute. Sebastianus went up and out of the cave with Azell. The cave was flooding. Buy the time, Sebastianus was out of the cave, it was filled to the entrance and the goblet had stopped pouring out water.

"Azell!" yelled Sebastianus. "What about the gaint?"

"Water destroys sand. Remember, Sebastianus?" said Azell.

Sebastianus thought back to when he was in Azell's garden. What he had seen."

Then Sebastianus saw a figure running. It was Cassius. "Pellitos!" yelled Azell. Then Cassius was pulled back by a light from Azell's wand.

"We can take care of this", said a soft voice. A man in a green cloak bigger that it should have been was standing there. He face was pale with no emotion. His big brown eyes showed gave Sebastianus a little fright. Then several more appeared. They were exactly like him.

"On behalf of King Osmani, you will be sentenced life at the Prison of Idanlesh, with the possibility of death", said the man with the soft voice.

"The Idanlesh guards", whispered Azell.

"Oh", whispered Sebastianus.

Audax flew Sebastianus home as Ramus flew Azell home and Almasic with Titus. All was well. Liberius had been gone for a bit and Cassius was arrested. Titus had also told Sebastianus that Icarus was sentenced life in Idanlesh as well. But Sebastianus knew something was wrong. There was something odd. But Sebastianus would find out on his next adventure. He just needed to be patient.